Wolf Tears

The Horror of the Jester

Koos Verkaik

Outer Banks Publishing Group
Raleigh/Outer Banks

FIRST EDITION – August 2025

Library of Congress Control Number: 2025941090

ISBN - 979-8-9907093-7-9
eISBN - 979-8-9907093-8-6

We cried as do the wolves, without tears.
Wolf tears, intangible as life itself

1 -Rotterdam Cathedral

I stood there and read my own name on the shop window: Paul Brand.

The streetlight shining behind me etched my reflection sharply against the secondhand violins and classical guitars that were barely visible on display behind the glass. At five foot seven, I wasn't what you'd call tall, and I was definitely too thin. The belt of my coat was fastened tightly around my waist, and I buried my narrow, unshaven face in a woolen scarf to protect it from the bitter cold. My brown eyes peered anxiously out from under a lock of lank, black hair.

Why wouldn't I go inside?

Francis Beck was dead.

Why wouldn't I take the key out of my pocket and open the door?

Francis Beck had driven headlong into the concrete pillar of a bridge. The car was burned out, and the charred remains of the driver were subsequently identified as those of Francis Beck. On his fingers were the eight gold rings that he had worn at his last concert in the Rotterdam Doelen.

So why didn't I simply walk through my shop of musical instruments, up the stairs, through the lounge, into my bedroom, and go to bed? It was dark and cold, my breath swirled around my face like smoke. I kept my hands plunged deep in my pockets against the biting frost, but not for one moment did I entertain the thought of seeking the warmth and comfort of the house.

I decided to drop into a cafe to have a drink, and then perhaps wander through the deserted city. Who knows? By that time I might have gathered up enough courage to enter my own house.

Why was going into my own darkened shop and walking up the stairs proving to be such a problem for me? It was because time itself seemed to have played a trick on me.

On the pillow of my bed there lay an envelope, given to me by the New York composer, Francis Beck. That envelope contained a faded photograph on thick cardboard, with the name of the photographer from the Hoogstraat in Rotterdam imprinted on the bottom right-hand corner. Two men posed, seated in front of a painted backdrop in the photographer's studio. Between them was a small wooden table, on which stood two glasses and a bottle of wine. The man on the left wore a shabby three-piece suit. He had a narrow face and a thin, rather beaklike nose. His lips were thin, his eyes small and half-shut. His short, curly hair was sparse at the sides, and his eyebrows, which were lighter in color than the hair on his head, met just above the bridge of his nose.

He wasn't what you would call handsome, but he had a friendly face and a slight smile that played around the edges of his lips. The man on the other side of the table was around the same height and wore a suit that was a bit too small for him. And he had my eyes, my hair, my face. On the back of the photograph, in fancy lettering written in ink, were the words: *Francis and Paul, friends for eternity—April, 1932.*

And in 1932, I hadn't even been born yet.

In the warmth of the cafe, with a mug of coffee cupped in my hands, I thought about the short time I had spent with Francis Beck.

* * *

"Shall we take a break?" I suggested. "I'm beginning to feel tired."

Francis Beck stopped at once. He folded his arms and looked around. He wore a yellow jogging suit and white running shoes. His short curly hair was soaked with sweat. I stood next to him, panting, but his breathing was regular. Looking at him, you would never have dreamed that he'd been running nonstop for several miles.

I had first met him during a rehearsal of one of his pieces in De Doelen, and had discovered then that we were both fond of running. One Sunday morning, I had taken him along with me to the Rotterdam lakes just outside of town, where peace and quiet ruled, and recreational activities were enjoyed by those who were so inclined. Together we stood gazing out over the water at small boats with metal masts, and at windmills with motionless sails that sat on the opposite side of the lake. In the distance, etched on the horizon, we could see rooftops and a church steeple.

"Look at you! You could run a marathon. And you never sleep, Francis. Where do you get all this energy from?"

"The last time I slept was just before my fourteenth birthday. I'm now forty-two. I don't know anymore what it's like to close my eyes and drift off into a state of complete oblivion, or simply step into a dream that is all my own."

"It's certainly an intriguing predicament. If you'd like to talk about it—"

"Let's walk for a spell," said Beck, "and you can catch your breath. I would like to talk to you about it, actually. Touring the great cities of Europe makes me feel much less restrained—freer, if you will. I see so many new faces and contrasting landscapes. When someone suggested that I sometimes accompany the orchestra on the piano during performances of my own compositions, I jumped at the chance. Actually I find it very refreshing playing with a different orchestra every time."

He gestured towards the smooth expanse of the lake.

"London, Paris, Stockholm, Oslo, Copenhagen, and now Rotterdam. I'm looking forward greatly to performing with your orchestra."

We spoke Dutch, he with only a slight accent, adding that he could also converse with me in Spanish, Portuguese or French. Nothing further was said for a while, and I assumed that he had chosen to remain silent about his insomnia.

"I understand that while you were in London you played a piece with the orchestra for a quarter of an hour before the intermission," I said, in a clumsy attempt to open a topic of conversation. "It was said that a few hundred people had sudden stomachaches, and one person even had to be taken to the hospital."

The American smiled, but said nothing.

"In Paris, a large number of people became nauseous. They wondered what on earth could have caused it, but no one could say for sure. It appeared as if they had all seen something terribly frightful—all at the same time. One sufferer, attempting to describe it, said, 'Everything suddenly became very vague around me, and an image appeared in my mind's eye. It seemed to force itself upon me. I saw something lying alongside the road. It had apparently once been alive, but it was no longer possible to tell whether it had fur or feathers. It was a filthy, squashed mess, and it made my stomach churn.' I wasn't there myself, but the conductor of the French orchestra, a good friend of mine, sent me a newspaper clipping."

"In Stockholm, people who had never before laid eyes on each other suddenly fell in love," Beck told me. "In a concert hall you have so many strangers sitting next to each other, and if I had not switched my concentration to something else pretty damn quickly, it could have turned into quite an orgy. Just imagine what would have happened if I had continued playing. Heaven forbid! In Oslo, I took no chances; I played as well as I could for ten minutes without allowing myself to be swept up by my own hypnagogic images."

Francis stepped out onto a small wooden jetty, where loose layers of thin ice made a crisp, crackling sound as they rode the languid swell. Following him along the jetty, I was startled to see him sink suddenly to his knees, supporting his elbows on his thighs and burying his face in his hands. He didn't move.

A few long strides took me quickly to his side, and I put my hand upon his shoulder.

"What's the matter?"

"I'm afraid I'm prone to sudden headaches," he mumbled apologetically. "They flare up and flash through my head, and I have to sit down for a bit. I'm feeling better now, though. No sleep, the images that loom up out of nowhere, the headaches—they probably all stem from the same thing."

He stood up slowly, staring down at his feet. Then he shuffled past me gingerly, as if he were afraid of falling into the water, and made his way back to the path that skirted the lake.

"Perhaps we should quit running," I suggested. "There's a restaurant just over that humpbacked bridge a little further along the path. We can stop for a drink."

We walked on together.

Francis was only an inch or so taller than me. His small eyes were light green. His sharp nose, shaded by thick eyebrows that met above furtive, intelligent eyes, made me think of the uplifted, alert head of a bird of prey.

The dark blue jogging suit and thick sweater I was wearing made me appear more hefty than Francis. I am one of those heavy-beard types, and since I don't always shave on Sunday mornings, my face was dark with stubble from my sideburns all the way down to my neck. I stroked my chin and asked, "Hypnagogic images. What are they?"

"That's what I have always called them, although it seems they're only known as that when they appear before you at night, when you're drowsy and just about to drift off. When they appear in the morning as you begin to awaken, they're called hypnopompic, and are often marked by visions or fantasies. But day or night, it's all the same for me. Not everyone understands what I mean by this, even after I've explained it. That's a reasonable enough explanation for those who have never experienced this phenomenon. When cerebral activity is reduced, and other parts of the brain, such as the subconscious, become active, random images can often appear. Apparently they are not summoned up consciously in any way, but simply come and go, and you find yourself a surprised observer rather than someone who can control these strange images. Those who have never experienced it, though, really haven't the slightest idea what I'm going on about."

"I'm not surprised. What sort of images are they? Can you describe them?"

"They come at times of rest, when you're relaxing. They can be anything imaginable—a plane ripping through the clouds, for instance, or the sudden appearance of an unknown face. Dazzling colors sometimes fill my vision like an abstract painting that recreates itself into the multicolored, grotesque grin of a monster. A street, a building, a horse. Mountainous waves crashing onto the shore, columns of ants carrying a squirming slug to their nest, a huge hand adorned with a silver ring, which is manipulated back and forth by the fingers of another hand. Random images, following one another in rapid succession . . ."

We crossed the small bridge and came to a path lined with tall trees on either side, their bare branches arched above us like a military honor guard. The soles of our running shoes scrunched gratifyingly on the crushed shells that littered the path. We were silent now, and my thoughts turned to my extraordinary companion, the composer who was capable of transmitting images into the minds of his audience simply by playing an instrument—a mystic who used sound to create imaginary forms. I considered myself pretty damn lucky that the American millionaire had suggested we go jogging together, and I was determined to take this heaven-sent opportunity to learn as much about him as I could. I had picked him up at the Hilton Hotel in my car early that morning, and the plan was to stay together until after the concert that evening in the main hall of De Doelen.

Francis quickened his pace, and I followed.

"Are you all right? How's your headache?"

"I'm okay right now, thanks. But it could return at any time."

We jogged on alongside each other, and as I caught his eye for a moment, Francis grinned.

"There's something wrong with this old gray matter of mine. No kidding, I really mean it. I wouldn't want them to take a photo of my brain. I'd be too scared that it would show something that I'd rather not see. Apparently, my birth was difficult; it seems I was reluctant to make an appearance, and I was deprived of oxygen for a while. And I turned out to be a real sick kid, too. Picked up just about every childhood ailment in the book, and a few that weren't! I often lay in bed, burning with fever. That's how it started.

"We lived in New Jersey then, in a one-horse town, hunkered down between the corn and wheat fields. There was just one bar, with what folks liked to call a 'dance hall' built in, but we had another name for it, if you know what I mean. Anyway, this desirable, if somewhat shady, recreational facility was owned and operated by my father. We lived over the store. That's where I lay, listening to the music. The bass tones especially vibrated around my room. I heard music, saw images, sweated with fever, and drifted off into that state of drowsiness that lies between waking and sleeping. Kind of a 'twilight zone,' like the old TV show. It was terrific! I was happier lying feverish and still in my bed than walking down the street as fit as a fiddle.

"Content to slumber in the dim light, with music pulsating around my ears and hypnagogic images dancing before my mind's eye, I tried to combine images and sound. Eventually, what I saw began to adapt itself to the musical tones. That in itself was interesting enough, but then I figured it would be even more interesting if I could somehow manage to reverse this process."

"The musical tones themselves conjured up the visual imagery."

"Exactly. You, as a violinist, can perhaps understand that. Sound and image—both highly elusive terms. I really appreciate the feeling of comfort that I have discussing these things with you. You know, being so far from home, and meeting someone, quite by chance, that you find you can share your innermost thoughts with, often has better results than a visit to the psychiatrist."

"I'm a good listener," I said.

We both burst out laughing.

"The musician who can't listen has yet to be born," said Francis.

I pulled off my sweater. The setting sun shot its parting rays through the windows of the lounge that was situated in front of the restaurant. A waitress brought us coffee, cake and a glass of mineral water.

"Are you sure you don't want anything to eat?" I asked the man sitting across from me at the small table. "There's no nutrition in water. Or did you have breakfast in the hotel?"

"No, I didn't eat anything at all this morning."

"Tsk. And you've done all that jogging, too."

"I never drink coffee, tea or alcohol, nor do I smoke cigarettes. And I'm also very careful about what I eat. I have no idea what effect stimulants might have on my brain, and I'm not the least bit curious to find out. I have never experienced the pleasure that is said to be had from drinking or smoking."

Francis took off his jogging jacket. Under it he wore a short-sleeved cotton shirt that revealed long, thin arms. I had already removed my own thick sweater, and now, clasping my hands behind my neck, I leaned back and gazed out of the window. A large grassy field led down to the water's edge. Behind the leafless trees I saw the dike along which we had just jogged, where a solitary cyclist now peddled.

Francis recommenced his tale, stopping now and then to take a sip or two from his glass. He didn't look at me, but his green eyes seemed to grow paler in the sharp light of the sun-drenched lounge.

"I used to prefer being alone. If I felt well enough and was not confined to bed, I liked to go for long walks beyond our little hick town. The wind rustling through the corn fields was music to my ears; I could listen to it for hours on end. But my favorite spot was Robert Bragg's old auto graveyard. The site was filled with pyramids built with the bodies of just about every make of wrecked jalopy: old Fords, Buicks, Plymouths, Dodges, you name it. It was usually pretty quiet in there, and I often climbed to the top of one of those rusty pyramids and looked out like some toy soldier on guard duty across a sea of metal painted with every color of the rainbow, to the wooden house were Robert Bragg lived. I withdrew into myself and enjoyed the images that appeared before me of their own volition.

"I recall one particular Saturday I spent there. I had stretched out on the hood of a huge Chrysler, lying with my back against the busted windscreen. Suddenly, the wind blew my hair back, the sky turned gray and rain threatened. Then, below me I heard the plaintive mewing of a cat. I stood up and peered down from the pyramid of wrecks to the ground below. A kitten, black with just a small patch of white on its neck and no more than a couple of weeks old, was sniffing around, probably looking for something to eat. I knew the creature wouldn't be Bragg's. The old guy didn't like cats much and besides, he had a big dog, an aggressive Alsatian cross, who wouldn't tolerate another animal within a mile of the house.

"I was thirteen going on fourteen, and decided then and there that I wanted that little cat to keep me company when I was sick and forced to stay in my room. So I slid cautiously off the hood and clambered down the heap of wrecks. But when my foot touched the ground, the kitten was startled, darted off under the cars and let out a shrill cry that sounded altogether different from the throaty meow of a fully grown cat.

"I dropped down and crawled after it under the cars, but my movements scared the little thing, and it took off again. I followed it. Now, a big guy would never have made it, but I did—I kept my head down and wriggled forward on my stomach, between broken exhaust pipes, wheels, old tires and lord knows what, never noticing that it was beginning to grow dark up above in big-people land.

"The kitten kept up its mournful cries, and I followed the sound. But the farther I went, the more trouble I had finding a way through the tangled heap of metal. The weight of the topmost vehicles had crushed the suspension of those at the bottom, but I managed to slip between the chassis anyway—through open windows and doors hanging on their hinges.

"Stopping for a breather on the backseat of an Oldsmobile, I just lay there in that murky metal world, quietly listening. Then I heard the kitten again. I turned and slid out the other side of the car. It had no doors, and its caved-in roof left me with precious little room to move around.

"Thinking back, I wonder if rescuing that kitten was actually what was uppermost in my mind at the time. I mean—it was really a sort of adventure. A bit of a daredevil caper for a boy of thirteen, and I wasn't aware of any danger.

"Bragg had piled sedans on limos and pickups, and I was able to climb further in on my knees until I was under a massive truck. My shoulder bumped against a wheel so softly that I barely even felt it. But it turned out to be just enough of a whack to set the whole kit and caboodle wobbling. Something snapped, I heard creaking and cracking, and a storm of metal and glass broke out over my head. Everything suddenly crashed and thundered down all around me. I couldn't see anything, but I felt the undercarriage of the truck begin to press against my back so I squashed myself flat on my stomach on the ground, with my arms and legs outstretched, certain I was about to be flattened to death by the tons of falling metal. I took a deep breath and steeled myself against the instant that I would feel my ribs crack and my lungs burst. But the pressure did not increase. Everything that had been dislodged now stayed put. The only trouble was, so did I! I was pinned down, able to move my hands, feet and head just a little. I turned my head to the left and coughed out a mouthful of dirt."

Francis stopped talking and looked around him with a puzzled frown. I had tapped his wrist with my fingers to draw his attention to the waitress, who now stood by our table and was regarding him with undisguised fascination.

"Would you like another drink?" I asked. "I asked you earlier, but you were too busy talking."

"Thanks. Mineral water, please."

The waitress put his empty glass on the tray, along with my coffee cup and plate. She now turned to me with an inquiring smile.

"And another coffee for me," I said, and then once more turned my attention to Francis. "Please, do go on: You were pinned down there, under the wreck, and you could hardly move."

"Yes. While about three hundred yards away from me stood Robert Bragg's house, and he was probably sitting there with a beer, reading the paper and patting his dog. Further on you had Ben Lewis's place and the Russell's farm. And still further on was the town and our own house, where at that moment my folks were busy working behind the long wooden bar. Everyone was so close, but they might as well have been on the moon as far as I was concerned. I was afraid to move a muscle, for fear the truck and everything on top of it would suddenly collapse. Later, when I decided to risk working myself free, I soon discovered that any move was doomed to failure—or worse. At least I could still breathe and move my toes, fingers and head, but that was all. Strange as it may seem, I remember I felt quite peaceful after a while and knew that I wasn't going to let myself panic.

"I thought about death for a minute, but just couldn't accept the fact that my time had come. I was only thirteen, for Pete's sake! On the other hand I also realized that I wasn't going to get out of this mess without some help. My mind wandered. I saw myself lying under a colossal pyramid of wrecked vehicles, the topmost one of which reached up to the clouds and was covered in snow, like some lofty mountain peak."

Francis shivered a little and picked up the glass of mineral water that had just been placed in front of him. Tentatively, as if he were in great pain, he ran the fingers of his other hand through his curly hair, then drew them down over his narrow, pointy nose. His headache had apparently returned, but after a moment or two he relaxed and continued.

"Phew! That was painful. It came like a dazzling white flash, but it's gone now. Where was I? Oh yes! I know it sounds weird, given the circumstances, but I recall thinking about that kitten again. Where did it come from? Did it belong to the Russells or Lewis, or had some passing motorist stopped and abandoned it on the highway? I stared sideways into the twilight, and it didn't take much of an effort to reach a state of mind in which all sorts of images began appearing. That semiconscious, halfway world, remember? As soon as the images, visions, optic fantasies—call them what you will—began following one another in rapid succession, I tried to bring order to the chaos. I wanted to somehow control them, hold onto certain images and make others disappear. I had played this game before, and was steadily becoming better at it. Wretched as my situation was, there was nothing to distract me now. I felt totally alone in the vast universe.

"I then added something to this psychic mixture that I had only recently discovered—rhythm! Cautiously, I raised my hands, resting my elbows on the ground. My fingers found the undercarriage of the truck, and I began to tap on it with my nails.

"The rhythm affected the sequence of images; the sound directed my thought processes. Initially, my physical senses also became acute—my nostrils were assailed with the acrid smell of oil, moldy soil, and the fetid reek of damp, half-rotted auto seats—but as I sank deeper into myself (as I like to put it) I no longer smelled anything. Then, suddenly, the image of the kitten loomed up before my wide-open eyes, as big as a tiger.

"Head to one side, feet still, fingers raised to the rusty belly of the truck, I tapped away all the images that filled my vision, and I concentrated on that little lost creature, drawing it closer to me using all my senses. Up to then, my only experience in this twilight realm had been of a strictly spiritual, metaphysical nature. But the tiny, wet nose that I now felt nuzzling me was real! And there was no mistaking the bristly reality of those whiskers that tickled my skin, nor the tactile lick of its rough little tongue on my nose.

"The kitten pressed close to me, nestled under my chin and lay there quietly. I felt its belly swell softly with every breath. I dropped my hands. Who's to say how long I had tapped against that metal with my fingers? I fell asleep, and when I awoke again, the tapping sound was multiplied a thousand fold; it was raining hard, and water rushed down on all sides. I slapped the ground with my open hands and the water splashed over my face, reviving me a little. The kitten, soaked through and trembling with the cold, still lay curled up under my chin."

"Do you know how long you were asleep?" I asked.

"No idea. Fifteen minutes, an hour, half a day—but I awoke with real fear. When it first happened, when the truck pressed down on me, I didn't feel afraid. But now it dawned on me that I hadn't fallen asleep in bed or dozed off in some safe place, and I began to tremble like the kitten. My cheek lay in rainwater, and when I turned my face from one side to the other, my nose filled with mud, and I had to sneeze hard in order to clear it."

He took a couple of deep breaths. Staring straight into the sunlight through the patio windows, his thoughts had transported him back to the boy he had once been, pinned to the ground by tons of twisted steel and asking himself how long the rainwater would continue rising. He rubbed his hands up and down his long, thin arms, as if a sudden chill had invaded the cozy warmth of the restaurant.

"I stretched out my arms and grabbed hold of a rusty piece of exhaust pipe. Drawing it towards me, I started drumming on it with my fingers.

"I hummed in rhythm with it. Most people are used to thinking in words, while primitive peoples find it very easy to think in pictured images. Little children are also very good at it. I was now a skilled envisioner. As I have already told you, I used to combine the music that drifted into my room from the bar downstairs with the images in my mind, but while pinned beneath the wrecks I succeeded, for the first time, in creating the music myself and then exerting its influence on the images that invaded my senses. It worked very well and wasn't at all tiring. On the contrary, it invigorated me. I could make the kitten appear—perhaps I projected its image in the twilight, or the drumming and humming and image-forming transmitted a message into that little brain behind the saffron yellow eyes."

He gave a spontaneous laugh.

"I'm often told I've got cat's eyes—smaller but with that touch of yellow in the green—and as for the nine lives . . ."

He tailed off, as if that was another story, for another day, and then continued.

"Anyway, using my hands, voice and spirit, I succeeded in drawing that little creature to me time and time again. I repeated this exercise as often as I could. The small, wet body snuggled up against me, and the creature made a sound that came pretty near to purring. Later, when he was called Yo-yo and grew up, he learned to purr just like the big, contented cats."

"You got out from under, then, with the cat?"

"Yes, Paul, yes! Yo-yo lived for twenty years, fathered baskets of offspring and took up a place of pride on my father's bar. The customers were real fond of him. He was a damn good mouse- and rat-catcher too."

"Robert Bragg's auto dump," I persisted. "How did you get out from under the truck? And how long did you lay there?"

"Well, it was Saturday afternoon when I first got trapped in a place where even Bragg's dog couldn't reach me, and I didn't get out until Monday afternoon. I lay there on my belly in the mud for over forty-eight hours."

"Without any food."

"Without any sleep either. I kept drumming on the metal pipe with my fingers, and used my voice, even when my throat had become sore and I was terribly hoarse. My first composition lasted more than forty hours, and I remember vividly how my body started to hurt because I didn't really have enough room to fill my lungs properly. Singing, humming and drumming, I slipped into a sort of trance. I have no idea what the drop in temperature was when the day gave way to night. I was feverish and can't recall feeling the difference between the beads of sweat trickling down my face and the cold rain streaming along the undercarriage of the truck and dripping onto my forehead.

"I had learned to let musical tones send me on mental flight. I had learned to influence, change and control the images that invaded my mind. I now put these skills into action for a special purpose. Drumming and singing, I chose one of the numerous images that passed before me and saw myself in my bizarre predicament—lying under rusty steel in complete darkness. And when I changed the rhythm of my finger-drumming, I saw Robert Bragg in front of me, sitting in his rocking chair by the fire, gazing into the flames, idly stroking his dog and looking up attentively now and then.

"When he emerged from his house on Monday afternoon, he paid little attention to the truck driver who had come to tell him he had about twenty auto wrecks with him. Nor did he listen to another man who asked him if he could look around the scrap yard for a few parts for his old Dodge.

"'I need bumpers and a new door, and one or two engine parts,' the man told him, but Bragg didn't hear him.

"He strode purposefully over to his massive crane. As if hypnotized, he climbed into the cabin, switched on the engine of the impressive, cranelike machine and yanked it into gear. The caterpillar tracks shuddered to life, and he drove straight towards the biggest, highest heap of scrap in the yard. And I, pinned down in that shadowy, dank trap, knew he was coming. I saw him clearly before me—I saw the gray eyes in the blank face and the confident action of his hands on the gears and levers. The long jib rose high above the heap, and the giant claw suspended from it was slowly let out. As delicately as a crocodile picking up her eggs in her mouth, the great jaws of the claw closed over the uppermost wreck and hoisted it up. Bragg then played a little game; he picked up each wreck and set it down out of the way, where it slowly formed another heap. But never was there the slightest danger of a vehicle falling back onto the big heap and causing it to collapse.

"There are various tales told about what happened that day, most of them recounted after the event, in my father's bar. Folks asked why I hadn't yelled for help, so a potential rescuer could possibly have heard, and then been able to locate me from the sound. Some compared me to a bird who, frozen in terror, forgets that it can fly. But, as you know, I was in no kind of state to yell. My chest was pressed to the ground, and I could only hum and sing.

"Others claimed that Robert Bragg discovered me quite by accident while he was busy setting his crane, searching for a wrecked Dodge to salvage for a guy who stopped by looking for parts.

"Someone who witnessed everything first-hand was Stan Manselli, a police officer who was out looking for me. Apparently the police had been searching for me everywhere, and Manselli had heard my brother say that I could often be found snooping around the scrap yard. He had left his car parked at the yard with the door open. When there was no response to his calls, he jumped up into the cab of the crane and yelled into Bragg's ear, 'Have you seen any sign of Beck's boy around here?'

"'What do you think I'm doing right now, picking apples? Can't you hear it? The metal's singing, the trucks are talking. I know exactly where he is, and I'm going to get him out from under!'

"Stan Manselli didn't understand a word he said. He certainly didn't hear any singing metal, and no images appeared before his eyes—he only noticed how extremely carefully Bragg hoisted one auto after another between the steel jaws of the claw, and set each just as delicately down twenty yards away.

"Manselli was a big, fat man, with a black moustache and shrewd, dark brown eyes. He crossed his arms over his broad chest and followed Robert Bragg's skilled maneuvers with manly respect.

"The truck driver and the guy with the Dodge stood next to him.

"I continued my musical improvisations, feeling secure in the knowledge that everything above my head was going smoothly. Manselli and the two men couldn't hear anything—but then, I wasn't drumming and humming for them. I was doing it for Robert Bragg, who was applying himself to the task at hand as meticulously as a surgeon with his scalpel.

"At last, he breached the wall of wrecks; the crane was throttled down into silence, and only the mangled truck was left hulking over my head. Now the men, too, heard someone singing softly to a metallic beat. Manselli, realizing that I must be pinned under the truck, sprang into action. He dropped onto his hands and crawled across the muddy, soggy ground, without a thought for his spotless uniform.

"'Pass me a spade!' he called to Bragg. "'The boy's here! He's alive! But he can't get out from under the truck. He must be pinned down somehow. How the hell did he get himself in there in the first place?'

"To the cop's surprise, Bragg started up the motor of the massive crane again. Swinging on its hoist chain, the massive claw descended over the truck. The officer shot back onto his feet and raised both hands in urgent protest.

"'You damn fool! Turn off that motor! That truck is way too heavy! One wrong move could be the death of that boy. Do you hear me, Bragg?'

"The claw continued to descend, but no longer swung back and forth. Manselli nervously stroked his black moustache with the fingers of his left hand. His right hand went for his revolver, and he pointed it straight at Robert Bragg.

"'Did you hear what I said?'

"The muzzle of the gun moved upwards and Manselli fired a single warning shot into the air, but Bragg showed no reaction to it. The great steel jaws of the claw closed over the truck. Heaving and snorting like some medieval dragon, the crane began to tilt forwards. Bragg worked the levers skillfully and stared straight in front of him. The bed of the truck was raised clear off the ground as the rusted cabin broke loose and fell to one side.

"The police officer slipped his revolver back into its holster and ran forward. He picked me up and pressed me to his big, warm, comforting belly.

"'Francis! Oh man, how'd you get yourself into that mess?'

"Bragg, the truck driver and the Dodge guy came running over to me. The Alsatian-cross dog also came bounding and barking towards us from the porch of the wooden house.

"I folded my arms across my chest like a dead pharaoh, holding my bleeding, torn fingers rigidly apart. Tucked carefully on my chest, under my arms, was nestled the lost kitten that I later named Yo-yo, who was to be my loyal little friend for so many years.

"This traumatic experience proved to be a turning point in my life. Never again would I know true rest, never again would I experience the solace and comfort of sleep. I would go on to learn how to compose music and play instruments—from the piano to the violin, from the organ to the trumpet. And from that time on, I increasingly found myself thinking in images rather than words.

"But first I had to be taken home in Stan Manselli's old black and white Chevy.

"Leaving the truck driver and the guy with the Dodge at the scrap yard, Robert Bragg said he'd come along too, and quickly slipped into the back seat—knowing full well that when my father learned he had rescued me, drinks would be on the house.

"Only when I finally got home did I let go of the little black cat and begin to feel the pain surging through my fingers."

For a while we sat opposite one another in silence. I took a sip of my coffee and found that it had gone cold. Francis breathed a deep sigh and continued his story.

"That's the way it was. It's etched on my memory — which is not surprising, when you think of the drastic effect it had on my life. I live alone, I never married, I write music for myself and for others, I transmute images into tonal chords and play games with absurd concepts, with weird and wondrous thoughts—"

"Such as?" I interjected.

Francis jiggled his glass and watched the mineral water slop back and forth.

"Well, take this water, for example. It can set me to thinking. Maybe this very water I'm drinking now was also drunk thousands of years ago by a mammoth. We only have a certain amount of water on earth, and that must serve us for all eternity. So who's to say that there isn't a tiny drop in this glass that didn't once find its way into the innards of a mammoth or a woolly rhinoceros? Thoughts like this become visual, from pictures I once saw, and then I sort of flesh them out from my own imagination."

"Ah-ha! You mean things that are impossible to prove, but could very well be true nevertheless. Right? Something that springs to my mind in that context is the vast gold treasure of ancient Egypt. The gold that fell into the hands of the tomb robbers was melted down to cover their tracks, and in time found its way all over the world. You can't exclude the possibility that the gold in one of the rings on your finger contains a tiny amount that was part of an adornment that once graced the body of a citizen of ancient Memphis or Thebes."

Francis looked at me long and hard and then slowly nodded his head.

"Exactly! That's a pretty good example, Paul. But come, shall we press on now? I'm really glad that you listened to my story."

He stood up and pulled on his sports jacket. "What do you say we run another couple of miles, and then head back to Rotterdam?"

"Fine," I replied. "We need to be back in time to get in some more rehearsal before the concert this evening. Personally, I can't wait to experience what happens when you conjure up images with your music. After all you've told me, I'm naturally eaten up with curiosity. Could you give a demonstration?"

"In the main hall of De Doelen? With the entire orchestra present?"

"It would be really extraordinary—totally mind-blowing!"

"Very well," said Francis, as we left the restaurant. "But can we drop by my hotel first, so I can change? And I've got something there for you. An envelope, but you must promise not to open it until after the concert. Okay?"

Francis broke into a run, and I followed him. We sprinted across the bridge and along the lakeside path. I tried to breathe through my nose as long as I could, but was soon forced to open my mouth and fill my lungs with the icy-cold but refreshing air. When we finally stopped, I noticed that the American's breathing was not at all stressed. We gazed out once more over the lake, and he pointed to a spot in the distance.

"Gouda must be over in that direction," he said.

"How come someone who lives in New York, and is visiting Holland for the first time, knows where a town such as Gouda is?" I asked, puzzled.

"Because I happen to know that Stolwijk is quite close to Gouda," he answered matter-of-factly, which was intriguing, but didn't help me a lot.

I was even more intrigued when he proceeded to clean his nails with the prongs of the fork I had used to eat my cake in the restaurant, and had put back on the plate. Then he flung the fork out towards the lake, sending it dancing and slithering over the thin layer of ice encrusting the bank, only to plop into the water farther out.

"That's also become a habit of mine," he remarked. "I'm forever walking off with all sorts of things."

"What is so special about Stolwijk?" I asked, ignoring this latest demonstration of his odd behavioral patterns.

I was getting used to Francis Beck's eccentricity by now.

"Okay, I'll try to explain. When I told you my theory about a drop of mineral water, you reacted so well, telling me about the ancient gold and all that, that I thought maybe you were beginning to remember something."

"What are you talking about?"

"Maybe I'm mistaken. Its better to wait until the time arrives for you to open the envelope. Anyway, you asked what was special about Stolwijk. Well, way back in the fifteenth century, it was the home of two extraordinary alchemists named Isaac and Johan Isaac Hollandus. They knew exactly how the philosopher's stone was made, from which the elixir of life was produced. It is said that they were father and son, but if they possessed this secret of eternal youth, you must ask yourself: How could anyone tell which one was the father and which one was the son? Perhaps the father looked much younger than his son, or they might even have been brothers, or not related at all. But they definitely lived in Stolwijk, performed miracles and left written proof of their work."

"This sort of thing intrigues you, doesn't it?"

"And what about you? Aren't you just as curious?"

I gave a little shrug of my shoulders, attempting to seem cool. I was running up quite a sweat trying to keep pace with this fleet-footed man. To be honest, I hadn't understood all that much of what he had said. We jogged a while longer, and then I drove him back to his hotel.

I waited for him outside the Hilton Hotel, and when he reappeared and slipped into the passenger seat, he handed me an envelope. Later, I would remove from it the photograph that was taken during April in the year 1932. Ten minutes later we joined the members of the orchestra in De Doelen.

* * *

The composition we played contained a constantly recurring theme. The plaintive sound of the violins swelled over the auditorium, and the kettledrums beat the air, followed by a quieter section that was dominated by the gentle strains of the harp. It was a particularly graphic piece that made me think of a sea as smooth as glass, where a slow buildup of rippling waves swelled the rolling wall of surf until it crashed onto the shore in a mighty crescendo, only to ebb gently back over the sand and return to the waiting waters.

We rehearsed with the full orchestra. The conductor let us play until Francis Beck took his place at the grand piano. I had already informed the conductor that the composer was going to enable us to actually see images via his music.

The musicians played softer now. Most had closed their eyes and opened their minds to whatever impressions the piano music would give them. The piece had not been specially written for the piano, but from the moment that Francis began to play, the chords he evoked from the keys became the carriers of the composition, and our instruments acted merely as a background accompaniment. We supported his playing and allowed ourselves to be carried away on the powerful sound of the Bechstein grand in full flight.

The auditorium was empty. Not a single seat was occupied. We were playing only for ourselves. We repeated the same theme over and over—but no longer did I picture still waters slowly rising into tidal waves. I rose up out of my body and looked down on the illuminated orchestra circle, with its great organ and the row of chairs behind it, all gradually becoming smaller. De Doelen and I floated somewhere in midair. Hearing with my ears was replaced by receiving with my brain. I no longer saw through my eyes, but through my mind. Sounds were transmuted into images. I looked down on Rotterdam as if I were in a plane.

Beck's hands glided over the keys, casting a spell which sent the orchestra up to the heavens, where they had a bird's-eye view of the greatest port in the world, the ships that lay at anchor in the Nieuwe Maas, and of the Willemsbrug that linked Rotterdam South to the city center. We soon began to drift back to earth, coming to rest on the Schouwburgplein, a square just in front of De Doelen. With an aerial photograph of the city still fixed upon our retinas, we continued playing automatically, but needed some time to adjust ourselves to the fact that the square was now bustling with people who looked very different from ourselves. Some wore little more than tattered rags, while others dressed in colorful clothes. There was work going on all over the square. Everyone seemed to be busy helping lay the foundations of a large building of some sort. A team of more than a hundred laborers dragged a huge cart filled with heavy stones. Masons set their iron chisels against the stone blocks and tapped them gently with large wooden hammers, while lads carted burning lime and sand for the mortar-makers. The whole square buzzed with activity, and on a place that had never boasted anything like this in its entire history, something incredible happened. To the ascending chords of the grand piano, there arose a beautiful cathedral of breathtaking grandeur.

We looked at the master builder, at the blacksmiths, the plasterers, carpenters, glaziers, stonemasons, scaffolders, sculptors and slate workers, and at the many revered master craftsmen with their apprentices, whose combined skills attended the growth of the great building. Men trod along treadmills to hoist the building materials. Tall pillars and flying buttresses were constructed, built by fragile human hands. It all happened in front of our eyes—we saw the cathedral rise, from the foundation to the roof, and our music was instrumental to that growth. We crafted it around the pianist, and heard it echoing across the forty-yard-high vaulted ceiling.

We now became aware of more intricate details. Falling chips of masonry revealed holy statues being freed from the rock—as if the figures, kneeling in prayer, had been imprisoned in stone for eons, waiting for the blow of the artist's hammer to break away everything that enclosed their form.

Gargoyles—monster heads, whose gaping mouths were meant to drain off the rainwater—now gushed with blood and colored the entire cathedral red.

The workers shinned down the ropes and wooden scaffolding. The great doors of the cathedral were opened, and the master builder led a huge crowd of people out. Screams could be heard above the music. The secret of the structure was revealed. A hand pulled a stone from one of the walls, and everything collapsed.

Just as the chancel of the Beauvais cathedral had caved in back in 1298, marking the demise of the great medieval architectural period, so now fell the building on the Schouwburgplein in Rotterdam, with an earsplitting crash—accompanied way off in the background by the resounding chords of a grand piano.

The fallen gargoyles continued spouting blood. A man lay under the rubble with his arms outstretched towards me, and I saw Francis Beck lying there. I saw myself moving towards him. He cried for help, and I began to remove the debris from the pile stone by stone. It was a hopeless task, but I hadn't the slightest intention of giving up.

Just as Robert Bragg had hoisted the wrecked autos out of the way with his crane in order to rescue the trapped boy, so did I heave those stones from the pile to free the man.

My jaw dropped in amazement when I saw Francis stand up, shake the rubble from himself like a dog shaking off water, and walk towards me. The clothes he wore resembled those worn in medieval paintings. Something moved under his leather doublet, and for one horrifying moment I thought his heart had burst out of his body and was beating under his clothes—a thought that was strengthened by the blood that covered him, spewed out from those grotesque stone monster heads. But then he produced a young black cat, held it out towards me with both hands and laughed amiably.

My violin produced sweet and gentle sounds. For a moment I saw the Schouwburgplein before me just as it had always been, with the theater on one side and De Doelen on the other. Restaurants, terraces, vegetable stalls abounded in the surrounding neighborhood. Then I saw Francis Beck, bending tautly over the keys, his fingers pounding out an impassioned closing sequence to his astounding work. Next, I became aware of the sweat-soaked faces of my orchestral colleagues—their expressions of disbelief, their dazed awakening from the dream.

I felt their eyes staring at me.

I was the man who had dragged Francis Beck from under the rubble of the Rotterdam cathedral and had taken the black cat that he offered me. If only they knew that I understood as little about the entire bizarre happening as they did. Our conductor walked towards the piano, or rather, he tottered unsteadily towards it as if he were drunk, placed a hand on the American's shoulder and stammered, "Have we all had the same experience? Have we all seen a cathedral built to perfection, only to see it all fall apart again?"

"Everyone saw it," said Francis.

We could hear his voice clearly. It was now completely silent in the hall.

"How in heaven's name can anyone possibly bring about such a thing?"

The man behind the piano straightened his back and placed his hands on his thighs.

"There's a well-known anecdote about the English and their marvelous gardens. A foreigner once asked a gardener how it was that his lawn always looked so immaculate. 'Regular and thorough weeding and mowing,' answered the Englishman, to which he added after a short pause, 'and that for century after century!' Time is the perfecter of art."

That evening we played Francis Beck's music to a packed auditorium. Just before the intermission he seated himself at the piano and played a short piece with sublime virtuosity. After the concert he appeared to have vanished into thin air. A few days later I was to hear he had met his death in a burning car.

* * *

After stopping at a cafe for a cup of coffee, I braved the bitter cold night again. It was quiet and deserted, the sort of atmosphere where you find yourself listening to your own footsteps. I quickened my pace and hurried back home. I had put the photograph back into the envelope and decided that I wouldn't take it out again—ever.

Francis Beck had disappeared.

I had the feeling that I must learn to live with countless questions, the answers to which I would never know.

 # 2 -The Pressure of Life

I slotted new frets onto the fingerboard of a guitar, and when I examined the result I felt sure that the customer would be more than satisfied. Then I set about restringing the instrument. As I adjusted the tuning pegs, it struck me that this was the only job I'd done today, and I hadn't sold a single thing. My income was in a decidedly low key, and it didn't look as if it would be hitting any high notes in the foreseeable future either.

I had a good view of the shop from my workbench. The stringed instruments gleamed softly in the warm glow of the overhead lamps. Violins hung in a long, soldierly row on the wall, and under them stood guitars, contrabasses, cellos and even a single, elegant harp. I didn't know very much about wind instruments, and I normally bought one only when an orchestra colleague assured me that the resale would be profitable. I did keep the odd trumpet, oboe, flute or clarinet in stock, and from the ceiling there hung a mighty tuba that was beyond repair and unable to blast anyone's ear anymore, but now served to catch the eye of the passers-by.

After I had put the guitar away, I returned to my workbench, leaned back in my old chair, cupped my hands behind my head and thought about Francis Beck, and about the people who had paid him their last respects. In addition to the musicians and a few representatives from the press, there were a couple of American mourners present.

"Why wasn't he taken back to the United States?" I had overheard someone ask.

"Apparently he left specific instructions with his lawyer covering this eventuality," was the response. "No fuss, no mass gathering of admirers. Everything was to take place right here, and in silence. He didn't overlook a single detail. And since he had no close relatives, the owner of the music publishing company that has all Francis Beck's compositions in its keeping anticipates inheriting his entire estate. With the exception of his house in New York, which is to be sold, plus what remains in his bank account—all those proceeds, I understand, are to go to some charity or other." A timpanist from the orchestra and a journalist were discussing this, and I gathered that the latter had gotten this information directly from America.

I put my feet up among the tools on my workbench and pondered the fickle finger of fate.

Right now, there was some institution, society, fund or whatever, that was about to receive a couple of million dollars out of the blue because a composer had driven himself to death against a concrete pillar. Charitable thoughts on the luck of strangers don't come easily, and if there was one thing I could have used myself right then, it was definitely a large legacy.

Then I noticed someone standing outside the front door of the shop. A man in a long overcoat was peering in through the glass. It was still bitterly cold outdoors, so I wasn't surprised that he wore a woolly knitted hat and a scarf wrapped up to his eyes. He had both hands plunged into his pockets and leaned sideways, bending to open the door with his elbow. The door swooshed slowly shut behind him. He shuffled unsteadily forward across the shop right up to my workbench, where he stood swaying a little. I swung my legs onto the floor and gripped the arms of my chair defensively.

The eyes of the man looked directly into mine. I noticed the narrow bridge of the nose, the fair eyebrows that met in the middle and the short curly hair peeking out from under the knitted hat. The eyes were green. My fingers tightened their grip on the wooden arms of the chair, my toes curled and I pushed myself back on my heels. I now turned my eyes from the man to the tools laid out between us on the bench. Small, razor-sharp knives lay there for the grabbing, if necessary. I couldn't imagine why the man standing before me would want to attack me, but if he did, I could at least defend myself. The fact that he kept his hands in his coat pockets also had an unnerving effect on me.

If he wasn't Francis Beck, then he was probably some villain after my cash or one of the more costly instruments. But the suspicion, however incredible, that it was indeed Francis grew steadily stronger. I recognized his voice immediately when he said, "Ah, yes. I've always associated you with the smell of wood, glue and polish. Hello, Paul. If you're not expecting anyone else today, I suggest you close the shop and invite me up to your apartment. I've got a lot to tell you, a lot to explain."

Standing up, getting out my keys and nudging past him, I felt myself suddenly begin to tremble. I put out my hand, intending to steady myself on his shoulder.

"Don't touch me!" he cried out. "I'm standing on shattered legs."

This tidbit served the purpose of further stupefying me. I walked on with difficulty, turned the key in the lock, stopped and took a couple of deep breaths. The moment I approached him for the second time, I noticed how very cautiously he lifted one of his feet.

I switched off the light in the shop and mounted the stairs. I heard him shuffling across the floor behind me. He followed me. Step for step, painfully slow, he began to climb the stairs. It was as if I had the devil himself on my heels, and I hurriedly switched on the light in the living room and sat down on the sofa.

He remained standing in the middle of the room, swaying slightly to and fro on his feet.

"Is it really you?" I began. "Or are you someone else? You have Francis Beck's eyes and his voice, but I can see little else of you, all muffled up in that coat, hat and scarf. Do sit down, please, and let me see your face!"

Totally thrown and distracted, waiting for him to make a move, I looked around my familiar room: I'd never made much of it really. I often worked on my instruments here, and tools were scattered all over the place. The table was strewn with violin parts. Rows of books lined the wall, spilling over into stacks on the wooden floor. I'd never got around to buying a bookcase. My only other visible possessions were a low wooden chest, a coffee table and a three-piece suit. The man stood in front of one of the easy chairs and finally took his hands out of his pockets. The hands dangled loosely this way and that, as if they were attached to his forearms with elastic.

"My wrists are broken," he grunted, "and my ankles are in the same state. Have you ever tried to unfasten the buttons of a coat with fingers that you can scarcely move? Give me a hand here."

Unable to believe what I was hearing, I stood up and unbuttoned his coat, which he shrugged off by flexing his shoulders. He wore a white shirt heavily stained with blood. His upper body swayed backwards, while his feet remained in the same position, and I heard dry, cracking noises, like the snapping of small pieces of bone. Then he collapsed onto the easy chair and in a voice as broken as his body, stammered, "My hat and scarf . . . take them off for me. . . ."

I gently removed the knit hat from his head. His short hair was covered in a helmet of dried blood, and his forehead was black and blue. I undid the knot and unwound his scarf with even more care and trepidation. The skin on his chin was badly grazed, and his lips were swollen.

"I'm afraid this is all getting to be a bit too much for me," I gasped. "I'll have to sit down for a minute."

"Well, this is what you get when you drive your car headlong into concrete." He grimaced, trying to summon a laugh from his mutilated lips.

"Nobody can walk on broken legs," I reasoned, trying to hold onto my sanity and ward off that tightening in my throat that threatened my breathing again.

I didn't understand how I had had the presence of mind to close my shop and go upstairs with this man.

"There must be ten thousand people in this world who are mourning the death of a composer tonight. I can imagine that the New York media are giving it plenty of prime-time slots and front page space. I witnessed a cremation! So who the hell is sitting here opposite me?"

He opened his mouth, and I saw a scarlet tongue gingerly moisten the broken lips. Then he began to speak.

"Just stop and think how you have reacted to all this so far. Anyone else would have rung for a doctor, an ambulance—or simply panicked. Don't worry about me, Paul. I'll be fine. It is all a question of time. And that's something we've got plenty of. The photograph that was taken in 1932 isn't the only clue I've given you. In fact, I've been trying to jog your memory all along. Get me a glass of water, will you, but keep listening to what I tell you. Okay? And don't worry about the physical state I'm in. I thought maybe I'd triggered your recall when I spoke about the mammoths and mineral water."

"I remember that very well, because you mentioned it again later. And I responded by telling you something similar I'd imagined about the gold of Egypt that was melted down."

"You and I, Paul, have melted down more gold than you could imagine in your wildest dreams. Believe me, you are not 'forty something.' You are older by a couple of hundred years, and that makes you just about my age."

I had just fetched a bottle of mineral water from the fridge, and I was unscrewing the top. I felt myself trembling again.

"I have almost total recall. It's a mixed blessing," I heard him say behind me. "You, however, have finally discovered a very simple trick to help you withstand the pressure of time on your mind. You have suppressed your past. If you think I'm making this up, tell me what year you were born in, what your father did for a living, and where you spent your youth."

"I—" I started to say, when he broke in.

"How long have you been living in Rotterdam?"

Wolf Tears

"As long as I can remember. Or rather, maybe twenty or twenty-five years or longer!"

"Where did you come from?"

I gave no answer, but poured a glass of water and put it on the coffee table in front of him.

"There was a significant clue in the answer I gave to your orchestra conductor—time is the perfecter of art. Those who possess a musical talent and see hypnagogic images pass before them need more than a lifetime to learn what I have mastered!"

Suddenly and forcefully, his arm shot forward. The hand flapped back and forth, and the fingers ticked against the glass. By manipulating his shoulder, he somehow managed to get his thumb and fingers around it, but as he lifted it to his mouth half the contents slopped over. It took a lot of effort to get the glass to his lips, and when he drank I noticed blood trickling down the inside of the rim. Only then did I pull myself together enough to help him drink.

"I told you about my youth. New Jersey. A one-horse town. Well, I wasn't born in New Jersey. I never had a bedroom above a bar. The automobile graveyard is likewise a fiction. Robert Bragg, the Russell family, Ben Lewis, Officer Manselli with the black moustache: they're all imagined characters. It all revolves around the theme—that's what matters."

"And Yo-yo, the black cat," I cut in, feeling a growing anger because he'd lied about a tom cat that was supposed to have lived for more than twenty years.

"It's the theme that matters," Francis repeated. "And you see why? You only show anger now I've mentioned the cat. That creature came back when I seated myself at the piano. I built a cathedral for you that never really existed, and then I allowed it to collapse. I had hoped that my version would trigger your memory. Once, Paul, we really did work together on the construction of a church. And this time I am telling the truth! A black cat used to hang around the building site for days on end, and we both got pretty attached to him. One day a wall collapsed, and I became trapped. You pulled me out from under the rubble, and I can still see the surprise on your face when I got out, holding the cat in my arms. We both laughed because you seemed to be more concerned about the cat than about me."

I raised my hand, palm upwards—questioning:

"Okay. Suppose your absurd story is true this time. Then why didn't you tell me right away that we'd known each other longer than—"

"Than many lifetimes in a row?" he broke in, finishing my question with an involuntary laugh that split open his injured lips. They bled anew; with a side twist of the head, he wiped them off on the top of his shirt.

"I have done my damnedest to help you remember certain things of your own accord. If I'd told you straight off who I was and who you were, you would only have marked me down as talented but completely deranged. Right?"

"I still don't know who you are."

"You don't know who you are yourself either! Your memory only goes back twenty-five years. You've suppressed everything—but you'll have to face the truth sooner or later, because danger is lurking everywhere. Just look at me. Or do you imagine I drove that automobile into a concrete pillar for a joke? Then, to add insult to injury, grabbed an innocent passer-by, shoved him behind the wheel, and set fire to the whole kit and caboodle? You all paid your final respects to someone who was out to get me, and not for the purpose of composing a sonata for him—oh no! And if he had known who you really are, maybe he would have come after you instead of me."

"So the fire was necessary to make it impossible to identify the remains," I prompted.

"Exactly. It was my automobile. I had rented it. The man wasn't much taller than me, and my rings fit his fingers. Nobody doubted the fact that I was the man behind the wheel."

"But perhaps your pursuer was of a different blood type?"

His green eyes widened, and he stared meaningfully at me from the ravaged face.

"You can take it from me that no one knows my blood group! As a matter of fact, blood plays an important part in all this. Mine, and yours! I've already spoken to you about Isaac and Johan Isaac Hollandus."

"You mean the two alchemists from Stolwijk. The fifteenth century. Father and son. The elixir of life—all that?"

"Yes, I spoke of them because I'd hoped it would help you recall your own buried past—then you would understand. I never knew the Hollanduses. But there were three other people who had the elixir of life in their possession, and those I know only too well: namely, you and I and the man who currently calls himself Rainer Miethe. The old fox imagined he was immortal, but is in a bad way these days. Our eternal friend now fears for his life and so has his heart set on hunting us down."

"I never heard of anyone called Rainer Miethe."

"You've known him as long as I have."

"How can I believe that I am so old?"

"You don't believe it. It still needs to enter your consciousness from the hidden recesses of your mind. For the present though, it would make things a lot easier if you simply took my word for it, Paul. The elixir of life! Every atom of your body and mine is worth its weight in gold to science. Rainer is ill. Dangerously ill. He has acquired the taste for eternal life and will move heaven and earth to cheat death. He knows that we still enjoy excellent health, that my brains are in good working order, and that you have gone to ground, as it were, and are fettered at present by what we must call 'loss of memory,' for want of a better phrase. Now are you beginning to understand a little?"

I shook my head.

"I'm trying, but—the idea—it's too crazy!"

"Listen. There is a belief in an afterlife. There is a belief in reincarnation. Millions of people believe in life after death and rebirth into another body. I think you would be open to a discussion about that, right? We could talk for hours about belief, religion and life after death. But if I tell you that there is also such a thing as an eternal earthly life, you dismiss it at once. The raven lives for seventy, eighty years, my friend, while the sparrow dies after only a few. Yet they are both birds of a feather!"

It needled me that I really wasn't able to go back into my own past more than twenty-five years. My life was off track, that much I knew. I only had to look at the man sitting opposite me, with his broken body and lacerated face, and the scarlet stains on his shirt, which darkened and spread even as I watched. He was silent now, so I took his glass to the kitchen, rinsed it clean and filled it with mineral water. I helped him to drink some more. He took small sips, and then signaled me with a blink of his eyes that he'd had enough.

"If I read you right, you're asking me to give you the benefit of the doubt for the time being, yes? Very well. I'll listen and give serious thoughts to your words."

"That's great! I'll make it short. Is there anywhere I can stay where I'll be unnoticed?"

I thought for a minute.

"I've got a boat. It's moored quite near here. I can take care of food for you."

"That won't be necessary. Water will suffice. Could you moor the boat anywhere else?"

"I think so. You remember when we jogged along the Rotterdam lakes? You sank to your knees on that jetty when you suddenly had a headache? There's mooring space for boats there, and it's quiet at this time of the year. There's a gas stove to keep you warm and a tape deck with earphones. You can drift and dream for hours with those on."

"Sounds ideal. How soon can you fix that up for me?"

"In no time! I can even navigate there in the dark."

"That's settled then. I hope to be back to normal in a few days. You must get away from here too, Paul. I'll explain about Miethe in more detail later. Right now I'll just say that I suspected he had picked up my trail—the trail I had deliberately set for him by breaking my cover, as it were. He is aware of my talents. That's why I allowed my audience in America to experience the most fantastic things during my concerts and did the same thing in Europe. Strangers falling in love in the auditorium in Stockholm, something bloody in Paris—you know the story. Here in Rotterdam I had a gun shoved under my nose. That weapon is now lying in a ditch, and the man who threatened me with it spilled a lot of informative beans when I grabbed it and shoved the muzzle under his nostrils. Paul, I've earned a fortune with my compositions in the past years. For us! You will need to find someone to look after your shop temporarily. You can sell the entire business later and never return. As soon as we're on board I'll explain why you must disappear from here. We can leave right now as far as I'm concerned, and I hope you'll lend me your support, because I don't think I can get far on these legs."

"Do you need any painkillers? You must get some sleep!"

"Thanks, but I really don't need anything. And I never sleep."

"I know. Ever since you were fourteen."

"Yes, well that isn't entirely true. Near the end of the last century I suddenly found I no longer needed to!"

* * *

I lifted him up as if he were a child and carried him downstairs. His hands and feet dangled loosely, like a puppet's, every time he moved. Once outside I supported him as well as I could, and heaved a sigh of relief when I finally eased him into the passenger seat of my car. We drove to the outskirts of town, where my small cabin cruiser was moored. I carried him along the jetty and helped him aboard.

The gas stove soon warmed the cabin. I had laid Francis on a bunk bed. He was still wearing his torn, bloodstained clothes. I eased the shoes off his broken feet as gently as I could. Then finally—and thankfully—covered him with a warm blanket. His face glistened with sweat. Staring straight in front of himself, he began to ramble. His voice was weak, and he was forced to swallow repeatedly. The torn lips peeled painfully apart like red tissue paper, and every now and then he licked the edge of his incisor teeth with his scarlet tongue.

"It would be a ghastly coincidence if either one of us had the same blood group as Rainer Miethe. Can you imagine? Held captive. Unable to move freely about anymore. Blood transfusions. Your blood might help keep him healthy. You would be like a piggy bank. You would give blood again and again, over and over: the horn of plenty! Your veins would never run dry; you would continue giving just enough to keep Rainer Miethe in fierce fettle!"

He swallowed two or three times.

"We have come far, Paul. We have seen so much—so very much. After the epidemics of the plague halfway through the fourteenth century claimed millions of victims, new generations arose who desired eternal life. The elixirs of life were dangerous. They contained mercury. Those who wished to prolong their lives were actually slowly destroying themselves. But the elixir we had, you, Rainer and I—that was pure! It does not grant immortality, Paul! No it does not! Yet the lifetimes are long. And we have seen all those generations come and go, and have bound ourselves to no one. We remained childless and alone. For who would want to love and live with a wife, only to watch her swiftly age while you yourself remained the same? Don't worry about me. Perhaps you think I'll die, but I won't, you know, I will remain alive. We still have so much to discuss. But first you really need to regain your memory!

"Slowly, very slowly, we do grow older. Right now we look forty-something. When we drank the elixir of life, we had just turned twenty. It has taken us centuries to age twenty years. We are so young on the outside, yet so old on the inside. I can't put it simpler than that, Paul."

I started the engine of my small craft. Francis was still talking, but less coherently now, and I couldn't catch all his words. I stood behind the steering wheel as the boat cut cleanly through the dark water, cracking the thin layer of ice that rode the waves on either side of the bow. It wasn't that late, but on these winter evenings a murky pall hung over the lakes. I looked up for comfort at the brightly lit windows in the houses along the Rottekade, sailed up Oud Verlaat, on the watch for a suitable jetty to which I could tie up. I thought it would be best to make fast among other craft, so that my nameless boat would not attract attention. Boating people didn't hang around for long here in the winter, and only came now and then to check the condition of their own boats. I'd draw the cabin curtains before I left, and then nobody would suspect that there was somebody lying in the bunk.

I imagined that Francis would make use of my tape recorder to listen to some classical music on the earphones. On the one hand I couldn't help feeling that I'd return in a few days to find a corpse in the cabin, and on the other hand, weirdly enough, I could somehow imagine that the broken bones would knit together again, that the injured face would heal and the wounds on his body would disappear, leaving no scars.

The boat lay still, the motor silent. The gas from the stove streamed up with a clearly audible *phwishhh,* which, once set, kept going. The man on the bed was still talking, and now I could make sense out of his words.

"The pressure of life! You've lived through too many years to grasp it all now, Paul. There is no longer any depth in your thoughts. The way back is too long. For you, suppression seems better than remembrance. The photograph! The photo from 1932. We knew Rotterdam after the great fire of 1563. We knew the inner city before the bombardment in 1940 like the backs of our hands. We already had so much behind us when that photo was taken. But we were still friends! Forget the old-fashioned clothes we're wearing—just look at our faces. We were friends, Paul, and it is as friends that we must go forward. Where all this will end is, and shall probably remain, a mystery. But one thing at least is clear—we need each other. Look at me. At the state I'm in! Yet the thought of giving up life doesn't enter my head. Even for us, the day will come when we shall die. But until that time comes we must each take care not to become the victims of investigators who seek to know the secret of the precious potion we once received. Meanwhile we must, above all, be wary of our former friend, Rainer Miethe!

"Don't ask me what the precise year of your birth is, Paul. I can't even say with any certainty what mine is either. I only know that we're both around the same age and first saw the light of day at the beginning of the fifteenth century. If you ever recollect that stretch along your lifetime, the knowledge will probably hit you like a sledgehammer. Your wisest course would be to open your mind to the truth and prepare yourself for some unique and altogether devastating memories."

"The Hollanduses. Suppose you are speaking the absolute truth. Are we Hollanduses, Francis?"

"No. If we had journeyed to the lowlands in that time, we could have visited them and discovered for ourselves whether or not they were father and son, or brothers, or whatever. Or indeed, because of the elixir of life, perhaps the father was actually younger than his son, or they were both the same age and enjoyed eternal life."

"I can't fathom any of this. It overwhelms me, and I've got no idea how I'm supposed to react. But you're right on one thing: Try as I might, I can't form a picture of my early past. I can't remember my parents and know nothing about my situation before I was around twenty years old."

I flinched, suddenly taken aback by something that had never before entered my mind.

"Rotterdam," I heard myself saying. "Three elements of alchemy can be found in air, earth and water. The bombardment took care of the fourth element—fire. Why did this suddenly pop into my head for no apparent reason, Francis?"

He grinned.

"Because, as I hope, you are at last beginning to recall your past. I'm only too aware that I come across to you as this incredibly weird stranger, but never once did you start to panic. Certain reactions don't change, even if you have forgotten what it is that makes you respond that way. Maybe you could call it instinct—experiences that have been built up over centuries, resulting in a certain manner of behavior. Just suppose, Paul, that we still had the black cat that, along with me, you dragged out from under the rubble of the collapsed cathedral. What would happen to a cat that has drunk the elixir of life—that survives its legendary nine lives and lives on forever—if it were discovered? It would end up in a laboratory, undergoing scientific research, that's what! And if we don't watch out, that's where we'll end up too!"

"I don't know what to do right now," I said. "It's getting late, and I don't much feel like leaving my boat and going to the restaurant to phone for a taxi. We'll sort things out tomorrow. Anyway, you'll probably need my help. Your nutrition needs are few, to say the least, and there's enough food and drink on board for mine. I'll make myself comfortable on the other bunk. Then if you need anything, just ask me. I can put some music on for you, we can talk, or we can remain quiet. Hopefully I can get in a few hours sleep and, even more hopefully, you will look a whole lot better when the sun comes up."

"We're safe here," was Francis's response. "Yes, you tuck yourself up under a blanket, and then listen to me. I can't move my hands to beat out a rhythm, I can't tap my feet to measure out a tempo—but I can hum, and if you listen, I can tell you something about your early years. You will again experience the time when you roamed around as a hobo, a carpenter and later a maker of stringed instruments. Lie down, close your eyes and listen to my melody. Let the pressure of life become lighter, so that the world of the past will open up for you, and you will realize that you have a long life behind you. Give yourself up to the sound that I will create, and dare to divide yourself into the alchemical duality of the earthly toad and the eagle in the air—linked by a chain: the chain of body to spirit. I will let you see your life on earth as through the eyes of an eagle in flight."

I stretched out on the bunk next to him, drew the blanket up to my chin and listened to the soft hiss of the gas stove. I felt the warmth caressing my cheeks.

In the familiar surroundings of my own little motor launch I drifted to the gentle humming that came from the throat of Francis Beck—a sonorous melody that entered my subconscious when he exhaled through his nostrils, and fell silent when he filled his lungs through his bloodied, open mouth.

The pressure of life was released and gave wings to a wondrous lightness of being.

Memories welled up, the eagle looked down on the toad, and with my mind's eye I gazed into the depths of my own past.

 3 -Native Ground

The bird of prey moved away from the amphibian, but remained connected to it as though attached with a chain—just as during a mystical session, the astral body leaves the physical one and the connection consists only of an elastic cord rooted in the pineal gland—the third eye. Floating on wings of fantasy, I looked down at the world with the sharp eyes of an eagle.

Everything around me was of wood. Trees—branches, trunks and roots. The wood weeped, its resin falling like tears, and the smell tickled the senses of my spirit. I set my knife into the living wood, which caused more honey-colored tears to cascade down the rough bark. I was working in wood, and understood that Francis, who sent me these impressions, would hold them safe for me as long as possible. These were his hypnotic images, which he made visible for me with the vibrations of his unspoken voice.

It was the way he had shown me the Rotterdam Cathedral, where sculptors freed images from their stone coverings. Nevertheless, there was an important difference: those stonemasons had been strangers, and the man who cut this wood was myself.

The carved figures of Isaac and Johan Isaac Hollandus stood next to each other on the same base. They both wore hats, and the eldest one had a short beard. They stood a bit apart from each other, for I had cut them from two different trees whose roots had entwined under the ground. I had cut Jan and Hubert van Eyck, the painters of *The Adoration of the Lamb,* from the branches of an oak tree. A shock went through me when I beheld the wooden image of Albrecht Dürer in my hands as I carved the last of his long curls.

Michelangelo and Leonardo da Vinci were cut in much rougher fashion from the wood; it was obvious that I had never seen them in the flesh. Chips of wood flew in all directions as I began working on a rough tree stump, but soon it yielded its hidden image. Now it was an image that came in the form of the Hundred Years' War; although this awful conflict had ended halfway through the fifteenth century, and I did not feel closely associated with it, its presence forced its way out of me. Next was an oaken Christopher Columbus, who closed the century and, following the shape of the tree from which he was cut, bowed to me gracefully. His face, with determined jaws and bright eyes, smiled warmly at me, his creator. His thin hair and benign countenance gave way to that of Dürer, the painter, whom I had cut out with great precision. He looked fixedly at me and spoke to me in a deep but silent voice, which I heard nonetheless. His wooden lips were tightly closed, but if he had actually spoken I would have recognized his voice immediately.

The sound did not reach me through my ears, but flooded across my entire being, without my being able to tell where it had originated.

"Albrecht Dürer was born after you," I heard my mind's voice tell me.

The year of his birth was 1471, I remembered, and I saw him before me the way he was in his self-portrait from 1500. Yes, I was indeed older. With Francis as my guide, I had made a flight in time of six hundred years.

Away I flew from my forest of wooden figures, whose roots grew deep in their native soil, and who now stared after me with tears of resin in their eyes. Now I floated over a landscape normal eyes could not see, which was only visible in the mind of one being guided by someone adept in the psychic arts.

I was a vagabond, a woodcarver and a musician. My own native ground, the territory I had traveled over so many times, extended from Brussels to Cologne in the north and from Reims to Saarbrücken in the south. I felt myself come down to earth again and move with unbridled speed from east to west. I saw woods, rivers, villages and towns and recognized churches and castles scattered across France, Belgium, Luxemburg and Germany. I flew over the cities of Luxemburg and Trier and along the winding paths of the Moselle River, past the castles of Arras and Eltz, and back again, before I could see the river flow into the Rhine near Koblenz. I came down once more and felt my feet touch the ground.

The feeling came back into my entire being. During my flight, I had retained the sensation of sight, but had not been aware of the wind against my face or blowing through my hair, of warmth or cold, or of smell and sound. Directly before me I saw the double tower of a castle, and for one brief moment I thought I was standing before the open gates of Kasselburg, but then realized that I was too close to the winding river, and was not as far back in the Efel region as I had thought. This castle was smaller, and the double tower was of lesser proportions than that of Kasselburg, which was the equivalent of about eight stories high.

* * *

We slept outside, a bow-shot distance from the castle with the double tower. The time of the year was favorable for it: halfway between St. George (April 23) and St. John (June 24). Franciscus and Miethe lay on the other side of the fire, which had now almost completely burned out. I knew they slept just as lightly as I did. Right beside me lay Maria, the dancer, wrapped in her blanket, with her long, brown hair cascading over her naked shoulder.

We rambled through northern France and earned money in the cities by making music for the crowds. I played flutes, which I had cut myself from reed stems, and Franciscus was the drummer. Our ensemble always fascinated the audience, and this gave Miethe the opportunity to mingle with the crowd and make someone here and there a few coins lighter. Every now and then we worked at building or repairing churches. I had, when on our way from Metz to Saarbrücken with the intention of following the course of the River Saar to return to our native ground via Trier, cut two large wooden images for the abbot of a monastery. This had provided me with a considerable sum of money. The friars had watched with a healthy respect as the images of the archangels Michael and Gabriel took shape.

"This is brilliant and inspired work," said the abbot. "A holy fire is burning inside of you, and you instill the sparks of it to your creations. Do us a favor, and stay here for a while. Create an image for us of the damned who have been hauled off to hell and the angels who were fortunate not to have been. You will be rewarded handsomely. Give us inspiration to gaze upon when we wish to consider good and evil."

I shook my head.

"I cannot do so, father."

"And why can't you, Paulus?" he asked me.

"Because we must travel on. Franciscus, Miethe and I live by the day. We never stay long in one place. We come from France and are anxious to return to our native ground. Someday, when I am much older, and no longer haunted by restless feelings, I will remember this place and return to make everything for you that you have in mind."

The abbot tried one more time. "It is safe and warm within our walls."

But Miethe—big, strong Miethe—deprived him of all hope, saying, "Give us food and drink once more so that we may proceed on our journey with full stomachs."

"Paulus can create whatever he wants," said the abbot. "His knives are able to cut whatever forms his mind envisions. In this short time, I have come to know Franciscus as a man who has withdrawn into himself, one who is just as good a musician as Paulus and has a strong, rich mind. But, Miethe, pray tell, what are your qualities?"

"I am the man who shepherds the three of us through all dangers," Miethe answered. "I trust in my physical strength. There is not a thief or gang of robbers that will bother us as long as I can clench my fists and throw the first punch!"

"Do you trust in yourself more than you do in God?"

"My trust in God is great in fact, because it is He who has given me the strength to endure everything that comes our way, no matter what that may be."

We departed early the next morning, I carrying my knives and flutes, Franciscus his drum and the wine we had been given. Miethe walked in front. He was the biggest of the three of us, with his broad shoulders, strong arms and powerful legs. His long hair hung down past his shoulders like that of Albrecht Dürer. His eyes were light brown, his chin was round and heavy, his lips were full. He habitually walked as if in a hurry, and Franciscus and I often had trouble keeping pace with him.

What he had told the abbot was true. We tramped about the world aimlessly, and that world was full of dangers. With Miethe in our midst there was not much that could happen to us, for he was as strong as an ox and seemed to know no fear.

When we left the monastery with full stomachs, the bread and wine we had been given, and the money I had earned by cutting the archangels from wood, we were still friends. By nightfall though, things had changed. We now kept a wary, jealous eye on each other, for we had met Maria, and each of us had fallen in love with her.

She was more beautiful than all the women we had ever met. She made our hearts pound, we had eyes only for her and all that surrounded her. Nothing existed for us any longer, save Maria.

We had arrived in a small town, and I had taken out my flute and began to play while Franciscus beat the drum. We hoped, as always, that we would attract a large gathering of people, so that Miethe would be able to score once again by robbing the spellbound listeners. All the wine we had drunk along the way had made us loose and carefree. We seemed to be in an almost devilish rapture that brought forth our music in a harmony seldom heard. Our instruments and voices had never been better.

Suddenly, as if the tones of my flute and the roll of the drum had drawn her forth from some mystical nether world, Maria appeared in front of us. Like a spirit, nay, like a dream, she danced before us. Her bare feet glided ever so lightly over the pavement, convincing us that she was floating. She looked at us with her big, dark eyes, her long hair flowing around her and her full, round breasts caressing the cloth of her dress. She undulated her hips, her hands held high above her head with her long fingers spread wide. If Miethe had not fallen as deeply under her spell as everyone else who watched her, he could have stolen enough that day to make himself a rich man. Instead, he stared at her, entranced, and rather than use his hands for profit he used them to push the crowd of onlookers aside so that he could stand in front. He whipped the curls from his eyes and stood transfixed, his mouth agape.

But money came in anyway. Fortunately, we did not have to steal anything that day to turn a profit. Further, Maria's sensual dancing elicited an invitation for us all from a rich merchant to join him at an inn, where we were honored with the best seats in the house, near the fireside.

There had never before been a moment of hostility between us, but now I felt the tension and jealousy growing between Franciscus, Miethe and myself. Each of us would have claimed Maria for himself in a heartbeat, but she was not a woman who would allow herself to be bound to another so easily. She told us she was from Italy and was of noble blood. She claimed to have lost her friends during her journey and be in need of protection, although from what she did not say. She told us of high, snow-capped mountains, of cities with marvelous cathedrals, of kings and princes, and we believed not a single word of what she said, but hung upon the sweetness of her lips anyway. She decided to travel along with us. She drove us out of our minds with passion and lust, but she let none of us seduce her.

We went on.

With Miethe as protector of our small company, we had no fear of the dark, nor of the evil spirits living in the woods that we journeyed through, nor of the people we came upon from village to village and from town to town. Spring sang eternal in our hearts, and it was Maria who laid down the tune. And so we reached the windings of the Moselle on the eve of a big national holy day and feast, and we finally had the castle with the double tower within our sights.

I had carved a wooden amulet for Maria, and I was proud to see that she carried it on a leather cord in a place of honor between her firm, round breasts. To have been that lucky charm, to have been given the glory of the position of that amulet, I would have gladly traded away a kingdom. Franciscus had long and deep conversations with her, and Miethe tried desperately to impress her by showing her time and time again that he feared nothing and nobody.

We awoke early in the morning, just as the gates of the castle swung open and a group of riders emerged. I immediately recognized the man in scarlet attire who rode in the forefront. It was the lord of the castle himself, Count Kaspar von Karst, a great, bearded man with the stature of Miethe and the pride of noble birth in his eyes. He rode down amongst the villages in the valley, where the church bells were already tolling, to attend mass at the beginning of this holy day. Count Kaspar von Karst had gathered the populace into a large procession that showed neither favoritism nor segregation. There were clergymen led by their bishop, followed by the count and his noble guests. Then came a following of people from all around the county—farmers and civilians, from the richest to those less blessed. There were also several merchants mixed among the noblemen, and they were the count's most important guests—or should I say targets? They would be tasting his best wines, and he hoped to reach an advantageous business arrangement with one or more of them—today the wine of the county, which the count produced and which was the source of his wealth, would be traded.

Daylight had finally broken, and the slow tolling of the bells echoed in our ears as the morning mist slowly lifted. The contours of the proud castle became sharper now, and the large field in which we found ourselves glistened from the dewdrops, which also sparkled in Maria's hair. I put some more wood on the fire, and the flames blazed bright and warm again.

Previously in this region, we had picked grapes for the father of the count. We had worked hard and long on the steep slopes of the hillsides where, when we raised our eyes upward, we could see the upper part of the towers, and when we lowered our gaze, our eyes followed the eternal flow of the river.

Now we were back; the old count had died, and Kaspar ruled the land, which yielded so much wine that he could afford to live in comfort and luxury. And we, well we were just as poor as when we had left.

Kaspar von Karst, we knew, was descended from robber knights. It was said that his ancestors had taken part in the Crusades and that they had come home with great riches. Much gold shone in the halls of the castle, and it was rumored that the count purified his wine in gold and silver goblets, all inlaid with precious stones. I could not say if this was true or not, for I had never entered the castle and had only contributed to his wealth by gathering the grapes from his land.

The sun drove away the dew, and it began to get crowded on the field between the castle and the slopes down through which the grapevines ran. Yesterday, everyone had only labored for half a day, and they now prepared themselves for the eating and drinking that would soon begin. Beggars, the lame, the unfortunate blind, farmers, village people, all the citizens of the county now ascended the mountain on which the castle was built. The gates were opened again, and large trestle tables were placed outside. Breads, sausages and myriad other foods were displayed upon them. Pourers tapped wine casks and put out mugs, decanters and jugs. Four guards placed themselves in front of the open gates to prevent uninvited guests from venturing too far in. For, despite the show of the procession, it was a fact that this holy day would indeed be celebrated on two different levels: the common people, the hungry wretches, the poor and the lame had to stay outside, while the clergymen, the nobles and the merchants were all welcomed into the home of the count.

After the church bells had fallen silent, the procession made its way back uphill, with the Bishop of Trier at the head. We were standing at the edge of the field and saw the procession approach over the road, whose boundaries were marked by grapevines. Behind the bishop and the clergymen rode the proud Kaspar von Karst and his entourage of noblemen and wealthy merchants. At the very end of this parade were the inhabitants of the river villages, who later were to be seen swarming about the large field. For, like us, they were denied entrance to the castle.

The feast had officially begun, and everyone fell greedily upon the food and drink.

"You must play," Miethe said to Franciscus and me. "Let Maria dance! Show yourself, Maria. Make sure that the people have eyes only for you. Then I can walk around at ease and guarantee that the four of us will be somewhat richer in a just a little while."

I played better than ever before, for I played for Maria. Franciscus's drum rolls laid the foundation for my flute-playing, and Maria turned her lean body around and around, her bare feet hardly seeming to touch the grass. She opened the upper part of her clothing wide so that the people could gaze upon her luscious naked breasts swaying to the rhythm of the music. Miethe was now free to haul in the loot.

Later that afternoon, I gave a small part of that loot, a single coin, to an old man who claimed he could see the future. He sat on the ground in the soft grass and looked up at me with drunken eyes. When he spoke, it was with a mouth that had long ago ceased to retain any teeth at all.

"I am like the dog that smells the hare, but is no longer able to chase it down," he said. "I have eaten and drunk today as if it was my very last meal on this earth. I hope, my friend, that it will be a long time until you feel the same as I. Take my hands and help me up."

I leaned down and stretched out my fingers to him. He grabbed hold of them, and when he lifted himself up and stood unsteadily on his aged legs, I felt how light and fragile he was. His thumbs glided across my knuckles.

Then he turned the palms of my hands up towards him. He bent his head, upon which he wore a cap of worn leather with wisps of white hair sticking out. His face was covered with the stubble of many unshaven days.

"Death comes for all of us," I heard him say. "I am like the old dog that can no longer. But you—you will live forever!"

He gazed at me with his mouth open and then let go, falling backwards in the grass and making averting gestures as if terrified that I would attack, kick or beat him. He started to scream, shouting that I must be the devil's helper. I retreated, afraid he would catch the attention of the bystanders. But when I turned around, I saw that everyone was fascinated by quite something else.

A bear handler was having the greatest trouble controlling his huge bear, which he led along by a ring through its nose. Pigs were being roasted over the open fires, and the animal had probably been made hungry by the sweet aroma of seared flesh. The man pulled at the rope that was attached to the ring, and the bear lashed out with his mighty claws.

"Let him fight!" a cheer rang out. "Who will stand up to the bear?"

It was Miethe who accepted the challenge, striding up to the man and his animal. Cheering and roaring resounded through the air. I saw Miethe give a handful of coins to the bear handler, and when the crowd fell silent, he said, "This is for you if the bear wins, but I get back twice as much if I manage to keep him pinned to the ground while you count ten."

The handler grinned. "You've got yourself a deal, foolish sir."

Miethe was standing there, tall and proud. I had no doubt he was doing this to impress Maria. I was jealous and was sure the same wave of emotion passed through Franciscus. We would have done anything to win Maria for ourselves, and Miethe was obviously prepared to go to any length.

"His snout is tied down!" someone shouted. "That's not fair! Get rid of that rope!"

The crowd formed a wide circle, and standing in the middle of it, the bear handler removed the rope that was tied around the head and snout of the animal. Snorting, the bear rose mightily on his hind legs. Miethe pulled his knife out of his belt and removed his outer clothes and handed them to me. Then he walked up to the animal with long strides, while the handler moved backwards until he was standing amongst the onlookers.

Maria held her hands in front of her face and stared between her fingers. At the same moment that Miethe sprang into action with clenched fist and punched the bear's snout hard, she closed her fingers.

The roaring of the bear drowned out the screams of the crowd. The great beast, who had trudged along with his owner for so many hundreds of miles, doing his tricks and fighting countless reckless men, shook his head and looked at his attacker with small, startled brown eyes.

He was used to the bustle of his carnival-like existence, and had learned to live with pain from the moment the ring was set in his nose. But, after all the times he had been provoked, challenged and beaten, something was different. For the first time he was able to open his mouth!

Miethe began to lash out, his fists pounding into the thick belly and front legs of the animal. Just at the moment he was about to take a step back, the bear lashed out, its mighty claws swiping Miethe full across his broad chest and tearing his skin open. Miethe staggered, and the bear immediately fastened his teeth in Miethe's flesh. I saw Miethe trying to grab hold of the animal's large nose ring. If he succeeded, perhaps he could quiet the animal down. He caught hold of the fur. The bear was now standing on all fours and seemed determined to use his jaws to finish this fight. Miethe managed to climb onto the animal's back, throw his strong arms around his neck and try to pull his head up, with the intention of grabbing hold of the ring as soon as he got the chance. But the bear was stronger. Our friend was swung to the ground, and the bear's teeth again sunk into his skin. The bear shook his head violently from side to side, and we watched as Miethe's upper body became soaked red with blood.

Suddenly, a man broke free from the crowd and ran up to Miethe and the bear. He was a big man, holding a thick stick in his hand.

"Let them be!" I heard the bear handler shout. "It's an honest fight!"

The man paid no attention to the handler and began to beat the bear on the head with the stick. At this, the bear no longer bothered with Miethe, but stood up on his hind legs again and looked around, hurt, irritated and confused. He then let loose a noise from deep within that was not a roar, but more like a primal howl. He turned, his forelegs touched the ground again and he began to run towards the crowd, who, screaming in fear, gave way to the charging bear. For a brief moment I thought he would feast upon one of the roasted pigs, or perhaps one of the audience. But he ran past the crowd, past the roasted pigs, on past the walls of the castle and continued on his way up the mountain until he disappeared from view.

The bear's owner took the loss of his animal surprisingly lightheartedly. He picked up Miethe's purse, which was closed with a little thong of leather and cut it open with the point of his knife, and everyone looked on as coins and trinkets fell out onto the grass. He picked up one after the other until he thought the price of the bear had been paid and, of course, he also kept the money Miethe had already given him. He cast not even a passing look at the man with the stick who had hit the bear.

Franciscus and I ran towards Miethe. Maria sat down on her knees close to him and cradled his head on her thighs. The surging crowd closed in on us and, as inebriated as they were, stood there laughing and staggering on their feet, staring at the wounded man.

"Pick up your friend's money before someone else does it," the bear handler advised me.

I knew he was right and began to search for the coins and trinkets in the grass. As I collected the money I realized that Miethe had been financially unscrupulous to Franciscus and me. He had given each of us a mere pittance and had kept the lion's share of the loot for himself. I wondered how long he had been walking around with such wealth hidden from us.

"That necklace belongs to me," a voice boomed in my ear.

I raised myself to my knees and found myself looking up at a man who was wearing clothing decorated with elaborate stitching and a fur-trimmed coat. He had a noble face, and although he was smiling, his eyes were icy cold. He held a knife in his hand, the point almost touching my throat.

"Give it back," he said.

I handed him the golden necklace I had slipped into the purse just seconds prior.

"And now I shall punish the thief," he said. "A knife right through his heart is the only thing he deserves."

Three things were painfully obvious to me at that moment: one—this man really was the owner of the necklace; two—he was too wealthy to try and bribe; and three—he was definitely in a mood to kill someone. I quickly rose to my feet and pointed at Miethe, who was lying there covered in blood.

"He has already been convicted and punished, sir," I said. "You have your possession back. Don't spoil the feast any further with a thrust of your knife. Leave the man to his fate. He lies here, paying a heavy penalty for his actions."

The man considered what to do, looked at Miethe for a while, and then looked at me.

"When he recovers from his injuries, if he does so at all, he owes his life to you," said the man. "You are right. I would only be putting him out of his misery, and that he does not deserve."

He walked away, and I squatted down again to pick up the last coins. I fastened the purse to my belt and tried to help Franciscus and Maria stop the flow of blood and bind up Miethe's wounds.

* * *

A group of young men had decided to leave the field to hunt the bear. We had moved ourselves to the walls of the castle, and I had hidden the purse under my clothes. Miethe leaned his back against the stone wall and drank wine to ease the pain. The upper part of his body was covered with scratches, but apparently his injuries were not so bad after all. The bear had bitten him on his upper left arm, lower on the same arm, and on his right shoulder. The claws had narrowly missed his carotid artery, which certainly would have resulted in his death. Franciscus and I sat in front of him playing the drum and flute. Maria was dancing again, and she smiled about all the attention she was getting. Someone had requested us to play and have Maria dance and we did so, hoping to show our best side. We were afraid now and wanted to avoid any problems since everyone now knew that Miethe was a thief and was one of us.

We figured our friend would recover from his wounds; they did not seem at all life threatening. Because of his duplicity and deceit, though, he was no longer a factor in the quest for Maria's affections, so now my competition for her favors was limited to Franciscus. The melody I played was slow, with long, shrill whistles alternating with each beat of Franciscus's drum. I could not coax a song filled with cheerfulness from my flute now, even though I was gazing upon Maria's naked breasts, which heaved and swayed to my tune, only momentarily covered by her long, flowing hair. Her hard, brown nipples teased me as they poked through the strands of silk cascading from her head. She danced with her arms outstretched and fingers spread, gazing at the blue sky as her feet rustled through the grass.

All across the big field all forms of entertainment were being provided. There were jugglers, acrobats, actors, magicians and musicians. But not one of them drew as much attention as Maria.

There was a sadness in my music now. A sadness which had its roots in the understanding that Maria would accompany us no further on our travels. She had felt safe in our company of friends, trusting in our camaraderie and Miethe's enormous courage and strength. Now, though, the seeds of mistrust and been planted in our fragile garden, and Miethe was barely able to protect himself, never mind others. His injuries had made him more of a burden than anything else.

Suddenly, I saw the man in the fur-trimmed coat again, standing between the onlookers. He was the only one in the crowd who was not staring at Maria. The necklace I had returned to him was hanging from his neck. He quickly stepped aside, and four large men pushed forward to stand beside him. They all had long knives stuck in their belts, and one of them held a club in his hand. They talked amongst themselves, watching Miethe all the while. The situation was painfully clear to me—the man with the noble face would not soil his hands on the punishment of a mere pickpocket, so he had enlisted these men to help him with his dirty work. I knew that Franciscus and I would be involved in this equation, and that these thugs would expect me to hand over the purse filled with gold. I decided that if they wanted it that badly, they would have to cut it free from my cold, dead body. Franciscus and I looked at each other, and I knew that he also realized the danger we were facing. I dared not look at Miethe, for I was afraid to read the fear in the eyes of my once strong but now defenseless friend.

Not too many hours earlier, an old man had predicted an eternal life for me; but right now I questioned the validity of that prophecy as I saw the man with the necklace nod. Upon his signal his four henchmen drew their knives and came towards us. Maria, still dancing with her blazing eyes turned towards the heavens, seemed oblivious of the fact that anything was amiss. She existed in her own sensuous, swirling world, cut off for the moment from the rest of the world.

Flute and drum fell silent. Maria's otherworldly gyrations finally ceased, and she rubbed her eyes as if she had just been awakened from a deep, deep sleep. We knew that Miethe would never escape with his life from this battle, but Franciscus and I still had a chance of surviving, so we decided to fight to the bitter end. I thought my best plan would be to try and reach the open gates of the castle. Perhaps they would not dare to follow me in there. I rose to my feet, let the flute drop and grabbed for my knife.

"Stay close to me, Franciscus," I said.

Someone started to scream, and a confusion of sounds arose from the crowd, whose overall mood had changed greatly since when Miethe had done battle with the bear. The four men had come within a few yards of us. Then, oddly enough, they paused in their attack. I figured that if I took to my heels quickly enough, I could run to the gates of the castle and make it into the inner court before they caught up with me. Perhaps then I could get some help from the guards. As I looked aside, silently calculating the distance to the gates, I suddenly, and quite unexpectedly I might add, found myself standing eye to eye with Count Kaspar von Karst.

He was considerably taller than me, and the loose, scarlet clothes he wore made his stature even more impressive. His dark beard was full of leftovers from the feast. The hair on his chin glistened—whether from sweat, slobber or wine, I was unable to tell. He was accompanied by several noblemen who were in much the same condition. The people in the immediate area bowed to him in a show of respect and stepped back. The four men who had intended to attack us put away their arms and retreated quickly.

The count was not even aware of the fact that there had been the threat of a fight. His attention was focused completely on Maria, who was standing there like an artist's model, showing off her body. She boldly resisted the count's lustful stare with a proud and defiant expression. As he crossed his arms over his broad chest, I heard him inhale deeply and then breathe heavily out again through his nostrils.

"You will dance for me, and only me," the count said to Maria. "Walk along with me. I am going for a stroll to see that all are having a good time on this holy day.

Afterwards, you shall be a guest at my table. I offer you the seat right beside mine. What is your name?"

"Maria Delaruelle," she answered, while looking him in the eye haughtily. "In Venice, the mere mention of my name is sufficient to open doors that would remain closed to most others."

I stood with my mouth open as I watched the count come up to her and put her hand on his arm. Together, followed by the small company of noblemen, they began their short walk across the field. Franciscus and I quickly gathered up our belongings and then lifted up our battered friend and draped his arms around our shoulders. Miethe's feet dragged over the ground as we followed Kaspar and Maria. We figured that as long as we stayed within the vicinity of the count, we need not fear another attempt on our lives. Franciscus's drum was hanging down his back, and with every step he took it swung against Miethe's body.

"Let go of me!" Miethe moaned. "Put me down on the grass and let me be. You cannot drag me around like this. I feel as if my wounds are about to burst open, I will lose too much blood!"

Concerned for our own personal safety, we ignored his pleas. We would stop and stand still when Kaspar von Karst halted to drink a mug of wine, to taste the succulent, roasted meat offered to him or to simply have a brief chat with someone. We went on when he, with Maria still on his arm, continued his stroll. Finally we had completed a round trip and had returned once again to the gates of the castle. At this point, I left Miethe and Franciscus alone and stepped up to the count. After showing my humble respects and making a deep bow to him, I said, "Sir, Maria will dance for you in a way that she has never danced before. We are her accompanists. Allow us to step inside with you, and rest assured, you will have the devotion of the finest musicians in these parts!"

Immediately the count turned to Maria and said, "Do you need them?"

"I don't need anyone," she answered. "I can dance just as well without music."

My eyes blazed angrily when I looked at her. How many miles had we traveled together? We had shared everything with her and left her to lie in unmolested peace when she slept near the fire. We had bought sandals for her bare feet and had clothes made for her half-naked body. Kaspar turned and walked on in the direction of the gates.

"But with their music I dance much more defiantly, of course," I heard her say. "And your guests will be delighted with their playing."

Without looking back at her or anyone else, the count made a gesture with his hand.

"Inside—all of you!" he said.

* * *

It was hot, dark and smoky in the great hall of the knights. Meat was constantly roasting, and the wine goblets were never empty. We had eaten pies, made music, watched the swirling temptations of the dancing Maria, and then again drunk much more wine than was probably good for us. Miethe lay stretched out on the stone floor near the fire, inside a ring of clergymen and noblemen who paid not one bit of attention to him, even when they tossed gnawed bones across him into the flames.

High on a platform, with his back against the wall, Count Kaspar von Karst looked out over the entire hall. He sat there in his splendid clothes as if he were the German emperor himself, and if one were able to steal a glance into his eyes, they would see enormous pride and ego betrayed there. With his chin raised high, he took the big hall in at a glance. In his hand he held a golden goblet encrusted with jewels—the only piece of crockery worth anything in the great hall. All the other guests drank from stone or wooden mugs, and the meals were served on trays of baked dough.

Maria had been given a seat of great honor. Like his empress or his queen, she sat next to Kaspar and, smiling all the while, allowed him to rest his hand on hers. I had heard that the count's wife had recently succumbed to a serious disease. Observing Maria and Kaspar that night, I knew that in the near future the count would be announcing a second marriage.

Miethe suffered from physical pain, but I suffered from mental pain that hurt me no less. I could play my music no more, and threw my flute into the fire.

There was a jester in attendance to entertain the dinner guests, and he was as drunk as they. On a normal night, the things he was saying about the count and his entourage would have cost him his head. As it were, the count was as drunk as the jester, and he laughed as loudly as anyone at the jokes and barbs that were directed mostly at himself. The jester put his arms and legs around one of the hand-painted support pillars and climbed upwards until the points of the fool's cap he was wearing brushed against the ceiling. "Now I sit higher than even you, my lord," he shouted. "I can keep a sharper eye on you now and see what you are still capable of doing, now that you have had filled and emptied your goblet so often tonight."

"You may be sitting higher than me," the count shouted back, "but you still won't be able see how I am about to amuse myself!"

He lifted his legs, pushed with his feet off the side of the table and fell backwards, chair and all, dragging Maria along with him. The jester, needless to say, could see exactly what was happening under the table. It was obvious to him, and everybody else in the room, that the count was enjoying a quick feel of Maria's voluptuous body. Not a man in the room, and probably a few of the women, could avoid feeling jealous of the count's good luck. The jester climbed down from his lofty perch and looked around with half closed, drunken eyes.

"A woman! Please, a woman for the jester too!" he shouted. "For who am I, not to follow the example of the count? Who am I not to enjoy what my lord enjoys?"

At that moment Franciscus nudged me.

"Miethe can't hold on much longer under these conditions," he warned. "It is far too hot, crowded and noisy for him in here. It's dark outside. If we leave now, we can escape from the man Miethe robbed and his four thugs."

"And what if the count won't let us go?"

"I have seen other people take their leave without a problem. At least we can try. I have rolled Miethe onto a carpet. It will be easier for the two of us to carry him that way."

Kaspar von Karst had finally regained an upright position. Maria wrapped her arms around him and pressed her face into his beard. I couldn't leave without taking one long, last look at Maria. With long strides I walked through the hall, past the feasting noblemen, clergymen and merchants. Apparently it was not only the jester who felt obligated to honor the count by following his example. All around the room men and women were having an excellent time feasting on each other with little or no concern as to who was watching. I climbed up onto the platform and stood directly in front of the count's table.

"Sir, we have played for you, and it has given us great pleasure to do so. We have been greatly honored to have been your guests and have enjoyed the party. Will you allow us now to leave? Our friend is badly injured and is in need of medical attention and rest."

He made the same sweeping gesture with his hand as when he had invited us to come inside.

"Do as you please."

I looked into the dark eyes of Maria. She gave me a short nod with her head, glanced at the count's treasured golden goblet standing on the table, and then looked at me again. She leaned towards the count, kissed him full on the mouth and let one hand slide down over his belly towards his crotch. With her other hand she waved at me—"goodbye and begone," the hand said. It was her parting gesture. Her long hair, wet mouth and roving hands made it impossible for the count to see what was happening around him. Maria would keep him busy long enough to assure us a safe retreat. I was standing with my back to the people, and it didn't look as though anyone was paying special attention to me. The jewels on the cup sparkled in the light of the torches that burned in iron sconces on the walls. I reached out and felt my fingers close around the cool gold. I lifted the goblet, drained the wine from it and then stashed it away under my clothes. Count Kaspar von Karst moaned softly as Maria's hand explored between his legs. At the moment I was robbing him, he was having the time of his life. And he would never know that she had made it all possible.

"Hurry!" I said to Franciscus, after finding him in the crowd. "Leave your drum behind. We have to lift up Miethe and get out of here, now," I told him.

Without questioning, he helped me lift the carpet on which Miethe lay, and we started off. I had hidden the stolen goblet under Miethe's legs and hoped for the best.

As we were about to leave the hall, an armed guard stopped us and demanded, "Halt and tell me where you are going and what's in the rug."

We put Miethe down and opened the carpet. The guard could see the blood from Miethe's wounds seeping through the cloth with which we had bandaged him.

"His illness and fever grow worse and will probably lead to his death. Don't get too close to him, if you want to stay alive a bit longer yourself! I think he might be contagious."

The man recoiled in fear and let us pass. I looked over my shoulder and saw that Maria was still keeping the count amused. We walked quickly across the inner court and through the gates and, still carrying Miethe, crossed the large field, now almost completely deserted. A few people sat on the ground and nodded by the dying fires.

"Where are we to go now?" asked Franciscus. "Miethe is heavy, and we're not going to get too far."

"Quite the contrary, my friend," I said. "We're getting out of here. Head into the woods. We'll walk all night long if we have to. For you see, Franciscus, I've got Count Kaspar von Karst's golden goblet tucked away under Miethe's legs."

Franciscus suddenly had no trouble at all with the weight of the carpet and began walking so fast that I had trouble keeping up with him. I just hoped that the edges of the carpet wouldn't slip out of my fingers.

"You stole the goblet? You actually got a chance to take it right under his nose?"

"Maria distracted him for me."

"Tell me—do you really have the goblet with you?"

"Yes. Yes. I have the goblet. But he has Maria. I would throw it in the river if it would bring her back to us."

"He is going to be furious," said Franciscus. "Someone told me that the goblet is very old. It was brought as spoils from a crusade. It must be his most valuable possession."

"Now Maria is!" I snarled out. "Save your breath, friend. We have to get as far away from here as fast as possible."

Fear gave us strength. We both knew very well what would happen to us if the men the count would undoubtedly send out after us crossed paths with us. Miethe was heavy; it wasn't easy carrying him over fields and through woods and bushes. At first I had a good idea where I was headed because, although it was very dark, I knew my way around here. But the farther away we got from our native ground, the more difficult it became to make a wise choice when we came to a crossing or when the path forked. And there was always the risk that we might follow a twisting road that would lead us back towards the castle instead of taking us further away from it.

At daylight, we laid Miethe down in the grass at the edge of a wood and sat down next to him, panting and sweating. Crows and magpies flew from branch to branch, a deer ran through the wet field, an owl flew past us silently and disappeared between the trees, searching for a place to sleep.

Miethe said he hurt all over. He was burning up with fever and needed help badly, and soon. We heard the sound of hooves and threw ourselves flat on our bellies; a moment later a small group of men rode past. Although I knew we were wanted men now, I did not regret at all that I had taken the goblet. "The count's men probably won't find us," said Franciscus, thoughtfully rubbing his thumb and forefinger along his pointy nose. "But they'll tell everyone they can to watch out for us, and whoever turns us in will be amply rewarded. Two men carrying a dying third one. Easy enough to remember."

"Then leave me behind," said Miethe. "What's the difference whether I die here or a day's march further up? I should not have fought the bear. I have been foolish and reckless."

Franciscus said nothing, but I disagreed. "Nonsense, Miethe. Everything happens for a reason. One thing leads to another, and everything has to lead to something else."

"What are you talking about?" asked Franciscus. "When we first climbed up to the castle of Kaspar von Karst, we were men without worries. Now one of us is gravely wounded, and we have a fortune in our hands that is going to get us killed. Yes, everything has to lead to something, Paulus: everything leads to death!"

"Not me. It was predicted that I would have eternal life. Yesterday, on the field."

I took the goblet out from under Miethe's knees. The jewels sparkled in the light of the rising sun.

"The stones shine as the eyes of Maria," I said in a subdued voice. "Let's be honest; all three of us loved her, and now we've lost her. And Miethe of course, Miethe had to fight the bear. He had to show off his strength to her, just as we played our best music for her and did everything else we could to try and please her."

I turned the goblet over in my hands.

"It is an exchange. The stones for her eyes, the gold for her body. It is done, and we can't go back and change things. Here we sit, with blood and gold, and apparently it was meant to be this way."

* * *

For two days and nights we continued on. With numb fingers we held the carpet within which, Miethe, now deadly ill, lay in complete delirium. Walking through the woods as much as possible, taking the least-used paths, we had managed to stay out of sight and undiscovered by the count's men. By skirting farms and villages, we had been able to avoid anyone who could have betrayed us. We lived on what the land had to offer us: fruit of the forest, clear water from little streams and the meat of a number of different birds. Franciscus and I could each throw a stone precisely and a fairly lengthy distance. Miethe could only drink a little bit of water. His strength faded visibly, and his sunburned skin began to pale. The strongest of the three of us had become the weakest. The gold under his legs kept us on the move, for we knew that if we managed to get outside Kaspar von Karst's sphere of influence, we would be rich! Slowly but surely, Franciscus and I began to realize that Miethe was not going to make it. He should have been carried straight from the castle to one of the villages along the Moselle, where a surgeon could have properly cleaned his wounds and given him something to bring his fever down.

Miethe lost consciousness, and his face had become so white that I was sure that he had bled to death. Only when we stood still and listened could we hear his breathing, and only then if there were no other sounds to interfere.

Miethe was doomed, and we were nearly exhausted, but we stayed together. My brain no longer registered fantasies or daydreams; all I could think about was the pain in my hands as they clutched the carpet, and my sore feet that no longer even felt the ground upon which they walked.

I looked up as we came upon a clearing and a crossroad in the forest path.

There ahead of us, between two trees, the roots of which were so huge that they rose above the ground, sat a little man. He wore a gray habit, and his hair and eyes matched the color of his robe. On his feet he wore sandals of leather. His face was small, and gray stubble covered his chin. There were greasy, black stripes on his cheeks, and his hands and nails were filthy. He laughed at us without friendliness or joy, and we saw that his incisors were big and yellow, like those of a beaver.

"There is no time to lose, the fire has to be kept burning," he said to us, as he sprang to his feet and stumbled over the roots at the crossing. "Let me do all the talking, and everything will be clear to you."

We remained standing there. We set Miethe carefully down on the ground and wondered what to do about this strange, little creature.

"What fire are you talking about?" asked Franciscus.

"That, you will see later," said the little man. "It is better that you come with me right away. I can help your wounded friend. Horses are faster than men, especially two men carrying a third. The theft of a golden goblet has started a roundup of suspects in the area, but where I live no one will be able to find you. I have been waiting for you. Your arrival is quite important. Exchange safety for gold and be assured of a good life."

Once again, we lifted our burden and followed the little man, who took one of the four roads. After a few yards he chose a small side path. I had to let Franciscus go first, and we really had to hurry to keep up with the little man. Every now and then he stopped to pick up dead branches, and soon he had a considerable bundle of wood in his arms.

"My name is Alexander," he said, without turning his head. "I have the remedies to heal your friend. He needs rest, but you will have to work hard."

The path wound to the left and then to the right. We walked around trees and through thick brambles. And now, as we finally neared a place where we knew we would be able to rest for a bit, we realized just how exhausted we were. Our hike had taken a long time, and we had traveled a great distance. I knew that we could never find our way back to the crossroads again where we had met Alexander.

In a little clearing in the forest stood a cabin. Its wooden door stood ajar, and the smell of burning wood found its way to my nostrils. We entered the structure and were surprised to find that the small building was being used merely to hide what appeared to be a steep, descending flight of countless steps. We followed them down, under the ground, and came into a big room.

Flames burning under a smoke hole evoked a hellish vision of purgatory. Alexander threw the branches he had gathered into the fire. Strange looking pots and glass containers hung above the flames. An aroma of sulfur and other, vaguely familiar smells accosted my senses. The room was filled with sealed crucibles and decanters, and in a corner was a pile of straw, which, I assumed, served Alexander for a bed. The only audible sound in the room was the crackling of the fire. Not one sound from the outside world could be heard down here.

Alexander motioned for us to lay Miethe on the straw. When we had done so, he produced a knife and started to cut away the clothes and the blood-soaked bandages. He began to rub the wounds with a truly awful smelling liquid from a little stone jar, and as he did so he said to us, "The two of you must sit by the fire and rest. Your arms must hurt terribly from carrying your big friend all this way. Now you know just how heavy the weight of friendship can be. I want you to give me Kaspar von Karst's goblet so I can remove the jewels and sell them. The gold I will keep, for I need it to complete my experiments. I have been very busy with a major undertaking—I am trying to create gold from inferior metals. Yes, the venerable realm of alchemy is my domain."

Alexander fell silent for a bit, as if to give us the chance to ponder what he had told us. Perhaps he thought we would question his motives and ask him why he thought that of all people, we would turn our stolen treasure over to him.

Whatever his plan was, we were too tired to speak a word or indulge him in any further conversation.

After he had tended to Miethe and spread a blanket over him, he poured wine for us and gave us some old, hard bread and a few pieces of smoked meat. He kept a watchful eye on the fire and meditatively looked into the glass bulbs hanging above it.

He then told us, "Everything must remain closed, so that the healing sprit cannot slip out. It's all a matter of dissolving and solidifying, of endless repetition, putrefaction, ascending, multiplying. The fire must burn constantly. The alternation of the elements requires patience. You will stay here with your friend, and I shall explain to you how to tend the fire. It is imperative that you stay awake tonight regardless of how exhausted you are. I have not slept for many a night myself. I will be off early tomorrow to sell the jewels. I'll return as soon as I can with all the supplies I need." He nodded thoughtfully. "This is the way it must be"

"Why should we give you something as valuable as the goblet? Especially considering the fact that it is just about the only thing we have?" Franciscus asked Alexander.

The little man's gray eyes blinked, and he scratched his stubby beard with his long, dirty fingernails.

"There are three great theories that I am working on," he said, as he sat down next to us and pulled up his dirty habit, baring two dirty, calloused knees.

First there is the wisdom and the deep understanding of divinity. One with all, all with one. Beggar or king, man or insect, living creature or silent stone—everything is the same once the gates of wisdom have been opened. I have not come that far yet. Second there is the quest to make gold out of dross. The precious out of mud. With this one, also, I am not far along the road to success. I need much more money and much more time for my research."

"No wisdom and no gold," I said with a sigh. "So what have you achieved then, Alexander?"

His long nails scratched at the dirt on his knees.

"The third and last one, my doubting friend! The elixir of life itself! He who drinks from it will become an immortal. Its elusive solution has cost me many years of my life. I scraped together all the ingredients, from all over the world. I had to determine for myself the most favorable points in time for boiling, hardening, mixing, aging, with no help or consultation from any other living soul."

He pointed at the smoke hole above the fire. Behind the veil of fumes venting towards the ceiling, I saw a wooden cage hanging down from a chain, the bars black with soot. Small eyes stared at me from behind the bars, noses with whiskers moved up and down in curiosity, and long bare tails hung down.

"These rats enjoy the gift of eternal life. And there are others! I put a few drops of my precious potion in the pool from which my horse drinks. The frogs, the salamanders, the little fish and the water beetles in that mystical pond no longer die, and as long as the horse drinks enough of the water, he will live to be older than the oak I recently planted. The potion of immortality: the first work I could complete. It is a major accomplishment, but now the other goals must be attained—the creating of gold from base metals and the mystic union with the divine. When these are mine, I shall rise above all that is vulnerable and earthly."

"And have you taken a sip of your potion yet, old man?" Franciscus wanted to know.

"No sir. That honor belongs to you gentlemen. You shall be the first humans to experience life everlasting!" cried the little man. "Immortality—in exchange for the goblet of Kaspar von Karst."

* * *

Alexander left us, riding off on a beautiful black horse.

We tended the fire and let the flames lick along the pots, bulbs, pans and all the other strange hardware hanging there. We explored our surroundings, both inside and out. We found a small path that led to another clearing in the forest not far from our present location. Alexander had built a stable for his horse in this clearing.

There was also an herb garden and a pool of crystal-clear water. In the barn we found food and wine. Back in his underground workplace, just behind the rat cage, hung sausages and hams. We made ourselves at home and wanted for nothing. For the first time in a while we felt safe.

Alexander could call himself a rich man now; the goblet was worth a great deal. But still, the goblet, as beautiful as it was, was no match for the beauty of Maria. The presence of jewels could not compare with being in the company of my splendid dancer. The three of us missed her greatly and would have gladly traded any riches to have her back. But now we were looking at the possibility of immortality, of eternal life, and we looked forward to it with a burning desire. We figured Alexander would return to his hidden lair sooner or later.

And then, there he was again, just walking down the path one day. Behind his horse walked a donkey, heavily laden with mysterious supplies. The old alchemist went straight to the fire and told us that we had done good work during his absence.

"The time is not yet ripe, but soon I will have obtained the secret to making gold," he said.

The next day he took us to the pool. He dropped to his knees and began to dig with his hands in the ground at the waterside. He dug up a jar, which was sealed with a tapered, wooden stopper. We stood behind him and watched, and waited. Miethe, whose wounds were healing quickly now thanks to the ointment, stood in the midst of our little crowd and laid his hands on our shoulders.

"You first, my friends," he said. "I will wait for a couple of days. I have been ill, and I must be patient."

Alexander pulled the stopper out of the jar. A nasty smell pervaded my nose and throat and made my stomach contract until I thought I would vomit. Miethe and Franciscus could not hold it back and stood there retching. Alexander came and stood in front of us and offered us the jar.

"A mouthful will do, boys. This is the end result of so many years of work. This is what the earth can yield when a man has walked the divine way and taken the time to understand the nature of things. This was all there for the taking if one only had an eye for it. Who's first?"

I took the jar from him. With both hands I lifted it and brought it up to my mouth. I had expected it to be a thin liquid, but what touched my lips was a thick, syrupy substance. Just one mouthful, and my tongue began to tingle. The magical brew slid past my teeth—the taste was more awful than the stench. I gave the jar to Miethe, who immediately passed it to Franciscus, who looked at me for some time, as if he expected me to do something to interfere with his actions. Or maybe he thought that I was about to drop dead on the spot. Only after I smiled at him did he bring the jar up to his lips and let a portion of the contents slide down his throat.

"Now I have everything I need for my experiments," said Alexander. "The goblet has certainly brought me luck. This has been a good, fair deal. Everybody is getting something they need. You see—everything is connected. Now time no longer has a grip on you, my young friends; for you have absorbed the purest energy that Mother Earth has to offer."

* * *

I drank, I rose, I flew. Below me I saw the double tower of the castle of Count Kaspar von Karst. Higher and higher I went, till I could climb no higher and finally descended into myself. I lay on the bunk next to Francis Beck. His lips were closed, and he was no longer humming.

"Francis," I whispered, "I saw a forest of wooden figures standing with their roots in the ground. Why were their tears made of resin? Answer me," I demanded. "Why do they cry resin?"

"Mortals have tears," he said in a soft voice, while he blinked his eyes. "Their life is short and oh, so hard. Their strength comes with their years, the fruit grows into a tree. But eventually a turning point is reached, and sooner or later the storm will arise that will blow the tree over."

I stood, turned off the gas stove, and remained standing there for a while staring at Miethe. His breathing was calm now, and he seemed to sleep peacefully. I was tired and knew that I must sleep. When I finally laid my head down to take my rest, I tasted the horrible flavor of Alexander's immortality brew on my tongue, and it was by no means pleasant. But then, there she was again, Maria, dancing before my mind's eye . . . and my lips smiled.

4 -The Patience of the Watchman

We knew all the tricks to hiding things; we stole, and then we hid the things that were not ours. Gold coins and jewelry were the easiest to hide and to trade later, but we had hidden other objects of value deep in the ground, behind walls, in deep pits. Over time our treasures earned interest. We would wait so long that they had become antiques before we tried to sell them. And then they were worth even more! We traded often with antique dealers, and we never had to undersell because they knew, they understood that we were connoisseurs, and were usually able to give more information about our wares than the details you would find about them in catalogues, specialist literature and encyclopedias.

Who, for instance, could tell more about a violin from the seventeenth century than I? I, who had built just such a priceless antique, a masterpiece without equal, full of a sound so soulful, it could only be explained in her construction.

At first, we had hidden our loot in one spot. But when we returned to the area later we couldn't find our hiding space because the neighborhood had changed so much over the years. That's why we became like squirrels, who hide their food in so many different places that they can forget some of them and be none the worse off. No doubt, treasures have been found here and there that we buried and forgot about.

We had always worked together, Franciscus and I. We had been friends for as long as I could remember. I found comfort in the thought that I wasn't the only one who lived from century to century and would never, ever die. Francis Beck, the New York composer, had disappeared, but my old friend Franciscus was alive and well and lying on the bunk in my boat.

I had gone out in the morning, leaving him behind. He had given me specific instructions.

"Leave your shop, leave your house. Arrange it quickly, and stay on the alert. It is difficult to say if Rainer Miethe knows about your home. He has been on my track for quite some time."

I looked at him with raised eyebrows. He lifted his head and leaned on his elbows on the bed. Since he had had a night's rest and I had washed the blood from his face, he looked much better.

"New York! I put money in a safe-deposit box there, but it might be too dangerous to try to get it out. Do you remember the secret storage spot near the Danube?"

Wolf Tears

At that moment a strange sensation came over me. I felt as if I were falling deep into time, and it scared the hell out of me! I grabbed onto fleeting thoughts and then let them go again. I was inundated with volumes of unexpected knowledge. I nodded affirmatively.

"What we have in New York, we'll save for a rainy day," said Franciscus. "Break loose from Rotterdam. Sell your car and buy another one. Wear clothes you would never normally wear. Drive to Germany."

"It's a ruin," I said, remembering. "The castle had already been destroyed when we arrived there. We leaned over its broken walls and looked out over the Danube. Remember? Not far from there, there is a fortune to be found, hidden under a heavy, flat stone."

"Could you find that spot again?"

"Perhaps. It's worth trying."

"There are mainly golden coins hidden there. It won't be hard to find a buyer for them. I really cannot tell you much more than that except that you go from—"

"From Passau upstream," I quickly finished the sentence for him. "Less than twenty or thirty miles away from it. Follow the river all the time. With the water at your left hand. Good heavens! What am I talking about? How long ago was that?"

"You know as much as I do, Paul. Neither one of us has ever been back there. Listen to me carefully. Leave your home as soon as possible, but take your time on the trip. Take a few days to travel. Drive for short periods of time and deviate from the main roads. That's the only way you'll know if someone is following you. Also, plan to take several days, even a week perhaps, for your return trip. I don't know how long it's going to take me to be strong enough again to leave the boat."

He rubbed the side of his sharp nose and smiled.

"Who knows? Maybe I'll be ready to walk around in two or three days without any pain in my joints. Maybe I'll still be laying in bed when you return with the money."

* * *

I followed his advice. There were plenty of musicians who would gladly take over my shop and live in my house. I made a deal with a good friend of mine, a timpanist. He usually had some kind of business going on, and with the space I offered he could realize some new plans now. He even bought my furniture and my car.

I took almost nothing with me. I packed some clothes in a big suitcase, but not before I put the photograph from 1932 on the bottom. I had told my friend who was taking the house that he could have the books standing on the wooden floor of the living room along the wall. Before I left, I sank down on my knees and started to investigate the spines. Every now and then I picked a book from the row to take a better look at it. Downstairs I heard the new owner whistle a merry tune and rummage among the tools on my workbench. My hands began to shake when I discovered I had Italian,

Portuguese, Spanish and French books in the house, and I realized that I was able to read them all. I leafed through books written in Greek and Latin and understood every single word and every line my eyes came to rest on.

After a while, I went downstairs with the heavy suitcase in my hand. Walking up to the door, I reached out my hand and ticked the tuba hanging from the ceiling.

I took leave of the whistling timpanist and caught a taxi to a garage, where I would buy a secondhand car. I had left the smell of wood and glue behind. I hadn't become rich in Rotterdam, but I had had a good time here. It wasn't the first time I was leaving a place that had become dear to me. I still didn't know how I had come to be there, but I knew for sure now was the time to go.

* * *

On the first day of my journey, I left the freeway before I reached Frankfurt. I didn't follow a particular route, but drove from one village to another and stopped the car every few hours at the small parking places at the edge of the pinewoods. During the entire drive I watched my rearview mirror to see if I was being dogged. Now and then I would get out and just stand next to my car for about ten minutes.

In Rotterdam, I had bought an old Ford; when I handed over my driver's license to identify myself, I couldn't remember ever having picked it up at the city hall. When the salesman honestly told me I couldn't expect much more out of this car, I suddenly started recalling the names of countless makes and types of cars I had driven in the past. I thought of the ones I had bought brand new. I had bought my first Ford in 1927. It had spoke-wheels and open sides. Thoughts like this flooded in, and I had to concentrate quickly on other things to get my attention back to the matter at hand. Franciscus had stirred something up in me that I had let fall asleep. It was stronger than me, and I did not have the power to suppress it.

I was thinking about that when I took a walk through the pinewood. We had given guest concerts throughout Europe, and that had given me the opportunity to travel with the orchestra from Rotterdam. Not once had I remembered something from the past during those long, monotonous trips by bus or train. Now I had to breathe in deep and press my fingertips hard against my temples to come to grips with the memories that flooded my thoughts.

I thought about the cities I wanted to visit during my journey to Passau: Würzburg, Nuremberg and Regensburg. Würzburg brought the taste of wine to my mouth. I could see the different townscapes and the water of the river.

Nuremberg made me think first of horses, and then the face of Albrecht Dürer appeared, as it had when I had let myself be led by Franciscus. Now I rode behind him on a brown horse, and there were people everywhere around me. We rode to the north, to Aachen, to be present at the coronation of Charles the Fifth.

Now I knew why Dürer's picture sprang so clearly to my mind. I had shown him some woodcarvings I had made, and the master had been very enthusiastic about them. Franciscus and I rode along with his retinue, and when we split up after witnessing the coronation of the emperor, Franciscus and I moved on to the north again and arrived in the Netherlands, where I sold woodcarvings and sculptures. From the harbor of Rotterdam the whole wide world opened before me.

The thought of Regensburg made me feel the coolness of the St. Peter cathedral. I saw the old bridge over the Danube and districts without streetlights. I remembered that a portion of the golden coins we had hidden outside Passau had been stolen by Franciscus and I in Regensburg, from a merchant who had been too drunk to be able to watch his money.

The walk did me good. I was the eternal traveler who enjoyed covering long distances on foot. When I turned down a path at the other side of the wood, leading to a small village through a hilly landscape, I began to long for food and a drink. Not because they were necessities of life, for me anyway, but because the feeling of a full stomach would gratify me. I realized that I could live from the energy that came down to me from the immense universe and flowed through me. A glass of water every now and then would be enough for me. That's how Franciscus did it. Perhaps also, before long, the night would come when I would sleep for the last time, and it would be sufficient for me to rest only a few moments every twenty-four hours.

Franciscus had advised me to wear clothes other than I was accustomed to. The people who saw me enter the restaurant, across from the village church, noticed an unshaven man of about forty with straight, black hair, wearing an old sweater, worn trousers and brown leather shoes.

Because the kitchen was not yet open, I ordered a bottle of Frankish wine. I sat down at a large table, on the smaller side of a wooden corner seat, from where I was able to look over the entire room. Floor, ceiling, beams, bar, tables, chairs—it was all made of wood. On the walls hung deer heads, musical instruments, framed pictures of village feasts and the portraits of former owners and occupants of the building.

Something broke within me. I fought back my tears as I realized that I had a centuries-old past.

Someone sat down opposite me. An old man with pale blue eyes, he put a newspaper down on the table and looked at me searchingly. He started to talk to me, and I answered his questions in his native dialect. He wanted to know where I came from, and I told him that I lived in Rotterdam.

"Hearing your accent, I would have guessed you're from this neighborhood," he remarked.

"I speak the languages of all regions," I said. "From the present, from the past . . ."

The old man smiled. "Do you really know much about the German language?"

"No less than the Dutch, the French or the Portuguese languages," I answered, and noticed that the bottle was empty as I turned it upside down above my glass.

A little later I talked German in different dialects. The old man turned around and invited all those present to sit down at our table and listen to the stranger who spoke all possible vernaculars. Like a medium in trance, I promptly reacted to anything someone might say. A glass of beer was pushed towards me, and I went back far enough in time to make an enumeration, with an Old-Bavarian accent, of more than fifty different kinds of beer, from red ale to small beer, from wedding beer to wheat beer. I found it relaxing to talk this way. I made use of all the languages I knew, and it seemed to help me accept the fact that I was many times older than the gray-haired man who sat there opposite to me and listened to me open-mouthed.

After having spoken in dialects, I started to enumerate forgotten names, words and expressions. A man who had drawn up a chair and leaned his elbows on the table turned out to be historically well informed and knew a lot about music and musical instruments. I started to name all the different kinds of tools that were used in former days to build violins. He interrupted to ask me to repeat them slowly so that he could to write them down.

"I honestly believe that you are not playing jokes on us," he said. "Some of these names sound familiar to me."

A doctor, who was standing near the table with his wife, listening, asked me if I also spoke Latin.

"Just as good as Greek," I said and was soon translating a couple of sentences for him as he read aloud from a Latin paperback he just happened to have with him.

"It's all correct," he had to admit. "Where is it exactly you come from?"

I didn't feel like telling him the truth—that I was born in a village near the Moselle such a long time ago—so I produced my Dutch passport and driver's license from the back pocket of my trousers. Glasses of beer again were pushed over to me, and I automatically answered all the questions anyone asked me, without realizing what I was saying. As I talked I journeyed through time, and my mind became filled with many different thoughts.

There, at a large table in an unknown restaurant, in a village I didn't even know the name of, I finally realized that everything Franciscus had told me was true, and at last I became reconciled to it. There still existed countless gaps in my memory, but the black seas of suppressed experience from my past were dotted with islands of well-remembered adventures. Eventually I might be able to build solid bridges between them. For the time being I had come to terms with the awareness of my age and understood that this long, long road had begun with Alexander, the magician, who had poured eternal life to me out of a jar.

I heard people laugh.

Suddenly, I was startled by my own voice.

"Who am I? An old, childless man! The years gain momentum, and I have always been alone. I have no offspring and no relatives." My voice groaned and hissed. I spoke different German dialects together, and every now and then I used a Latin word or expression.

"*Terra enim est mater elementorum*—the earth is the mother of the elements. The magnum opus—the great work—has to be completed. And then, my friends, one gets the elixir of life!"

The laughter didn't stop. I put down an empty beer glass and saw that there was a plate in front of me on the table. I held a knife in my right hand. With my left hand I put down the beer glass and noticed how dirty it had become on the outside. I was eating like a medieval man, with my fingers and my knife. There was a large piece of meat on my plate. I folded pieces of grated carrot, sauerkraut and tomato in a lettuce leaf and put the whole thing in my mouth. The amazed faces around me, the laughter and muttering suddenly frightened me a little. I didn't belong here; I was an outsider, a wandering buffoon who did his tricks for a meal and a drink.

One probably thought I was acting so strangely because of the wine and beer. But the whirl I was in was caused by an overwhelming feeling of happiness. I understood now that there were other horizons outside my limited life as a musician and instrument seller and repairman in Rotterdam. Alcohol and other toxic substances could cause little damage to my body, which recovered quickly even after consuming great amounts. I remembered how I had behaved very unwisely two centuries ago and had been in a drunken stupor for some decades as a result.

"No one speaks so many languages and dialects," declared the doctor. "I have never seen anything so remarkable."

The old man, still sitting opposite to me, shoved backwards, chair and all, when he saw how I poured beer from a glass into an empty little salad bowl to wash my fingers in it. Wiping my hands on my sweater, I rose to my feet and walked up to the wooden bar to pay my bill. But the manager insisted that I keep my money in my pocket. "Please, come back soon! Are you staying here in the neighborhood? Not much happens around here, and you must have noticed how we all enjoyed listening to you."

For me, the show was over. I had better had be more careful, as Franciscus had warned me to be. Anyone who crossed my path could be one of Miethe's informants. Nevertheless, I was sure that no one had followed me.

I said goodbye to the people in the restaurant and went outside. Walking with my hands behind my back, I returned to the wood. It was already late when I reached my car at the parking place. I opened the door, got in and started the engine. I would search for a room to spend the night in at the next village.

Franciscus had told me to do everything at leisure. The journey should take a long time.

I had time. I had all the time in the world.

I had only needed a sweater on my stroll through the woods. The sun had been shining all day, and the temperature was some degrees above zero. In the next few days the weather changed—it began to freeze, and the sky turned gray. By the time I arrived in Passau, it had begun to snow heavily. The old town is built on a spot where three rivers flow together: the Inn, the Danube and the Ilz. I found myself on the Danube side of the mainland and walked, face down and with my hands in my coat pockets, up the steep road that led to the Veste Oberhaus, the high castle from where I could look out over the entire city. The snow came down in heavy flakes on the land and water. Spontaneous memories can spring up when the circumstances are the same as those during a previous experience—if I had arrived in Passau in the summer, perhaps I would have looked down on the town center, on the spit of land between the Danube and the Inn, without feeling my heart beat faster all of a sudden. There was snow on all the roofs, but only a thin white layer dusted the round, weather-beaten domes of the church towers.

At the other side of the Inn I could see the Mariahilf monastery. I knew a flight of stairs lead up to it, climbed over the years by many a pilgrim.

The dark sky, the contrast of the white snow and the now almost black looking water, the mountains, the houses, the towers—all made a deep impression on me, and I knew I had seen it all before. In the eighteenth century, Franciscus and I had been here, looking for a place to hide some golden coins. In Regensburg, in a busy inn not far from the cathedral, we had robbed a sleeping, drunken merchant. Braving a snowstorm, we undertook the journey to Passau on horseback.

When we arrived in the city, our clothes soaked, chilled to the bone, we knew we were safe. We bought new clothes, found someone to take care of our horses, and then stuffed ourselves with food and drink. When we left the city again, the snow had stopped, and we rode upstream along the Danube, on the left side, until we came to a ruin. There we had found an ideal place to hide the golden coins. For later. For now.

* * *

The search wasn't difficult. Of course, much had changed throughout the years, but the road still followed the water, and the thick layer of snow gave the surrounding area a timeless look. I drove through several villages, and all of a sudden a familiar high, bare rock face loomed up. Blasted green plants rooted in cracks where soil had stuck between the whimsical forms of the precipitous face. The road upwards was icy. Every now and then the car came to a standstill, and the rear wheels spun on the ice. There was a side road leading to houses, and I turned off, drove a hundred yards farther and then parked the Ford. I thought it wiser to go the last and steepest part on foot.

The sun was shining again, and big, white clouds floated through the sky. Screwing up my eyes, I looked up and peered through my eyelashes. It seemed as if the nearby clouds formed a rich blossom in the bare branches of the trees.

Arriving on top, I immediately recognized the ruined castle, the outer walls of which were built right along the edge of the precipice. Via stone steps it was possible to reach a small ledge where the first floor had been. When I leaned over the broken wall, with my elbows in the snow, I saw the river far down below me. Here and there were houses, and I saw my car standing along the side of the road. It was in just this way that I had stood here with Franciscus so very long ago. It was all so clear in my mind now, that I even remembered what we were talking about. I also knew, without having to turn around, exactly how to reach the spot where we had hidden the coins.

That day we had discussed our phenomenal good fortune and agreed that it must to be wonderful to have children. Children to love, children to see grow up, children to share everything with.

"We would outlive them, should we have them," Franciscus had pointed out, and then we both stared silently at the river for quite some time.

"That is why we have been spared from having them," he said. "All those years I never had a woman tell me she was pregnant."

I went down the steps and walked away from the ruin. Following a small path, I recalled that there had once been deciduous trees where I now saw only pines. After about a mile and a half, I reached a crossing, turned to the left and came upon a spot where someone had hewn great chunks of stone from the rock; possibly to use for the walls of the castle.

The most plausible way to hide our treasure would have been to hide it in one of the subterranean caverns in the area, but we had discovered a hole, probably a test hole dug by quarrymen to see if the rock there was suitable to use as building material. The hole was no more than two feet deep, and I had been able to touch the bottom with my fingers if I lay on my stomach and stuck my arm down there. The hole was sort of square, and the longest sides measured just over a foot. We had put the money in a linen bag and lowered it down. Then we had covered the hole with a big, flat stone, which we had tooled to make look like it was part of the ground there.

I recognized an irregular-shaped peak rising up from the snow; I knew the stone was not far from that spot. I quickened my pace, knelt down and began to push away the snow with my hands. I took out a pocketknife, opened it and scratched with the blade over the ground. The steel slid less than half an inch under the stone and stuck. I had found the place! I held the shaft firmly in my right hand and hammered on it with my left. The blade slipped under the stone. Using the knife as a lever, I pried the stone up just far enough to get my fingers under it, after which it took no great effort to shove it away from the hole. I lay down, with my face pushed into the snow, and put my hand inside. My nails scratched over the bottom. I didn't have to grope around long to realize that the hole was empty. Our gold had disappeared! I got down on my knees and took a lighter out of my pocket, leaned over, struck the flint and held my hand down in the hole. The stone had closed the hole so perfectly that in all this time, not even any water had seeped in. The flame of the lighter made it possible for me to see the bottom, and now I was sure that our fortune was no longer there. I thought about going back to Holland as fast as possible, to warn Francis Beck about his safe-deposit in America. Without bothering to cover the hole again, I got to my feet.

The entire journey had been for nothing. I stood there on that high, snow-covered rock and felt lonely.

Everything that had been so familiar to me I had left behind in Rotterdam. It suddenly became of the utmost importance to me that the engine of the old Ford did not give up and that I get back to my boat, where Franciscus lay recovering from his wounds.

I heaved a deep sigh and turned around, only to find myself looking straight into the eyes of a middle-aged man. Light blue eyes. Short gray hair, a small face, lips pressed together resolutely. A green coat, light green corduroy pants and big, brown leather climbing shoes. And in his hands, a rifle, aimed at my stomach.

"So there you are," the man spoke in German. "I didn't actually believe that you would ever show up here again."

He aimed the barrel of the weapon a little lower.

"Just remain standing there very still. The moment you move, I'll shoot your balls right out of your trousers!"

"Who—" was the only word I managed to produce.

Miethe? Rainer Miethe? No, Miethe had curly hair and was taller than this man. He was also more muscular and broader in the shoulders. Miethe's eyes were dark. I did have not the faintest idea who this man could be.

"Finally the waiting turned out to be worthwhile," the man continued. "Let me introduce myself to you, friend. My name is Walter Fabry, and today is the day of the great freedom. Now, thanks to you, I have my pile.

Money, a house and oceans of leisure time. Really, friend, I can finally leave this place. No more watching and waiting. No more sitting and staring through my field glasses. Oh, how I learned to concentrate over the years! Who would come to lift the stone? Who would go straight to his goal and kneel there? It is always so very quiet here. Not many people come to this spot. But everyone who showed up here was a suspect. During the daytime I was on guard, and at night there was always one of my dogs in the neighborhood to sound the alarm. Welcome! And now tell me, friend: who are you—Franciscus or Paulus?"

"My name is Hubert Nagel," I said, in German with a light Bavarian accent. "I am a medievalist, and this entire year I am doing research along the Danube. Places around ruins, like here, get my special attention. May I ask you sir, who you are and why do you aim a weapon at me?"

"I am the man who will shoot your balls off the moment you take a single step. But I already said that, and I already told you my name," said Walter Fabry. "But wait. Let me arrange it so that we can discuss this a bit more easily. I need move my rifle only a moment for that, and then I'll be able to drag you home and know for sure that you won't walk away from me—simply because you will not be able to walk, period. And for arguments sake, if you, by chance, turn out not to be the man I'm looking for, you will stay crippled for the rest of your life, but if you are the man I'm looking for, you'll be able to walk again in a few days."

With a quick motion he turned the rifle upside down and clasped his hands around the barrel and the butt. Stepping forward and sinking to his knees, he slammed my foot with the heavy wooden butt of his gun. I felt my metatarsals break. My stomach contracted and, raising my head, I held my breath. There was no one present on this snowy height who could help me.

A second blow broke the phalanges of my toes.

"We don't experience pain like normal human beings," said a voice in my head, which I recognized as that of Franciscus. "Sometimes I realize that I am bleeding and don't know from where because I am not aware of having cut myself."

I looked down at Walter Fabry, and it suddenly seemed as though I were an outsider looking in at this scene and not really involved in it at all. The butt of the rifle came down on my other foot several times in succession. I imagined that my shoes were now filled with a bloody mass mixed with bone grit. I rested on my heels and started to rock to and fro and then began to sway. Fabry danced around me, holding the rifle barrel with both hands. He was like a crazy lumberjack who makes cuts in a tree from all sides. I began to see everything in a blur. I saw only the green of his clothes and the gray of his hair as they went by when he hit me again. He crushed my heels and my shins. To keep myself in balance, I spread my arms and swayed on my broken heels. I must have looked very much like a scarecrow in a storm. I fell to the ground, face forward, and was flipped onto my back. Fabry's head appeared above mine, upside down. He slid an arm under each of my armpits and began to drag me, my smashed feet trailing through the snow.

"I expected you to start screaming," he grunted. "If you had, I would have pushed your face in the snow till your lips were frozen. Then I wouldn't have worried about you making any more sounds at all."

He panted, staggering backwards in a bent position as he dragged me along. A couple of times he let me drop, to straighten his back and to take a rest.

I felt a strange tingle in my feet that soon crept up my legs. I closed my eyes and felt myself lifted up again and dragged away. I lost consciousness. Later I recalled that I had heard the barking of hounds and felt a wet nose nudging my throat and a tongue licking my cheek and ear.

* * *

When I came to, I was in a big living room. The man had taken off his coat and sat opposite me in a big, leather armchair. I sat in a similar chair, my numb, broken feet propped on a table. Thick carpets lay on the wooden floor. Three hounds stretched out in front of the roaring fireplace. There were pictures and rifles on the walls. A window offered a view of a snowy garden, bordered by pine trees.

Walter Fabry rose to his feet and took a bottle of white wine from a cupboard. He opened it silently with a corkscrew, poured two glasses and put one in my hand. He sat down again and raised his own glass.

"Wine from the Moselle, friend! Must be familiar to you. Wine from your native ground. The man who longs to see you has been living there for years now. Take a sip. It will do you good. And I— well, I will drink because I have something to celebrate. Come, drink! Tell me your name, then, for I don't feel like calling you friend all the time. Is it Franciscus or Paulus? Is your name Francis Beck or Paul Brand? If you are Franciscus, Rainer Miethe will be completely surprised, for not so long ago someone almost caught him in Rotterdam. Tell me your name, put all your cards on the table, and then I will be honest with you too and tell what you want to know."

We both took a sip. I held my glass in my hand, he put his down on the table.

"Paul Brand. I am Paul Brand."

My feet were tingling again. It didn't hurt, but I did feel a headache coming on. I knew Franciscus got these headaches quite often. When he did, he doubled up in pain and hid his face behind his hands. He had told me it seemed as if there were flashes of lightning under the crown of his skull.

"Aha! Paulus. The woodcarver, the violin builder, the man who has remained trackless for such a long time. It was known that Franciscus had established himself in

America. He became a composer. In Rotterdam he supposedly was crashed to pieces and burned beyond recognition in a car accident. Miethe doesn't believe a word of it. The story goes that you didn't hide yourself intentionally because you were unaware of your own long past and lived an uncomplicated life somewhere. Do you know how long I have been guarding here? Thirty years!"

He pointed at the hounds near the fireplace.

"Don't ask me how many dogs I have trained to watch the hole and the stone. In fact I didn't even believe anymore that someone would ever appear. For before I came to live here, there was another who guarded here, and he himself followed someone else. Perhaps the first watchman was posted here a hundred years ago. It was made clear to all the watchmen that the men who were expected to show up would give the game away by a certain deed. Whoever lifted the stone from the hole had to be Franciscus or Paulus."

"Why are you telling me all this?" I asked.

He heaved a deep sigh.

"In the first place, because you can not escape from me, now that I finally have you. The only way to get away from me is to get down on your belly and drag yourself out using your hands. You will scrape your knees, and your feet will get heavy, and—"

"And in the second place?" I interrupted him.

"I can tell you whatever I want, because I'll be turning you over to Rainer Miethe in no time at all. But I mainly want to talk to you because I finally, after thirty years, sit face to face with the man I actually didn't ever expect to meet. My patience will be amply rewarded, however. This house, this beautiful, big house, will be in my name, and Miethe will pay me for so many loyal years of service. Paul Brand, you have made me a millionaire!"

I looked straight into his light blue eyes. He didn't evade my glance; his small lips smiled.

"The patience of the watchman," he said dreamily. "I already had resigned myself to my fate. I knew that soon I would have to give a younger man the use of the house, and I would have to content myself with a small pension."

"How could someone know if we did hide our money here?" I wondered.

"Miethe was in Regenburg, followed you to Passau, followed you to the ruin, saw everything. He was still healthy then. Now the situation is quite different. The man is dying. What he needs is blood."

"Maybe my blood type is different from his."

"So what? This isn't about a normal blood transfusion. This is about your blood. Through your veins flows something that makes you immortal, that repairs your broken bones. Miethe is powerful, he is rich, his sources are inexhaustible, but he needs your blood."

"He told you all of this?"

Walter Fabry nodded.

"He calls me every day. You hear a lot, Paul, when you get the same man on the phone every day, for thirty years at a stretch, who urges you to stay on the alert and convinces you of the importance of your task."

For the second time he pointed at his animals.

"I used to be a policeman in Trier. I was approached by someone who worked for Miethe. When I proved to be as loyal as those three hounds put together, when I solemnly promised to keep my eyes open all the time and never, ever slacken my attention, I was told that I could earn a house in Bavaria and a fixed salary. It all seemed so beautiful, but it turned out to be tedious. Now I finally can leave this place. After I have brought you to Miethe, I will go on vacation, and then it'll be a long time before I come back here. I am the watchman who was lucky, gathered in the harvest and soon will be spending a whole lot of money."

"Do you believe all those stories about immortality?" I asked.

"I have believed them for thirty years, since I was at Rainer Miethe's home. It is like a museum in there! Everything he ever stole and kept is on display in the rooms of the building. But it wasn't the old objects that convinced me. When I looked him in the eye, I saw an age that goes much further back than the simple life of a man. Even then, he already didn't look all that good. Nowadays his appearance must be horrifying."

He fell silent for a moment and took a sip of his wine. Then he continued, "What I did to you, with the butt of my rifle, that would have brought down any other human being. You sit here in front of me as if nothing happened."

"And now I am going to be Rainer Miethe's guinea pig, and he hopes to recover through elements of my blood."

"Almost right," said Walter Fabry. "Almost right. Yes, he will feel strong and healthy again soon, that is true. But there is something that seems to be of much more importance to him."

I raised my eyebrows.

"Quite often he has mentioned the name Maria Delaruelle."

I bolted straight up in my chair. The glass slipped out of my hand and broke into a million pieces on the wooden floor. My feet slid off the table. A tingle crept up through my legs, and the slight headache became worse. It made it impossible for me to think clearly any longer.

Maria Delaruelle. Her name bridged centuries. When the headache began to ease off a bit, I carefully put my feet back on the table.

Fabry said, "The mention of her name caused quite a shock, didn't it?"

He got up and began to pick up the pieces of broken glass. I remained silent. Something I had suppressed forever had come flooding back into my memory.

* * *

Miethe had passed the jar to Franciscus, after I had brought it to my mouth.

"I will wait for a couple of days," he had said. "I have patience, friends."

How was it exactly? Franciscus and I had left Alexander's underground workplace. We had had enough of that little magician with his stubby beard, his big yellow teeth and his dirty gray habit. We went back out into the world, and time told us that the hour of our death would never come.

Miethe, indeed, had patience. He became the devoted pupil of Alexander, bent over his books, kettles and hermetically sealed vessels. Together they searched for a way to make gold. One day Miethe, realizing Alexander couldn't teach him anything new and deciding to keep all the knowledge to himself, killed the magician. He threw Alexander's body into the pool in which the immortal fishes swam and then mounted the black horse and rode back to the Moselle.

It is unclear how long Miethe lay hidden in the area before he got the chance to kill Count Kaspar von Karst as well, but the day finally arrived when he spied their horses standing at the edge of the woods. The count, wanting to be alone with her, had gone out for a ride with Maria Delaruelle unaccompanied by his retinue.

When he was found the next day, Kaspar von Karst sat there on the ground, leaning against a tree. He had been stabbed through his chest with his own sword. The point had been forced so deep into the trunk, that it took two men to pull it out.

Miethe had taken Maria to Alexander's hiding place. He dug up the jar and pulled off the stopper. They both took a swallow from the syrupy substance, and Miethe believed her when she told that they would be together forever. But one day she left him. And now she must always hide from the man who has eternal time to bring her back again.

* * *

I looked up and saw Walter Fabry holding up a new glass of wine in front of me.

"I don't know where she is," I said.

"Possibly," he said. "If you don't, Franciscus will. Miethe thinks that one of you has always maintained contact with her."

He could be right. Maria was our contemporary. She had stolen our hearts, and my feelings for her were timeless. I wished I could have the use of my full powers of memory now, because I didn't know if I had ever seen her again after I had left the castle with the precious goblet in my possession.

"The whole thing boils down to his," said Fabry. "Miethe wants to extend his life. Anyone who has lived as long as this clings to his earthly existence fiercely; you should know that better than I. He would do anything to become young, strong and healthy again. But he wants more. He wants Maria, his great love. He has fathered no children. He has said that Maria and he should raise a family. She is like him, like you, like Franciscus. He has told me about immortal descendants. About children who could live for at least five hundred years. You carry a secret. It is not so strange, after all, for him to reward a man like me so amply. I'm not bringing him someone who's just an old friend. I bring him life! And he will undoubtedly have ways to find out if you know where the woman is."

I put my feet on the floor and tried to get up— Franciscus had arrived at my house in Rotterdam with broken ankles. My feet were numb and immediately gave way. I didn't even want to think about what my socks would look like when I took off my shoes.

"Tomorrow you can get out of that chair," said Fabry. "Then I'll drag you outside and put you in my car. Together we'll take a ride to Rainer Miethe."

* * *

I couldn't sleep that night. I would never sleep again. I dreamed with my eyes open, and every now and then I became aware of the presence of Walter Fabry, who still sat opposite me and struggled to stay awake. Sometimes, when I looked up for a moment, I saw him dozing off. The feeling in my feet had returned. The pain wasn't that severe now or so constant. I almost forgot about it. Whenever I closed my eyes, I saw Maria in front of me. We were people from another time and I longed to be with her. With her I could talk about things no one else would understand.

"We would outlive them," I heard Franciscus say again. "That is why we have fathered no children."

Maria was one of us. Maybe Rainer Miethe was right? Could a man and a woman who had drunk from Alexander's jar raise a family that had a future of many centuries?

I would have given my blood to a friend, but Rainer Miethe was no longer my friend. If I could help Franciscus with my blood, I would. Miethe had become a merciless man. He had killed Alexander, his great master; he had stabbed Kaspar von Karst with his own sword. Since then he had lead a life of violence and thought only of himself. It didn't surprise me that he was a rich and powerful man now. How he felt about me was easy to guess. The hatred was perceptible in my feet, from my broken heels to my crushed toes.

* * *

Walter Fabry waited until it was light outside. He rose to his feet, had a good stretch and looked out the window.

"It has been snowing all night long," he said. "I'm not used to making long drives anymore. That's why I don't like to leave in the dark. I'm going to make some strong coffee, and after that, well, I have a lot to arrange. You came here by car, didn't you? I have to get it and put it in the garage so that no one will know you have been here. Where is it?"

"At the side of the road, beneath the ruin," I said. "It is an old Ford. You'll find it parked in the last turnoff. The keys are in my pocket."

It was useless to withhold this information. He could use the butt of his rifle one more time to force me to tell him these things.

"Good," said Fabry. "I'll walk to it and take the hounds with me. Then I'll drive your car to someone I know who won't care if the car has Dutch plates so that I can leave my hounds with him. When I come back, we'll take my car out of my garage and put yours in. By then it should be time to go to Rainer Miethe. He can have you, and I can remind him of our agreement. Soon I will be spending money like water."

I had no mind for strong, black coffee, but I drank two mugs with him. He went to turn off the main valves in the house, closed the shutters here and there, and finally pulled the telephone plug from its jack.

"In case you managed to reach the telephone and call someone," he said. "You are still able to crawl, that is why I have to tie you up. So I'm sure you will remain sitting right there, like a good fellow, while I'm out. How are your feet? Aren't you in pain?"

With his fist he hammered on my shoes. I didn't feel anything in my feet, but immediately got a stinging headache. He placed my hands on my lap and tied up my wrists. He fastened my body tight to the back of the easy chair. He checked everything one more time, called his hounds and left the room, the telephone in his hand. I heard the slamming of a door and the barking of the hounds.

Through the window I could see a gray sky and a snow-covered garden. The branches of the pine trees, at the opposite side of the garden, hung down, heavy under the weight of the snow. I stared for a long time and thought about Maria Delaruelle.

I was startled when all of a sudden a figure appeared in front of the window. A man of about my size, dressed in a red ski jacket, peered inside. He had a beaked nose and green eyes. His small face was unshaven. Short, curly hair stuck out from under a red, knitted cap. My heart began to beat faster. It was Franciscus, it was Francis Beck.

"I am alone!" I cried out at the top of my lungs. "I'm alone here, Francis!"

He nodded, took half a step backwards, lifted his left leg and kicked the windowpane to pieces. He kicked again and again to break off the remaining vertical, sharp fragments.

His feet were healed, like my feet also would heal. The man who climbed through the broken window was healthy and full of energy. Walter Fabry had not taken into account that a second man might turn up—after thirty years of waiting and watching, he had never imagined that another immortal would follow the first. I took a deep breath and was surprised by my own words when I said, "What do you know about the whereabouts of Maria Delaruelle?"

"Idiot!" he hissed. He was already busy cutting my ropes loose with his pocketknife. "Fill me in. The important things now, Maria later. Am I in danger?"

I told him in ten short sentences what he needed to know. He needed even fewer words to tell me that he was feeling pretty good and had recovered quickly from his injuries. He had been traveling behind me to make sure I arrived safely and was able to find my way back to the place where we had hidden the golden coins.

Then he took a rifle from the wall and began to search for ammunition. He found some in a drawer in the cupboard. He went back to the window. "I'll wait for him outside."

"Are you going to murder him?" I wanted to know.

"Of course not. I know how to handle a rifle pretty well. He gets a bullet right through one of his feet. Then he will know the pain he has caused you. And then he can tell us where we can find Miethe. It is about time that we know where we stand with our friend. Your car must not be found here. Erase all tracks, remember? We've always done things carefully. No doubt we'll find a place somewhere, where we can let the Ford roll into the Danube unnoticed."

"Maria—" I started again, but he didn't respond. He stepped out through the window, and I could hear his footsteps in the snow.

I waited. Two hours later I heard the sound of a motor. A door opened and slammed shut. I could hear it all very clearly through the broken window. The voice of Walter Fabry sounded surprised. "What—stop! I—"

Then a shot rang out and, I heard Fabry scream.

This time Franciscus entered the house through the front door, hung the rifle back on the wall, and said in a businesslike voice, "I need something to bandage his foot. The man is bleeding like a pig. Then I'll have to shovel the snow away. The red of his blood stands out too much against the white."

He winked at me.

"This time I'm the one who has to support his friend. Believe me, Paulus, after three days or so your feet will bear you up again, and it will seem if this lunatic never touched you. You will forget how he used his rifle to crush your bones. I suppose that Fabry treated you that way by order of Miethe. I gave him a taste of his own medicine. It's only a graze, and he doesn't even need a doctor, but I have no doubt he will do everything that I tell him to and answer all my questions."

* * *

At just about noon, we drove away. Franciscus had driven the Ford into the river and now was sitting behind the wheel of Fabry's jeep. Fabry himself sat on the back seat and constantly whined that the pain in his foot was unbearable.

"We have to find another car today," said Francis. "Sooner or later, someone will discover the broken window and warn the police. When they don't find Fabry at home, they will start searching for his jeep. We have to think about everything, Paulus."

I nodded.

"Do you know that I didn't sleep at all last night?" I said. "Furthermore, I have noticed that I'm no longer dependent on food. These are very strange occurrences, indeed."

We drove along the ruins and went down to the river. It started to snow again. I didn't know where Franciscus would go to now. My feet tingled, but I no longer suffered from the headache. I closed my eyes. As far as I was concerned, he could drive for as long as he wanted to. Just as long as he stayed until I was able to step outside without the help and walk on my own two feet.

5 -The Jester

Halfway through his drive, Andreas Pallasch had a very strange experience. He saw himself sitting in the cab of his truck, chin uplifted, fingers wrapped loosely around the steering wheel, staring out the windshield.

He had started out at the loading platform earlier that day, filling his truck with empty bottles that were to be transported to the wine makers in the area. Andreas was following the course of the Moselle River upstream, in the direction of Trier, when he began to feel very strange and quite uncomfortable. He felt as if he were losing all control over his muscular system and his mind was beginning to play tricks on him. From his lofty vantage point, he looked into the cab of the truck, through the side window, and saw the back of his own head.

There he sat, all two hundred and forty pounds of him, his big, plump body in the driver's seat, no longer under his command. With a sudden, great spasm his head snapped back, his neck muscles swelled and knotted up, his fingers locked around the steering wheel with a grip of steel, and his right foot slammed on the brakes. The clinking and banging of his cargo of bottles and the screeching of the tires as they tried to grab the road reached his ears at the same moment the truck came to a standstill. He felt his senses coming back under his control and started to think clearly again. His body no longer was a spiritless lump of meat that he was merely an observer to—he could see the world through his own eyes again.

The motor was dead.

With a trembling hand, Andreas stroked his short hair. He began to smile as he sat upright and leaned to the right to have a look at his face in the rear-view mirror. His round, red face shone with perspiration. Andreas Pallasch gave himself a wink and then looked at the road again.

He didn't understood exactly what had happened to him. For a brief moment his head had been as empty as the bottles he transported. From somewhere outside his body, high above the roof of the truck, he had looked down upon the fat man driving his truck as if he were a stranger. He had seen the winding road before him, the river flowing by on the left, and the hillside vineyards on the right with the thousands of sticks upon which the vines of grapes grew.

He wasn't at all worried about the fact that something really weird had just happened to him that he could not explain. Something else occupied his mind now. He, or at least the way he rationalized recent events to himself, had been wiped out for a moment; his whole being had been virtually erased. The act of slamming on the brakes had the effect of jarring him back to his senses, and he now seemed to be much more conscious of his inner strengths. It was as if his spirit had tapped into some new, inner resource that enabled him to hear, see, feel and smell better. He was extremely aware of himself and his physical surroundings. He felt excited and satisfied as he looked around and noticed that the world seemed to be more beautiful than ever. He had made this drive countless times, but this time he saw things he had never noticed before. The leaves on the vines were raised up in silent worship to the summer sun, and he could see the young, green fruit so sharply that he could count the individual grapes even as he drove past at a speed of forty-five miles per hour. The surface of the Moselle was as smooth as glass and wound up, out of sight, behind the mountains, high in the sky, and looked as if it might have its headwaters at the rim of the sun, where heaven's liquid gold flowed down into it.

A short while later Andreas was finally relaxed enough to slow down a bit. The reduced speed better fit his frame of mind. He was driving through a small village and decided to stop at a filling station for gas. He got out, unscrewed the gas cap and took the hose from the pump. He fastened the handle of the hose to his tank and deeply inhaled the scent of diesel while he waited. He was just standing there, looking around, with his hands shoved deep into the pockets of his overalls, when he saw someone come out of the filling station's small office.

It was a woman.

She was young, with long, silky blond hair and big, gray eyes. She wore a short black dress and a tight-fitting red jacket. Opening the door of a BMW, she lowered herself down onto the seat sideways so that her long, shapely legs were still outside the car.

She turned her head and gave him a quick glance.

He could tell by the double H on her license plate that she was from Hamburg. Suddenly, she pulled her legs into the car, closed the door, started the engine and sped off. As she drove off, Andreas ran to his truck and heaved himself into the cab. The gas hose was still attached to his truck as he started it up, stepped on the gas, popped the clutch and turned out onto the road. The hose stretched and stretched until the metal spout shot out of the tank in a spray of diesel fuel.

Andreas Pallasch couldn't remember exactly what the woman he was following looked like. He was chasing an image formed primarily around his brief glimpse of her legs. Long, smooth legs that vanished, all too soon, into the car behind a slamming door. With his engine roaring and the bottles banging in the back, he left the village. He followed the BMW, which accelerated rapidly, but he was still able to make out her taillights. He stared down the road through squinted eyes. The sweat trickled off his head, down his neck and into the collar of his overalls. He felt very much alive and was bursting with energy. Never in his life had he felt so strong, so vital, so virile.

Andreas knew this road perfectly. Almost daily, he drove this route along the river, from town to village, from wine merchant to winegrower and back again, carrying his cargo of bottles.

"Once I force her car over to the curb," he thought, "that girl from Hamburg is mine. And it doesn't matter at all where I have her; in her car or in my cabin, either will do! I want her, and I know it won't take too much effort to get her!"

He was so lost in his thoughts that he did not even notice that his old truck was slowly catching up to the BMW. He didn't look for an explanation for his sudden feelings of lust and violence—the urges were there, and he was going to satisfy them. With the gas pedal to the floor, he took the bends in the road as wide as possible and made use the other side of the road to get his control back.

Panting, Andreas breathed through open mouth; the salvia dripped down his chin like some rabid animal. He let his hand slip off the steering wheel and into his crotch to squeeze the throbbing hardness in his pants. He drove through Karst, a beautiful, scenic village between hillside vineyards and the river, drooling and squeezing his genitals.

Then his frame of mind started to change, and things were no longer quite as they had seemed. The excitement faded, and he closed his mouth. His chubby cheeks lowered as his eyes widened. He drove through the main street of Karst at full speed, but he had lost sight of the BMW. He thought about the woman. He was sure he had seen her get into her car and that he had gone after her. He knew he had almost caught up to her and was about to force her to stop so that he could relieve his lust within her. But neither was there a BMW with a double H on the plates nor an attractive blonde to be found anywhere. He sped along, faster and faster, until it was almost impossible to control the truck. H wanted to slow down but couldn't move his foot. It was as if the lower part of his body had become paralyzed; as fear tensed the muscles of his arms and stomach, he felt his erection begin to shrink.

Every time he hit a bump in the road, it seemed as if the truck would float into the air and then dance back to earth on the rubber of the tires. The road took a sharp curve towards the riverside, and he was out of Karst. Here the road ran straight until it came to the next bend of the Moselle, about a half a mile farther ahead.

He saw someone, a man, standing in the middle of the straightaway.

The figure was still pretty far away, but Andreas's consciousness seemed to center on it. It seemed he had only to stretch out his hand to be able to touch the man.

It was as if something had slipped into his mind that colored his world, like drops of India ink dissolved in clear water.

What he saw, was so sure he saw, was a jester. He wore a leather fool's cap, green on the left side and red on the right, with two horn-shaped protuberances, tipped with copper bells, sticking out of the top. His clothes consisted of a jerkin and trousers, both made of little patches of black and brown leather all sewed together. His shoes had long, curled, pointy toes, with little bells on them that were a bit smaller than those on his cap.

Once more Andreas tried to slow down. He succeeded in moving his foot to the brake pedal, but at the very moment he touched the pedal, all the strength left his foot and leg, and the sole of his shoe pressed the pedal way too lightly to put the brakes into operation.

He was approaching the jester at an increasingly faster rate of speed. The figure in front of him seemed to swell up and become the size of a giant. The vague wrinkles in the pieces of leather that made up his clothes appeared like deep ploughed furrows now, and all Andreas could see through the windshield was black and brown. For an instant he had control of his senses again and was able to step on the brakes. The truck began to shake as he slowed down. The jester was directly in front of him and had become normal size again. For the first time he was able to see the face clearly. The skin seemed to me made of leather, with the same furrows and cracks as those little pieces that formed his clothing. He had thick, rubbery lips and a snub nose. His most striking feature, however, was his coal black eyes—the white of the eyes was lacking, and his eyes seemed to consist only of pupils. The jester stooped and ducked. Andreas tugged at the wheel. The truck, its brakes jammed, pulled to the right, threatened to crash into the foot of the stony hillside, and started to tilt and roll. Andreas looked to the side and saw the jester, still stooped, backing towards him. With his hands pushed backwards and his arms outstretched he grasped the truck and let it glide over his shoulders and fall upside down on the other side of the road. The truck smashed to the ground and continued to roll crosswise over the road, leaving a thick blanket of broken, green bottles behind. Andreas Pallasch's arms and legs moved pumped furiously around the cab of the truck, which was now like a prison cell from which no escape was possible, to prevent his head from smashing against the sides, the roof or the floor and breaking his neck.

It was the jester who pulled him from the wreckage. The truck lay on its side, and Andreas was dragged out through the broken window. A stench he could not place filled his nostrils, and the hideous, bursting face of the jester thrust into his own. Yellow teeth were visible between the split, rubbery lips. Andreas felt himself lifted up and tossed aside like a rag doll. As he flew through the air, he heard the ringing of tiny bells, and finally came to light on the green carpet of broken glass. He felt no pain but lay still, flat on his back, until he was positive that nothing was broken. As the tingling of the copper bells slowly weakened and finally disappeared, other sounds came to his ears. The siren of a police car, the screeching of brakes, the pulling of a handbrake, the slamming of two doors. Andreas sat up straight, looked first at the approaching policeman and then at himself.

Now the pain settled in as he discovered that his body was covered with cuts and bruises. His overalls were torn, and blood flowed across his skin along splinters of glass.

"You've been driving as if you had just drunk your entire cargo, Andreas," said Josef Reimer, one of the policemen. "What's the matter with you? You pulled into the gas station to fill up, and all of a sudden you left, without paying and with the hose still stuck in your tank."

Pallasch and Reimer knew each other very well. They were both from the same region and had even been schoolmates at one point.

* * *

Now the police officer sat on a chair in the emergency room of Doctor Hilde Steiner, and the driver lay naked on his stomach on the examination table. At first the doctor refused to allow the policeman into the treatment room, but Andreas had said he didn't mind if his old acquaintance accompanied him. The fact of the matter was, Andreas was embarrassed by his corpulent nakedness and felt more comfortable with someone he knew in front him. Even if that person was a police officer who was determined to ask him questions which he could not answer very well.

"I was chasing a BMW. I had been able to follow it for the entire time once we left town. I wanted to see if I was able to keep up with it. Speed against driving ability, as it were. After all Josef, you know I know every inch and curve of that road as well as I know the back of my hand and—"

"Don't lie to me lies, Andreas. We got a call about the way you were driving through town and caught up with you soon enough. You were alone on the road, Andreas; there was no BMW anywhere to be seen. What's wrong with you, man? You didn't react to our lights or sirens, and you gave us no room to pass or come alongside you. When we tried, you swerved into the middle of the road, and your truck started to sway from side to side. You can consider yourself lucky that it was so quiet on the road. But . . ."

He fell silent for a while and watched the doctor's activities.

She was a good-looking woman, in her early forties, with big, brown eyes and shoulder length, dark brown hair. She was busy disinfecting all the little injuries on Andreas's hairy thighs and calves and examining the cuts for splinters of glass. Reimer watched her work without noticing that every now and then her fingers trembled.

"But the strangest part was what happened at the end," Josef continued. "That crazy ride over the dead-straight part of the road. I watched as you slammed on the brakes and your brake lights lit up and then went out again as you tugged at the wheel and seemed to be doing battle with your truck. The truck slid crosswise across the road, rolled, lost the cargo—and then, all of a sudden, was actually off the ground, as if it had been lifted or pulled up. But even that wasn't the strangest part of this whole thing, Andreas. For what happened to you? We were nearby, our car standing with its front wheels in the glass, and then, there you were, waving your arms and kicking your legs, above the cab of the truck. It seemed as if you could fly! You were actually floating through the air. While your truck was still moving forward, you went in the exact opposite direction and came down in the broken glass. Impossible, yes. But my colleague and I saw it with our very own eyes."

He rose to his feet and looked at the big body on the examination table.

"And look at you now. Basically unscathed. Insignificant scratches. You should be much worse off than this."

Then he turned to the doctor.

"This is not the first patient who has been brought to you because of an automobile accident in Karst or the surrounding vicinity, Doctor."

Dr. Steiner gave him a piercing look.

"Yes, many odd things have happened recently," she replied. Her voice was clear but obviously concerned.

"I'm not even able to marshal all the facts," Josef Reimer continued. "My jurisdiction is outside of Karst, but when I put together everything I have heard and add to that what I have had to deal with myself, well . . .

"There was the man who almost drowned in the Moselle and claims to have fallen into the river from the opposite mountain, but between the mountain and the water there are two rows of houses, two roads and a good-sized piece of land. And then there was the tourist found sitting stuck between two boulders, and it seemed as though those heavy stones had been shoved together by a bulldozer. It took the police hours of back-breaking work to free the woman. She cannot remember how she came to be there and—"

"Will you please leave us alone for a moment?" Hilde interrupted him. "Soon you will have all the time you need to discuss the events with Mr. Pallasch."

The policeman nodded, put on his cap and left the examination room. He sat down next to his colleague in the waiting room, and there they sat and waited until Andreas Pallasch could put on his torn overalls again and come with them to make a statement.

* * *

Dr. Steiner looked at the fat man, who had gotten dressed and now paced up and down with his hands behind his back.

"If there is any thing you would like to tell me?"

He stood still. "What do you mean?"

"I imagine that it is sometimes easier to tell a doctor something in confidence than it is to tell someone who is going to write everything down and bring it before a court of law."

When he didn't react, she continued. "The stories Reimer told were quite something, but I also have something to add. Your injuries are indeed only insignificant little scratches. You are a heavy man, Andreas, much too fat. If what Reimer said was true, and you were actually floating through the air, then, with your weight, you should have hit on the ground much harder and suffered much greater injuries. The glass should have been imbedded much deeper in your flesh. Look at your wrists: those wounds are right near the arteries. If they had been just half an inch closer, half an inch deeper . . ."

In silent retrospect, she thought to herself, *Wounded. But not serious enough to be brought to a hospital. More work for the doctor. The umpteenth patient since . . .*

Staggering, Pallasch went back to the table on which he had been lying a moment ago and put his hands on the smooth surface. He hung his head, and, suddenly and briefly overwhelmed by a feeling of suffocating emotion and anxiety, tears began to run down his cheeks. After a moment or two he was able to regain his calm, and he wiped his face with the torn sleeve of his overalls.

"It was all so beautiful, Doctor. So very beautiful, but oh, so strange at the same time. As I was driving I got the feeling that I was able to look at myself from the outside and that something apart from my physical self existed that was also mine. Can you understand that? Am I making any sense at all to you?"

Hilde nodded.

"I eventually returned to myself, but from that moment on there was something extra, something that showed me how beautiful the world was. At the filling station I saw a woman who was so enchanting, so attractive, and so desirable that I had to follow her. It must have been a mad race indeed, considering that I ended up crashing my truck. But suddenly there was someone standing on the road. And maybe this will sound just as incredible and perhaps as insane as the rest of the story does, but it was a—"

A jester, thought Hilde Steiner, and she hid her hands quickly behind her back. They had begun to tremble again.

"A jester," said Andreas Pallasch. "A man who has bells on his fool's cap and shoes. The skin on his face was—was, well, broken—yes, it seemed broken. Burst, actually. He pulled me out of the cab of my truck, and when he got close to me I could not believe the stench. He smelled so very bad that I cannot even describe it.

"I had driven extremely fast straight towards him. The truck approached him at an oblique angle, and as I was right upon him, he lifted the truck up and threw it over him. I was dragged out through the broken window and thrown like a rag doll, amongst the pieces of broken glass. Doctor, I must seem absolutely crazy. I can't tell a story like this to the police, can I?"

"No, I wouldn't think so, Andreas. I don't think they'll understand at all. Come with me. I'll walk with you to the waiting room. I'm going to give you a prescription for some tranquilizers to help calm your nerves, and I'm going to tell Reimer that the bump to your head has caused you to block out certain things. I'll let him know that if he has any questions, he should direct them to me, that I am always willing to help the police.

"Listen to me, Andreas. I don't want you to worry about anything that has happened today or what the consequences may be. I know that is asking a lot, but it is best for you. I have studied psychiatry, and you can come and talk to me any time you want. Think about how much worse this would have been if that wild ride of yours had gotten someone hurt or killed!"

She held the door to the waiting room open for him, and as he passed her, she thought, *I will help you as much as I can. I must, for it isn't your fault at all. It has nothing to do with you at all. It's all about me. Just me.*

* * *

Hilde Steiner's father had been, just as his father before him, the town doctor in Karst, and now Hilde had her practice in the same old house. After she had passed the exams and was qualified as a medical doctor, she had decided to widen her knowledge of the human mind. She went back to school and studied psychiatry. After that, she lived and practiced in Munich, and did well there, but had eventually become homesick and longed for Karst—for the shelter and comfort of her native village. When her father died, and she had to decide between selling the house or living in it herself, Hilde went home and took over the practice.

That doctors cannot always work wonders, she had learned at an early age, when her mother had become terminally ill, and all her father could do was stand there, empty handed. That psychiatrists were not always able to free themselves from their own fears, she also knew, ever since a phantom from her youth had come back to haunt her. While practicing in Munich she had often discussed phobias with her patients, supported them and helped lift the burden from their shoulders. Occasionally a certain avenue of therapy seemed to help greatly and she was rewarded by seeing her patient mentally rejuvenated. She was witness to a smile and a laugh, where previously there had been only fear.

Hilde Steiner took off her white coat, hung it over the back of a chair and sat down behind her desk. She switched on a recorder, leaned backward and closed her eyes. Then she forced herself to talk, the same way she encouraged so many of her patients talk. What was spoken in therapy could be recorded for later use. It could be heard over and over again, thus permitting an accurate report documenting the case at hand. It was also an important tool for making comparisons at later sessions. She had never practiced this method on herself before and was extremely curious about two things: one, how honest she would dare to be with herself; and two, how her voice would sound. For all her professionalism, sophistication and life experience, she was still human, with human frailties and a fair amount of vanity. She had ample time until her next appointment and just hoped that she would not be disturbed by the telephone.

"I was still so very young," she began. She stopped speaking for a moment and, with eyes closed, shook her head disapprovingly. The ends of her hair whipped across her throat. "No, no, I've got to be much more clear!

"I was seven years old. It was in October, the wine month. It was a time of joy and happiness—there were feasts, parades, parties. Big bonfires were lit in the mountains, and I can remember, oh so well, how cheerful everyone was. A procession wound its way through the streets of Karst, a train of enthusiastic people who were celebrating because the harvest was done and the grapes had already been crushed. I stood there at the side of the road and looked up at the passing floats and at all the musicians and the men, women and children who followed. I saw my parents and many acquaintances go by. There were people in regional costumes, uniforms, disguises, all sorts of dress.

"And all of a sudden, in the marching crowd, the jester appeared! He danced and jumped. The bells on his fool's cap tinkled. His clothes were dirty and strange. The short jerkin and the tight trousers he wore were red and green—each side of him being the opposite color of the other. Every now and then he stopped and stood still in front of the crowd and held out his open hand. When someone put a coin in it, he danced and jumped along. Sometimes he received nothing, and then he would push whoever was unfortunate enough to be standing close to him. I watched, and I must admit I was a bit frightened, and did not understood why the people simply laughed and did nothing to defend themselves when he put his fists against their shoulders and pushed them backwards.

"I remember all this very well, as though it were yesterday.

"He came nearer. His face was covered with dirt, except for a few narrow furrows where the sweat ran down and left clean tracks. Not a single hair stuck out from under the fool's cap, but his eyebrows were so long and bushy that they almost reached the top of his forehead. Holding my breath, I stood silently, hoping he would not notice me, and simply pass me by. Suddenly he spun around on his heels right in front of me, sank to his knees and put his face right in front of mine. He held out his hand, and his mouth opened wide. The sourish smell of white wine wafted up to my nostrils, and I stepped back. He wheezed, jumped up and continued dancing along with the procession. He was like a creature from another world, and I stared after him until he had left the street."

Hilde opened her eyes. She could explain the thousands of fears and agonies of others and help them find the basis of their problems, and if she couldn't banish them, she could teach them how to have the courage to live with them. Right now it was she who needed the lesson in courage. Her eyelids trembled, and she stared through her long lashes as she took a deep, soul cleansing breath and continued.

"The next day I took a walk along a small path, between the vines. I wanted to go look at the flowers that had been brought to the old chapel as an expression of thanks for the good harvest.

"From up there one could see, far below, how the Moselle took a sharp bend at that point, not far from my home. I still remember my father telling me about a count of Karst who was buried not too far from the chapel. He had been killed by a sword-thrust some centuries ago.

"Halfway to the chapel, I heard footsteps behind me. They weren't the steps of someone who walked at a normal, constant pace. Sometimes it sounded like stamping, sometimes it sounded like shuffling. The sound of jingling bells reached my ears, and I knew it had to be the jester; I turned around and stood still.

"It was indeed the strange little man in red and green from the day before. With long jumps he went from the one side of the road to the other. He waved his arms, bent forward, clapped his hands and took little backwards jumps. I think it was then that I realized what mortal fear was all about."

Her brown eyes grew big as she stared at the door that led to the waiting room. The odd grains in the dark wood reminded her of the dirty face of the dancing jester.

The doctor shivered in fear. Her gaze traveled up to the ceiling, and she became aware of the great emptiness in the house above her. This big, old house, with so many rooms that she didn't even use all of them.

"I knew he had seen me. He began to jump around and turn somersaults back and forth. He turned upside down and landed on his hands, with fingers spread out on the road, and then magically sank through the pavement all the way to his elbows. Then he jumped up to his feet again. When he had come to within a few yards of me, he began to move in a catlike manner, his hands clawing the air, and his eyes rolling wildly in their sockets. The hands came nearer, nearer, until he touched me. He drew himself up to his full height, waved at me and shook his head so that the bells started jingling again. Perhaps he was drunk and didn't realize he was scaring a girl of seven to death. Anyway, only now do I fully understand how big a mistake he made that day when he bent down again and picked me up. He should have just gone away and left me alone, but no, instead he had to stop and tease me and lift me up. My face slid along his stomach and chest on the way up, and I smelled the sweat-soaked material of his fool's dress. My nose rubbed along his cheek and along the fool's cap. Higher and higher I went. He had lifted me way above his head, and I could see the bare grapevines, the chapel in the distance and the river winding far below.

"That was when I started to scream.

"I sucked air into my lungs as quickly as possible and then screamed as loudly as I could. I was lowered half a yard until the jester was holding me directly in front of him. With his arms outstretched he started to shake me. He pursed his lips and made a hissing sound.

"Why do I remember so well that the sun was shining and that it was unseasonably warm for October?

"Because memories remain strong after an emotional event."

These last words she said in a voice as if there was someone else in the room with her.

"Men suddenly appeared from between the vines, field workers who had been checking the state of the vine tendrils since the picking. They saw a man dressed like a jester, dancing and jumping around and making strange hissing noises, standing on the road holding in his arms a screaming girl. These men saw only that a child from Karst was being dragged along by a strange person in a dirty fool's costume. They ran up to us, and I felt two strong hands grab me around my waist. Right after the jester let go of me, someone punched him in the face. There was bewilderment in his eyes as he staggered to his feet, blood spurting from his nose. He fell to the ground, covering his head with his hands, pulling the long protuberances of the fool's cap down. The men kicked and beat him. He protected his face with his elbows, and he pulled his legs up to prevent getting kicked the stomach. The man who had wrenched me from his hands put me on the ground and joined the others. The jester had now managed to roll to the side of the road. He spun around and around there at the edge of the woods, and searched the front row of support sticks from along which the branches of the vines grew, looking for an opening, an escape route.

"They hurled abuse after abuse at him, and the beating went on. I heard the sound of sticks cracking underfoot, and it seemed to me to be the sound of breaking bones. But in fact the jester had somehow managed to pull himself free and escape into the vineyards. He sprinted down the steep slope, fueled by raw, animal fear. And above all the noise that day, the sound that reached me was the sound of the little bells tingling on his hat and shoes as the jester made good his escape.

"That, and the sound of my own screams.

"Someone had brought me home, but I don't know who. I was weeping softly now, the screams had stopped."

Hilde got up, switched off the recorder and took a deep breath.

"A sad childhood experience," she said in a soft voice. "Something that should never be able to come back — something you never forget, but also something you should be able to think about without feeling terrified."

She turned and started to walk towards the door, stopped, and said out loud, "Why? Why has the jester come back into my life? Why are people coming to me and telling me that they have recently had a bad experience with someone wearing a fool's cap? My God, Andreas Pallasch is such a simple man, he hasn't got enough imagination to make up such a story."

She sat down again and listened to her own, fearful voice issuing from the speaker of the recorder. She saw the entire event unfold before her mind's eye one more time. Afterwards, her mother had not allowed her to go out alone for an entire year. Her father had told her that he thought everything was due to a misunderstanding. "In former times," he said, "the jester was a well-known figure. And until recently there were still men roaming about who danced and jumped and held out their hand, begging for money. But this jester, it seems, was no more than a drunk who had gotten himself a jester's costume from who knows where, and joined in the festivities. He probably wasn't trying to scare you. He lifted you up to dance with you."

"What has happened to him?" she had asked.

"The fool's clothing was found by the river. I am sure he ripped it off at the first chance he got and will probably never disguise himself again. No one will ever know who he was, and so much the better."

Later, when she became older, she had gone to the small library in Karst to search for information on jesters. From the Middle Ages up to the eighteenth century they had filled an odd position. Hunchbacks, midgets, the physically deformed, eccentrics, lunatics and buffoons had all worn the fool's cap to entertain the wealthy. They were among the few who were allowed to tell their masters the truth. Their virulent mockery would go unpunished, their satirical barbs were rewarded with laughter.

There was more to the history of the jester, though, than simply being the rude clown. The brotherhood of jesters had its origins well before the Middle Ages, as a society of men who honored the gods and were held in high regard by their fellow tribesmen. Some jesters were allowed to break into houses and take whatever they wanted, without fear of arrest. Hilde had never found an explanation for this in any of the books, but she guessed that it was the way some local religious leaders had of making it clear that earthly possessions were without value and that the quest for heaven was the only thing of great importance.

The events of that day had not left her with any perceptible trauma—until she had returned to Karst and had declined an offer that someone had made.

Behind Karst, behind the hillside vineyards, there once stood a castle with a double tower. The village owed its name to the lords of the castle. The last count, Kaspar von Karst, descendant of robber knights, should have been buried not far from its chapel. On the site of the castle a new building had sprung up. Three stories high, with many rooms, it looked very much like an army barracks, with its tight walls and narrow windows. The owner never showed his face, but everybody knew his name was Rainer Miethe

And Hilde was convinced that Miethe had looked deep into her soul, put his hand inside her mind and pulled the jester out by his fool's cap.

* * *

It had all started a few months before the accident that happened to Andreas Pallasch.

Hilde Steiner had gone out running in the mountains, dressed in shorts and a cotton blouse with long sleeves. She did this not only to keep herself in shape, but because she loved to be among the surroundings of her native land and to be able to think while she trained her body.

While running, she looked back for a moment and saw a fat, little man who followed her at the same tempo. He was bald, his eyes were little slits, and his double chin moved to and fro with every step he took. He wore black sports shoes, black shorts and a white T-shirt.

That man will need a doctor soon, Hilde thought.

She had jogged along the river and now ran uphill along the vines, with the little man still trailing behind.

He'll never manage this, she thought. *If he wants to play with me, he is welcome to try. But with such a heavy body, he's asking for trouble—I hope he has a strong heart.*

Hilde herself was slender. She was used to running over long distances, and she was also a good climber. She increased the effort and turned on the speed. The incline caused her a bit of pain in her calves, which she didn't mind. When she looked over her shoulder after a couple of minutes, she could see that the man had caught up to her quite a bit. The T-shirt had worked its way up, and his round belly shook so that the dark spot of his navel went to and fro like the rolling eye of a Cyclops. She was a little out of breath herself now, but the road had flattened out again, and she decided to make a fast sprint. Surely that would force the man to give up his pursuit. Her surprise was enormous when he was suddenly pulled alongside her. With his short legs he had to take faster steps. No sweat dripped from the round face, and his skin wasn't flushed.

"Hell," she heard him say. "When we both decide to stand still for a while, we can a talk. There is something I would like to tell you. My name is Georg Wust."

He didn't even pant; his speech had come out without stammering. He bolted away from her so fast that she couldn't even think about matching him and then came to a stop about one hundred yards ahead. Breathless, she caught up to him. The sweat trickled down her face, breasts and back. While she tried to keep on breathing through her nostrils and forced herself not to show him how spent she was, the little fatso stood leisurely in front of her, with his hands on his back and his feet slightly apart.

"Doctor Steiner," he said, "my compliments. One can see that you're not doing this for the first time. You have such a beautiful figure, and it is very pleasant to watch you while you exert yourself like that."

Then he extended his hand and repeated his name.

"Georg Wust."

"I have never seen you before," said Hilde, gasping for air so she might she continue, "Where do you get all that energy from?"

"I am only the errand boy," he answered. "I was requested to speak to you in a quiet spot, and I had to run hard for it. I am a servant of Mr. Rainer Miethe, and he sees to it that his men are able to perform special physical tasks."

He pointed at a wooden bench farther along the road.

Wolf Tears

"Let's sit down there, Doctor. We'll have a marvelous view of the river, and we can talk. That is to say, if you can spare me a moment of your time."

The name Rainer Miethe had made her curious, but she walked with him to the little bench more out of exhaustion than a need to know. She took him to be around fifty, and when he sat down next to her, she noticed that his feet didn't touch the ground because his legs were so short.

"Georg Wust, in service of Rainer Miethe," she said. "That makes us fellow villagers. Your employer lives as a hermit in a big building with barred windows. Everyone knows how to find the house, but I don't know anyone who has ever been inside."

"You can come to live there," said the man. "You can sell your house to another doctor and put the money in the bank. It will obtain a formidable return."

Her mouth fell open and closed again. She wanted to say something, but instead let the man continue.

"Your practice will be reduced to the care of one single patient."

"Rainer Miethe," she guessed.

"Exactly."

She began to laugh. "What an absurd proposal."

"You're absolutely right. And it becomes even more absurd when you hear what your annual salary could be. A sum of money village doctors can only dream about."

"All right. An absurd proposal it is, but I am supposed to take it seriously, aren't I? Is that correct?"

"Yes," said Georg Wust.

Hilde breathed calmly again. She leaned a bit forward, and her eyes followed the long, straight rows of vines, down towards the river.

"Mister Miethe has to come to my office during consulting hours, I think. Just like everyone else. Is he seriously ill? Can he leave the house, or does he want me to visit him? How old is he?"

"The end is nearing for him. You know, he is a scientist. A great medical practitioner. But his memory has begun to desert him, and he never wrote down the most important things. Self-hypnosis brings no relief anymore. He doesn't know what to do anymore to extend his life."

"Where did he study?"

"Everywhere. His longing for adventure has taken him to all corners of the world."

"That's not what I meant. I'm talking about scientific, medical study. What universities did he attend? A scientist, a medical practitioner—I'm not getting answers to my questions. I also want to know how old he is and what exactly is the matter with him."

"You are someone who could work together with him very well. You know the latest developments in the medical field. You could assist him in the examination of his physical state. You could also help him with a blood transfusion. Everything you need for that, you will find in the house. There is so much equipment and so much laboratory space that we can supply you with a perfect clinic, a little hospital."

Hilde got up. She stretched her arms and took a deep breath.

"This is a useless conversation. If he is too ill to travel, I will come to visit him; otherwise, he must visit me during office hours or make an appointment for a later date."

The little man put his hands on the seat of the bench and swung his legs up in the air. Then he pushed off with crooked fingers and landed on his feet right in front of Hilde.

"He invites you. The biggest rooms in the house are yours. Besides being a doctor you are a psychiatrist. You studied psychology and understand the human mind. Rainer Miethe will be very happy with an all-round doctor like you."

He began to jump from one foot to the other and did it as easily as if he were a much lighter man. He began to clap in time and his voice sounded flat when he began to speak in short sentences.

"My master lives forever. His knowledge is great. My master gathered riches. His capital is immense. My master has power. What he wants will be done."

Suddenly he stood still. With his right hand he made an inviting gesture.

"Shall we run along for a while? In the meantime I can tell you something more."

Nodding, Hilde turned and jogged down the road.

She didn't know what to think of Georg Wust. Maybe he had a mental kink. The way he had jumped down right in front of her, clapping his hands, was highly peculiar. Now the fat little man was trotting alongside her.

"You used the word *master*. Isn't that very old-fashioned? Master and servant?" Hilde remarked.

"Old. Very old. Exactly! Just imagine. . . . Ah, during a run it is too very easy to imagine things. Walk relaxed, and let us think of special matters. There is a town, somewhere in Europe. A town, surrounded by walls, and within those walls life is bad. There is terrible poverty, and many people are so sick that the healthy have no time to take care of them all. Then comes good news: Ranier Miethe is on his way. The great healer! No one wants to wait for him at home. The gates open, and the crowd swarms out to meet the healer. He appears with a large entourage of fantastic sights. Musicians march ahead, followed by African elephants. The people kneel. Miethe approaches these poor, stricken people and here and there goes through a ritual of 'laying on of hands,' putting his hands on their foreheads. He hands out medicine. Exchanges take place—money for the healing hands and gold for a dose of powder. His power is great, and anyone who works for him addresses him as master."

"And you were there, when he worked these wonders? When did this all take place? Are you years older than you look?"

"No. No, it's not like that. I am from this time. But he has seen the centuries come and go. He has shown it all to me, for he has the ability to take someone with him to far-off days. But his are powers declining; the end comes in sight. Have I made you curious? Tomorrow is Sunday. Why don't you come by at around ten in the morning? Meanwhile, think about the fact that you can sell your house and practice for a lot of money, and that new and exciting times await you. I repeat: my master has power. What he wants, will be done."

Now the little man began to run so hard that Hilde didn't even attempt to keep up with him. She stood still in the middle of the road with her hands on her hips and watched him go.

I don't know how much of what he is telling me is true, she thought. *But if Rainer Miethe actually can work wonders, then Georg Wust is an example of it. No man on earth can run that fast. Not to mention a man with such short legs and such a fat stomach. His heart should not be able to take this; at the very least, he should be winded and sweating.*

Hilde turned around and started home. She walked along, lost in deep thought, as she headed back to Karst. She decided she would, indeed, pay a visit to Rainer Miethe the next day.

 6 -A Wooden Cogwheel

Throughout the remainder of the day, Hilde Steiner thought constantly about Georg Wust. What he had told her was implausible, if not totally impossible. His peculiar mannerisms, on the other hand, intrigued her. The way he talked, jumped from one foot to the other and clapped his hands could all be an act, but someone of his weight shouldn't be able to perform such formidable physical feats.

He certainly didn't explain things well, she thought, as she paced up and down in her upstairs living room. *But where Rainer Miethe is concerned, I should be able to put the facts together. He is probably very old. He has great power—what he wants done will be done. He is a scientist, an academic, a medical practitioner. His health leaves much to be desired; the little man mentioned blood transfusions.*

Equipment, a laboratory. Wust had said, "Miethe sees to it that his men are able to perform special physical tasks."

Hilde went to the window and looked outside. It was quiet in the main street of Karst. The two supermarkets where people from the neighborhood went shopping were situated outside the village. Along the main street stood rows of houses and buildings where the local government offices, a bank, the post office and several small shops were located. There were wine shops, a library and a few hotels. Hilde turned around and let her eyes take in the room. The old-fashioned furnishings, heirlooms from her father, dominated the room, and did not mix well with her own modern pieces of furniture, which she had brought with her from Munich.

My conclusion should be this, she figured. *Rainer Miethe is an ancient man and the master of many branches of science. He has the ability to make an athlete out of a man like Georg Wust. He is sick now and needs help. He has his sights set on me, and he is undoubtedly a man who is used to getting what he wants. I think I'll go and listen to what he has to tell me. Bit it all sounds so illogical. Very rarely do people get to be older than one hundred years.*

All I have said until now, I have based on one single, spectacular fact: Georg Wust runs twice as fast as I do, and that undoubtedly makes him the fastest man in the world. I take him to be fifty, his height must be not quite five feet, and his weight two hundred and sixty pounds. A lump of fat. A cannonball.

If someone besides Georg Wust—an ordinary man— had told me the same story, she decided, *I would not have believed a single word.*

* * *

On Sunday morning, Hilde drove through the streets of Karst, turned her Volkswagen uphill and drove along the rows of vines. The big house was built on a high slope, and she could picture how one could look out on the Moselle from the towers of the once great castle. Alongside the road that ran around the property an iron fence had been put up. She could have entered through the driveway and around the lawns, but she decided to park her car at the fence and walk.

She took her doctor's bag from the back seat, closed the door and walked in the direction of the house. After climbing a broad, stone staircase, she found herself standing in front of an oval, wooden door. She let the knocker, clasped in the jaws of a cast iron dragon's head, fall, and took a step backwards.

The man who opened the door was Rainer Miethe.

He shook hands with her, told her his name and smiled. He was tall and broad-shouldered. Thick, blue veins were visible under the skin of his arms and hands. He wore a sleeveless cotton shirt and leather trousers. Long, gray, wavy hair was combed backward and reached down his back. When he stepped aside, Hilde walked past him into a big hall with a floor made of rough stones. Only now did she take the time to really look at him, and what she saw frightened her. Within the sharp frame of the silvery hair everything became hazy, as if his face were hidden behind frosted glass. Eyes, mouth and nose were vague forms in light tints, and the smiling lips were gliding, trembling stripes above a white chin. The skin was smooth, but the eyes were unmistakably those of an old man. His handshake had been so cold that she had felt as if she were touching a piece of ice.

"I—I had expected Mr. Wust to open the door for me," Hilde remarked.

Rainer pushed his index finger on her forehead. A cold shiver went right through her.

"Georg Wust lives there," he said. "The eyes will see something that isn't really there, as long as the brain gets the right impulses."

His voice was dark, and the cavity of his mouth was black; Hilde could see no hint of either teeth or tongue. When he turned and started to walk through the hall, she observed that he did so with a plodding step.

"Blood runs as slow as syrup through my veins," he said. "I saw your fear when you looked at my face. It is only an illusion—a projection, or whatever you want to call it. You would be shocked if I showed you the reality."

She put her doctor's bag on the floor with an audible thump. The man abruptly stood still and turned.

"Hilde Steiner, you have put your bag down on stones that were used long ago to build the walls of a castle. You are standing with your feet on fragments from the past. My past. I will understand if you want to leave immediately, or if, on the contrary, you want to fire a thousand questions at me. Do neither of the two. Follow me through this house, and I will show you unimaginable riches."

The hall was unfurnished, a large space with high walls, barred windows and closed doors. Resolutely Hilde picked up her bag again and said, "I wonder why I came anyway. If you are in need of medical care, you need only to ask for it. If not, then it seems better to me that I leave. I am not interested in your wealth."

Rainer Miethe's laughter had an eerie, hollow sound to it; again she saw the black hole between his open lips.

"It is not difficult to guess your thoughts. You are confused. Who wouldn't be? You are a doctor, you are a psychiatrist, you are used to having a rational explanation for everything that happens in your world— for every problem there must be a reasonable solution. Now you are confronted by all this, and you cannot accept the situation. You are looking for something to grasp, an explanation that brings everything back to your reality and that has been documented in one of your precious medical books. But, well . . . a man like Georg Wust just doesn't fit into your sphere of reference, now, does he?

"All right, all right, I'll stay. I will let you show me around your house."

"You need time to become acclimatized. I will show you my all my collections and treasures. As we go from one room to the other, we will have time to become accustomed to each other. Call me by my name and try not to look at my face too often. After you have admired all my possessions, we shall talk about other things, including myself. I have a special method for that: you have only to sit down, relax and receive images that explain everything. Now, will you please follow me?"

With short steps, he moved further down the hall and came to a stop in front of a big double door. The way he moved made Hilde think of the measured, shuffling steps of a battery-operated toy robot. His arms moved along with his feet—the left arm swung backwards with a jerky, sporadic movement when the right leg went forward and his right arm did the same in unison with his left leg.

"Let's go downstairs. I keep my automobiles in the cellar."

He opened the doors and pushed a button. An interior door slid open, and together they went downstairs and entered a brightly lit room that covered the entire floor of the house. Three rows of thick pillars stood apart from each other and propped up stone arched vaults.

Between the pillars, parked in perfectly straight rows next to each other, stood automobiles of all different makes and models. The blazing lights reflected in the paintwork, chrome and steel.

"Not one car has more than twenty-five hundred miles on it," she heard Miethe say. "No scratches, no dents. Everything in the original condition. What you see here, is the most unique fleet of automobiles in the world. I bought every model myself as soon as it was available. Feel free to walk around."

She saw a small, three-wheeled Messerschmitt standing next to a Mercedes-Benz sports car, little Fiats, big Jaguars, Austins, Studebakers, Vauxhalls, Wolsleys, Bugattis, Alfa Romeos and Porches.

"All the truly beautiful cars are here," said Miethe, and she could hear his enthusiasm. "Especially from the period around 1950. The first imports from Japan— Datsun, Honda, Toyota—Daimlers in many different models, Buicks, Chevrolets and the big Cadillacs."

With her hands knitted behind her back, Hilde walked from one car to another and stood still every now and then to look through a side window and admire the automobile's shining dashboard.

"There also are older examples," Miethe told her. "Here and there you'll see a model of which it is the only one in existence. There is little moisture in this cellar, and the temperature is constant, so these cars will remain in mint condition forever."

Hilde began to feel more at ease. Since Miethe remained behind her at all times, she didn't have to look at him. She found something amusing about seeing so many old automobiles together in one place.

"Aren't you afraid they will get stolen?" she asked.

"I have given them a permanent place in my museum. After I brought them all inside, I bricked up the entrance and removed the downgrade. All the windows are barred, and all the doors can be closed securely. And if someone did succeed in forcing his way inside, he would have quite a nice surprise in store for him."

As she stood in front of an open sports car, an American Buick, all of a sudden Georg Wust appeared behind the wheel. The seat had been pushed way back to create enough space for the fat man. Hilde let out a scream and pressed her doctor's bag tightly to her chest.

Georg began to clap his hands and was about to say something, but his mouth suddenly closed again, and his chubby cheeks fell in. His double chin shrank, and his belly disappeared. He wore a white shirt that shrank as he did; the closed collar remained tight around the continually shrinking neck. Then he grew taller and became broad but not fat. He could look above the windshield of the Buick now without difficulty. A second later, he had disappeared.

"Let me out of here!" cried Hilde.

Miethe acted as if he hadn't heard her and said, "Someone could be really intimidated if I started all the engines at the same time, let them roar and shriek, let the automobiles shake on their suspensions and fill the cellar with the stench from all their exhausts. Hear, see, feel, smell—it's all possible."

Leaning shakily with one hand on the door of the Buick, Hilde asked, "Do I have a choice?"

Koos Verkaik

"There is still so much for you to see, and I also want to tell you my story. Come, we'll go upstairs again via another route."

As Miethe led Hilde away, she tried to calm herself. The palms of her hands had become moist, her feet felt heavy, the rhythm of her heart was accelerated and she was breathing way too fast. She thought of her Volkswagen, standing like a beacon at the side of the road. She thought of the expanding and shrinking Georg Wust and of the unreal, blurred face of her host. Balancing on the edge of panic, she was led into rooms on the ground floor, where she saw a library with thousands of handwritten books, showcases full of silver and golden utensils, shelves with pots and vases, a room with antique tools, and a music room whose walls were hidden from view by violins, lutes and other stringed instruments.

"Most of these are made by a master," said Miethe. "Paulus. He used to be a friend of mine."

They didn't visit the second floor. These were the living quarters, Miethe told Hilde, and there were plenty of rooms for her to choose from. Her hand glided heavily over the banister as they climbed directly to the third floor. There they passed a steel door, reaching up to the ceiling, which Miethe pushed against with his elbow.

"There my paintings hang, in the dark, from long steel ropes, next to each other and behind each other. If they are ever shown, the world of art will be turned upside down. It will not be difficult to prove that the canvases of Dürer, Holbein, Rembrandt, Rubens and all the others are real. What hangs behind this door is of incalculable value."

She hardly registered what he said. In her mind she was taking silent inventory of what tranquilizers she had in her bag. She never had been in need of them, but now she staggered on her feet. There were pills to deal with a situation such as this; why, she could even inject herself if need be—or she could run away. Down the stairs, through the hall, through the door, over that large lawn to my car. Then think about nothing anymore and sleep for a long, long time. . . .

Rainer Miethe opened a door for her, and as she passed him, he said, "You will feel calm soon. I understand if you have been caught off guard by everything you have seen. I have learned many a thing in the course of the years. I can calm you down by the influence of my will." Hilde wondered whether her feelings of trepidation were being telepathically received by Miethe or if she had simply given herself away with her probably more than obvious nervousness. She suddenly began to regain her composure and calm down, just as her host had predicted. The tension in her body seemed to simply disappear. When she once again looked up at him, she was no longer afraid of that blurred face with its ancient eyes.

They were in a room now that made her think of the laboratory of some ancient alchemist. Pots and jars were everywhere. An old wooden table stood covered with open books whose browned pages gave a hint as to their age, and large glass beakers hung from chains above open flames fueled by gas. Miethe pointed to the blue flames and said, "I don't worry anymore about the fire. In previous times you had to make sure that the fire was kept burning so that the heat remained constant. Now I don't have to stay and watch it; I have only to watch what happens inside my glass boilers."

"What are you making here?"

Sidestepping the question, Miethe remarked, "I try so hard to remember things. The old art requires precision. If you make a single mistake, you may have spoiled the work of many years. Come, Hilde, I'm sure the next room will be more to your liking."

They came to a door that opened silently when pushed. Inside, the room was brightly lit, and Hilde immediately noticed that the room was stocked with equipment one would see in the intensive care unit of a major hospital.

"Anything you could possibly think of, that is medically related, is in this room," said Miethe. "There are medicines and instruments, all stored in those cupboards there against the wall, and there is a large stock of equipment that is ready for immediate use. Behind that screen is an operating room where any kind of surgery can be done, and done with precision. This is my clinic, Hilde, and I have brought this all together to make my inevitable dying easier and to try and extend my life by a couple of precious years through some simple surgery. I am afraid to die. I cannot accept the fact that my life could be over in a moment, not after all these centuries. I have come to know eternity, and I want to go on."

Hilde nodded. "I don't know how you managed to calm me down, but I can think clearly again and am beginning to believe and accept the fact that you actually come from a distant past."

"I was born at the beginning of the fifteenth century."

"Before me stands Rainer Miethe, a man from the fifteenth century. A man who is powerful enough to show me people who don't even really exist. And you are also powerful enough to make me as quiet as a lamb, just by your will."

"Go on."

"You need me for something that will require my constant presence here, but I have no intention of giving up my home and practice. Why didn't you just use your power to make me do as you please and let me think that I was doing it of my own free will? You could have forced me, the same way you forced me to see Georg Wust."

"A strong tie must be brought about between us," Miethe told her. "When my spirit grows weak, I will not be able to force you to do anything that you would rather not do, nor will I be able to make you see something that isn't really there. That is when I need someone I can trust, who can arrange things for me, who will fight for my life."

Walking past a number of hospital beds, they reached a tall screen, which Miethe pushed to one side. He went past an operating table, to a metal cabinet, and opened a drawer, from which he took out a brand-new scalpel blade and a matching handle. He took the tiny knife out of its packaging and snapped it into place on the shaft. "Look, Hilde. When you first came in, I told you that my blood runs through my veins as slowly as syrup. In no way did I mean that metaphorically." He leaned against the little cabinet and slid the knife downward over the skin of his arm. Dark red blood appeared and trickled down in thick drops. Like congealing wax from a candle, the drops rolled over each other. The shining color quickly dulled. After a moment or two, he rubbed his finger over the trail of dried blood, and it fell apart in little fragments. He showed her his arm. There was no visible evidence of the cut he had made in his skin.

"How is it possible that I am still alive? Is it the strength of my soul, or is my body not as sick as I suspect? I know I can talk about my mental state with Hilde Steiner, the psychiatrist, and I can talk about my physical state with Hilde Steiner, the doctor. I was pleased to hear you were back in Karst."

At first, Hilde didn't react to what he said, because she was carefully examining the skin of his arm. Then she looked up and said, "What are you talking about? I have never met you before. We have never even seen each other."

He smiled. "You have so many patients, perhaps there is one among them who is not known by anybody, except for you."

Again she thought of Georg Wust.

"I understand; someone who doesn't actually exist."

"Exactly, Hilde. Listen, I have shown you my possessions and told you something about my condition. Now let's sit down, and I'll give you much more information in another way."

"You mean I should sit down and receive images. You told me about your ability to do that."

"Yes. We can go to the living room, or any other room. Have you seen a particular room where you think you would feel at ease?"

"I leave the choice up to you."

"All right then, come with me."

"Just a moment. I have a feeling you're keeping something from me. You want me to believe that you fitted up this big room all for yourself."

"That's correct. For myself."

"If there has to be a procedure done, if an operation has to get performed, you will need specialists. You will have more use of a surgeon and an anesthetist than of a doctor who accidentally studied psychology as well."

"Imagine if I had to undergo an operation. I would have to stay conscious and give directions, and it would have to be someone with a fast hand, lest I heal before the surgery is completed.

"Think of all the medical knowledge that could be obtained from my body! It would be too dangerous to have many people around me. My body is worth more to science than all my paintings and treasures combined. That is why I need someone I know I can trust. Can you imagine how much a man is worth who was born in the fifteenth century and is still alive? Who can demonstrate that his brains have evolved, not degenerated?

"I have to make sure that I stay alive until I have regained the secret for the elixir of life. Your dedicated help, my dear Hilde, could possibly bring you immortality!"

"The laboratory next door: you are searching for the elixir of life in there?"

"Yes, but it will take a very long time, and in the meantime, I must think of other solutions. Very soon I expect to receive a message about something I need."

Hilde thought long and hard about everything he had said, but when she began to speak, it was about another subject:

"Why do I count four beds if you live here alone and this room is just for you?"

The eyes flashed in his blurred face, and his long hair whipped across his cheeks and neck as he shook his head.

"I would have explained this to you in a little while, but I might as well tell you now. I am not completely alone here. There is someone else here who also needs your care. Her condition is more or less the same as mine."

"Who is she?"

He straightened his back, took a deep breath and answered, "It doesn't matter. I could tell you her name, but it would mean nothing to you."

"Then bring me to her."

"No. First we will sit down quietly. Then I will see to it that you understand everything better."

* * *

Rainer Miethe sat down in a wooden rocking chair, his arms on the rests and his hands hanging down limp. Hilde sat opposite him in a similar chair. They were in a room that was designed to be a library and contained mostly books about medical science. The barred window offered her a view of the lawn; in the distance she could see her car.

Between them stood a strange table. It was a massive, cylindrical block of wood with a serrated edge. In the middle was a hole about four inches in diameter.

"I had a master, Alexander," began Miethe. "He explained to me that the ultimate form a tree will take is already established when you put the little nut into the ground. The tiny nut will develop into a giant, with a proud trunk and wide branches and a complex root system. Also, the life expectancy of what is to grow has already been determined. The mighty oak gets old, the puny flower withers away quickly. The birth of a child is the first step on a road that will lead to death.

"But the elixir of life gives room to the body and spirit. Today you would probably call it genetic engineering, changing the cell nucleus. I don't have to explain to you what happens in the human brain as it gets old. In my life, there has never been anything worse than aging. For so long, I have been able to think clearly, study, read, absorb information and gain experience with no problem whatsoever. If somebody else. regardless of the circumstances, could get as old as I have, there would be no guarantee that his capabilities and cleverness could compare with mine. The power I possess has its origin in the elements of the elixir. The little nut and the big tree; the small amount of the elixir and the great intellectual faculties of its keeper.

"Now, close your eyes and relax. I am going to take you with me on a long journey."

* * *

Hilde was floating. The rhythmic creaking of Miethe's rocking chair carried her away. There was a moment when she lost all physical contact with the outside world. She could not hear, see, feel or smell; but still there was a presence—a deep awareness. There was darkness.

There was silence. There was movement. Then light illuminated her mind, and she was able to see again. At first she noticed only the movement of shadows, and then suddenly she found herself in a hall, where a big celebration was being held. She knew, somehow, where she was. Her body swayed to and fro on the rocking chair in the library, but her spirit was attending the wedding of Miethe and Maria Delaruelle. Count Kaspar von Karst was dead and buried, and the new lord of the castle had appropriated all his possessions, including his wife. The appearance of the mighty Miethe had made quite an impression. The people lay at his feet and worshipped him as a born ruler, and noble delegates and clergy from Trier had come to join in the festivities. They saw how he had gathered a band of faithful followers in a short time and how he had become a man who would not let anyone steal from him what he had stolen himself. He had taken the place of a descendant of a family of robber nights, and for the time being, he was being given the benefit of the doubt that he was up to the position.

In Hilde's mind, time crawled. The events around her took place in slow motion. People walked around her without even noticing her, and so slowly that she could see every single detail of their faces and clothes. It was a whirl of colors; she seemed to move through the crowd without any consciousness of her own body. She was present and understood what was happening. Now the movements of the people sped up, and now she was also able to hear them. They laughed, sang, yelled and screamed. Smiling with pride, Miethe and Maria sat next to each other and hoisted their wine cups up to their guests in a toast of gratitude.

Hilde was pulled away from the hall and floated up. She saw the castle with the double towers in all their splendor reaching up from beneath her. The river, her familiar river, was there, with all its curves and loops.

When she landed, it seemed to be in paradise. Around a pool, where fish lived that never died, were majestic, eternal trees. The animals that came unhurriedly to drink from the pool were not shy. They did not run away when a man and a woman approached and sat down in the grass. The man pulled a stopper from a jar, gave the woman the first drink and then took a draught himself.

The sun shone down on them from a cloudless sky, and around them was an aura of glorious white light. Brown and green frogs crawled from the pool in their direction. The little deer that had drunk from the water came near. The branches of the trees were filled with birds that looked down with curiosity.

It was quiet around them when Miethe and Maria embraced each other and toasted eternal life with a kiss.

Hilde had never seen anything more beautiful. She was full of the things that Rainer Miethe let her experience. She was a quiet, invisible witness of the event, but her body, in the room with the books, in the house in Karst, reacted to the emotions and events she perceived. First she had moved to the rhythm of Miethe's creaking rocking chair. Her eyes rolled around behind her eyelids, and every now and then she smiled, but at the moment a luminous circle appeared around the two people sitting in the gass, she reached out her arms and spread her fingers as if to protect herself.

The upper part of her body twitched with a start. The rocking chair came forward and she almost lost her balance. Her hands grasped the massive table, and she remained in that position, leaning forward.

Opposite her, Miethe caught hold of the armrests of his chair as if something had frightened him. The mist in front of his face evaporated, revealing a very old man. The skin on his face was lined and cracked, tight and hard, and the flabby skin under his chin hung down to his neck. His eyes stared dully in front of him. He covered his face with both hands and stopped rocking. The creaking rhythm stopped.

Hilde still perceived the pool, but something had changed. The sun had disappeared, and Maria Delaruelle was no longer there. A little man, dressed in a gray habit, sat down on his knees at the pool and held a hand above the water.

Hilde sensed another presence than Miethe. A flood of information inundated her, and she understood that the man in the habit was Alexander. A big fish poked its head above the surface of the water. With great love and tenderness, the old man stroked it with his fingers. He ladled some water into his hands and poured it over the silvery scales.

"You see, Miethe?" he said, without looking up. "I live in complete peace with myself. Even the water creatures know that they have nothing to fear from me."

Miethe loomed up menacingly behind him. He was barefooted and wore nothing more than a ragged old pair of trousers. Silently, he approached his friend and mentor, and when he was behind him raised a mighty sword.

"Miethe?" asked Alexander.

Alexander rose to his feet, and at the precise moment he did so, his companion, the fish, slipped beneath the surface of the water.

And Miethe struck out.

His long curly hair flowed over his shoulders, the muscles of his arms tensed, and he wielded the weapon with both hands.

Alexander's head fell into the pool, and his body fell forward. The hood of his habit lay flat now and was quickly turning a deep red color.

"Keep your hands in contact with the wood," Hilde heard an unfamiliar voice tell her. "It is not a table! It is a cog, a wheel as it were, a part of a machine!"

Miethe leaned back in his chair, closed his eyes and tried to concentrate. There was a battle raging, and it was being fought in Hilde's mind.

Wolf Tears

"Who's there?" Hilde heard herself ask, unsure if she were speaking aloud or only thinking the words. She had, for a brief moment, suddenly become conscious of her physical presence in the room, and of Miethe sitting opposite her, and of her hands resting on the wooden block, fingers spread wide.

"Later, we can talk of that," she heard the voice whisper. "Later. First, there is something you must see."

"Be off!" commanded Miethe. The awesome power of his thoughts held Hilde once again, and she was back in the castle. One of the partygoers walked passed her with a stone mug in his hand, and she could clearly smell the wine in it—

A split second later Hilde was back outside the castle, an unwilling, horrified witness to the murder of Count Kaspar von Karst.

The count had fallen asleep after a long, hard ride. He slept with his back against a tree trunk, while Maria lay in the grass, her head resting on his thigh. Miethe appeared and stood for a while watching the two sleepers. Then he picked up the count's sword and raised it above his head. With incredible strength, he shoved the sword into the count's chest and pinned him to the tree. The count never opened his eyes again. Maria jumped to her feet and tried to run to the horses, but she didn't get very far before she felt two immensely strong hands grab hold of her.

Her clothes were torn from her body, and she was pushed, naked and ever defiant, to the forest floor. There, not fifteen feet away from where the count sat pinned to a tree, Miethe raped Maria.

Now Hilde was receiving various short impressions that attempted to show her a softer, caring side of her host. He showed her goodness, unselfishness and an even-tempered man who gave money, food and clothes to the poor. He built churches and houses. He administered justice fairly in the great hall of his castle and satisfied all parties involved. Karst began to flourish and all the inhabitants lived happy, comfortable lives.

* * *

Dusk was falling in Hilde's dream world. As she floated away from the castle of Karst, she saw a guard open the gates, and out came Maria on horseback. She rode at a gallop and never once looked back at the castle's high walls, where she had become Miethe's prisoner. Night came to Hilde's mind, and in the distance she heard voices, but could not understand what they were saying. Her spirit soared, and when the dark gave way to light, she found herself in the middle of France, on the banks of a fast moving river where hundreds of workers were busy erecting a complex wooden structure.

Hilde had become conscious of her own body again, although she still inhabited her netherworld. She felt the heat of the sun and the gentle caress of the wind. She somehow knew what was going on here: they were building the largest hydro powered machine in the world. Large wheels powered by the quickly running water of the river would turn huge wooden shafts and cogwheels, passing the power on to machines all along the river bank, in covered spaces, in wood and stone buildings, and in the open.

A wonder would come to pass. Everything would start operating—from the winepress to the corn mill, from the sawmill to the forge, where giant bellows were moved up and down. Workrooms with hammers that weighed more than two hundred pounds would be set in motion. Hoists could bring up stones that were needed for the walls of the castle that was being built opposite the machinery and from where Ranier Miethe would be able to overlook all that transpired. A cable that spanned the river could pull a ship from one side to the other and back again. A paper mill would produce great quantities of the highest quality paper products. Artisans who worked in stone and wood would be enabled to perform the most precise tasks associated with their work. Never before had such a machine been built.

Miethe's name was passed from mouth to mouth. As the miracle machine neared completion he ordered his guards to speed up the progress of the workers. In the eyes of all, he was the great magician, the man who used the eternal motion of the flowing water to bring more than a mile of the riverbank to life.

On the opposite bank from where his castle was being constructed, Miethe had set up tents for visitors, who had come from all over France, Germany, Italy and Spain to witness the miracle with their own eyes.

Hilde walked along and studied the various activities. Oxen and horses dragged tree trunks along. Stones were passed from man to man until they reached the spot where they were needed. She stopped and stood still in front of two thin men, who wore not much more than a loincloths and worn leather footwear. The sweat ran down from their unshaven faces. Around the left ankle of one and the right ankle of the other were metal rings that were connected to each other by an iron chain. They were busy working a piece of wood, the wood that was the heavy, massive cogwheel on which her hands now rested in the room in Karst. The men put down their tools and looked at her. Someone else approached. It was a guard, who laid the whip across their shoulders time after time. They quickly and silently took up their hammers again and continued to work the hard wood.

"Who are you?" asked Hilde.

Without looking up, one of them answered, "My name is Franciscus. My friend here is called Paulus."

"You have been beaten so often, and I can see that you are also underfed. Rest and nourishment are what you need."

"We receive more lashes than most," said Franciscus. "Tomorrow our skin will be healed, and then the whip will split the skin once more. Everything you see here is the work of Paulus. He is the master builder! But Miethe gets the honor! We are working on the last cogwheel. As soon is this wheel is set in place, the completed hellish machinery can be put into operation. Our hands are bleeding, Hilde. The wheel is tainted with our blood. Our sweat soaks the wood."

"You—you know my name."

"Yes. This is the very last part of the machine! All of our power, all of our attention is necessary to complete this work. With our hearts and souls we work on the last component of the machinery. Our blood, our sweat. Somewhere else, far from here, in another time, you will press your fingers against the wood into which our entire being has been sunk. That is why I can talk to you and why I know your name. I know that Miethe's spirit has penetrated yours, I can feel it. He wants you to be a witness to his goodness, but it is all a lie. Hold on to the wood, and I will show you the truth."

The man with the whip approached again, but Hilde gave him such a withering look, he didn't knew how to react. Perhaps he thought Hilde was a noble lady, one of Miethe's guests, come to have a look at the construction site. Whatever the reason, he turned and walked away, the whip under his arm.

"You know things without me having to explain them to you," Franciscus continued. "Paulus and I are just as immortal as Miethe. We like our leisure, and prefer to live in anonymity. But Miethe wants to assert himself. He brings death and destruction, pure evil—and all this only to better his own situation. For five long years Paulus and I have been his prisoners and have dragged this heavy chain along between us. Now the last cogwheel is made. If you look at everything from a distance, Hilde—take a step back—you will see all kinds of strange things happen.

Night came and went again. Time had taken another leap, and Hilde was now looking at the river and the construction from a high peak. Somewhere, in one of the workrooms, Franciscus and Paulus fixed the cogwheel. On the river men rowed to the boxes in which the paddle wheels were placed and prepared to hoist the hatches. Along the bank, Miethe and his guests had gathered to witness the unequalled wonder of the world. Priests knelt down, fearful that devilish powers would be turned loose as soon as the hellish apparatus was put into operation.

Miethe gave a sign.

On the river, the hatches were pulled up. The wild water rushed onto the paddle wheels. Creaking loudly, the shafts and gearwheels came to life. For two thousand yards up and down the river, all the machinery became active. It was the genius plan of Paulus, who had brought about something that no one had ever thought possible. However, only he and Franciscus knew that the operation of the machine would be short-lived. The last cogwheel they had put in place would bring this diabolic contraption to an end. What should have been Miethe's most glorious hour would instead turn out to be the moment in which he lost face.

There had been much rain lately, and current in the river was strong. The bellows began to sigh, the sawmill began working as hoists brought up the heavy loads. Somewhere in another room, a shaft broke and chips of wood flew about. People began to scream, run outside and throw themselves on the ground. A thatched roof was torn open, and big, heavy parts of machinery hurled in every direction.

Franciscus and Paulus found themselves alone in a barn. Their regular guard had panicked and run off.

A beam equipped with protruding metal pins turned and brought up hammers that could split wood and break stones. Soon after the pins had finished gliding along the handles of the hammers, the iron hammer heads fell down. A pointed hammer head went up and down on a chopping block. Franciscus and Paulus put their chain across it and with the next hammer blow they were free. In turn, they put their remaining pieces of chain on the chopping block until only a few links remained hanging from their shackles.

The machinery destroyed itself. What had taken five years to build was lost in a matter of moments. Hilde watched buildings collapse, scaffoldings fall, and a ship on the river get pulled to the side and ripped to shreds on the rocky ground.

And there was more.

Hilde's gut feeling told her that the chaos at the riverside was directly connected to Miethe's life, that it symbolized all the wreckage he had left behind on his violent journey through time. And then Franciscus and Paulus, freed of their chains but half-naked, battered and exhausted, appeared in front of her to show her more than the breaking of wood.

In a rush of visions, they let her follow Miethe's track through time. What she saw filled her with horror. The whole world was his playground. He sided with the winning party in countless battles and plundered villages and cities. He sailed the seas as a pirate and set foot on every continent. Murdering for profit was his way of life, wealth his goal.

The breaking shafts of the machine became louder and louder upstream. And above the din rose a white, sunlit cloud, taking the shape of a beautiful, smiling woman.

Elusive and ethereal, the image of Maria Delaruelle hung above the destroyed landscape.

The wild torrents of water forced splintered wood down the river and created havoc at the banks wherever a wheel still spun. Workers and guests alike fled.

"We have to go," said Franciscus. "We are too weak to be a spiritual first fiddle. Slowly but surely, Miethe is getting stronger—he is beginning to get the upper hand. Farewell, Hilde!"

Suddenly Hilde felt completely alone. From atop the high peak she watched the havoc along the river. The surging water began to turn deep red. She closed her eyes to block out the sight of the life-giving water throwing its wreckage on the rocks.

* * *

Rainer Miethe had stood up. The haze around his face had returned. He reached across the wooden cogwheel and caught hold of Hilde's wrists. The moment her hands came loose from the wood, she opened her eyes and looked up at him in fear.

And in an apartment in New York City, the composer Francis Beck sat up in bed and rubbed his eyes with both index fingers. The dream he'd just awakened from was still extremely clear in his mind. His heart beat fiercely, and he had to take a couple of deep breaths to settle himself down. What he recalled most was the wooden cogwheel. A woman had put her hands on it, on the wood that had absorbed the blood and sweat of Paulus and himself. He let himself sink back until his head touched the pillow.

We had contact, he thought to himself. *The wood and the woman formed the medium that bridges distance and time. I know I would recognize her if I saw her.*

Hilde.

Francis closed his eyes and relaxed.

Far from New York, far from Karst, at his shop in Rotterdam, Paul Brand shook his head, as if to chase away unpleasant thoughts. He sat behind his work bench, busy restringing an acoustic guitar. He had the feeling that he had been daydreaming for some time, and now felt sick and dizzy. The daydream had left no memory of itself. Carefully he put the instrument down on the table, rose to his feet and went upstairs. There he opened the fridge and took out a bottle of mineral water. With the screw cap in his left hand he brought the bottle to his mouth with his right hand. As he drank, he felt tired, almost on the verge of exhaustion. His back stung as though it had been whipped, and his ankle also hurt, as if a metal shackle were pinching the flesh.

Paul Brand drank an entire bottle of cold water and then went downstairs again. He thought about how much more there was to his life besides his shop and the orchestra. He tried to put it out of his head and returned to tuning the guitar he had just outfitted with six new strings.

* * *

"Let me show you to the front door," said Rainer to Hilde. "I want to rest for a while. It is obvious that you don't want to stay here and that you are not even considering the possibility of establishing yourself here any time soon."

Hilde got up. She had a headache. As soon as she was in her car, she decided, she would take one of the pills in her bag. She followed the man, who although he moved his feet in an extremely jerky fashion, still managed to open the doors for her with slow movements.

"Once again," she said, as they walked through the empty hall on the ground level, "if there is a woman here who needs my help, I will gladly have a look at her." He shook his head and smiled weakly from behind a half-transparent mist.

"I'm sure," Miethe said, "that I need not remind you of your Hippocratic oath, Hilde. You are sworn to protect your patient's privacy, so you will not mention your visit with me to anyone. Am I correct, Hilde? You'll see—you will be back one day offering your services to me. Until then, goodbye. We will meet again soon."

The big front door swung open. It was Georg Wust who bowed deeply to her and stylishly invited her to re-enter the outside world.

"My master has power," he grinned. "What he wants will be done."

7 -Dog's Eyes

Her first encounter with the jester took place on the way home. Hilde had started the descent to Karst. She was driving fast and squeezing the brakes on the curves. She knew it didn't matter how fast she widened the distance between Rainer Miethe and herself, but fear held her foot on the gas. The Volkswagen zipped downhill, Hilde steering with her left hand and grasping the gearshift knob with her right.

"Don't panic," she said aloud. "Please, don't panic now. What just happened is unreal. There has to be a logical explanation for everything."

She felt dizzy again. So many different thoughts pervaded her mind that she wasn't able to concentrate on any one subject in particular.

Coming around a bend in the road she saw Karst lying in the river valley below her. The next curve brought back the high vines that hid the houses from view again.

Suddenly, a figure jumped into the road from among the vines. It was a man, wearing a leather cap with long protuberances. The left side was green, the right red. He wore a jerkin and trousers made of little pieces of black and brown leather. He leaped about on shoes whose toes ended in long, curled-up points with copper bells attached. Hilde clenched the wheel with both hands and slammed her feet on the clutch and brakes. With a blinding flash, the horrible experience of her youth, which she had always managed to keep locked away in her memory, was back to haunt her. Only now it seemed that rather than being just a vivid recollection, the jester was once again a reality. She was that little girl again, in an agony of terror as an evil-looking, foul-smelling jester lifted her high up in the air over his head. The car began to swerve, but she managed to keep it in the middle of the road. A bit to the right would have smashed the Volkswagen against the rocks, a bit to the left would have sent the car tumbling down the hillside vineyard. Just as she was about to hit the jester, he jumped up and turned a somersault, and she heard him land hard on the trunk.

Hilde stopped the car, opened the door and got out.

I drove straight at him! she thought in fright. *I didn't even attempt to avoid him!*

Tears streamed down her cheeks. She ran to the rear of the car and saw the jester lying on the ground. The copper bells on his feet jingled as his legs twitched spastically. He looked at her with big, coal black eyes. Thick, grinning lips bared yellow teeth, and blood ran from his mouth. She kneeled down next to him and quickly turned her head away as a horrible odor hit her nostrils. The jester shook his head. The sharp horns of his cap clicked against the surface of the road, and the little bells jingled. Hilde jumped to her feet to grab her medical bag from the back seat. Leaning inside the card with one hand on the seat, she stroked her throat with the fingers of her other hand, trying desperately to calm herself down. She took five or six deep breaths and finally felt prepared to deal with the situation. But when she returned to the rear of the car, the jester had vanished. She looked all around the area and saw nothing but high vines and bunches of grapes.

The great fear from her past had certainly come back with a vengeance.

Hilde was wondering what to do now, when the situation was taken out of her hands. A car pulled up to a stop right beside her, and scaring the hell out of her. The side window opened, and a man stuck his head out. She recognized him as one of the local inhabitants of Karst, but could not remember his name.

"Problems with your car, Doctor?" he asked.

She held her bag behind her back and only now noticed that the motor of the Volkswagen was still running.

The trunk was unlocked so she popped it open and put her bag inside.

"Just had something I wanted to put away," she answered and tried to smile.

She got in and drove away. In her rear-view mirror she saw that the other car remained right behind her. She kept getting the feeling that his tailgating was intended to rush her, until she looked at her speedometer. She realized that she was driving at barely more than ten miles per hour and didn't dare push the gas pedal any harder. As soon as the driver behind her saw his chance, he passed her on the left side of the road. As he went by, she couldn't help but notice the surprised, or perhaps it was confused, expression on his face.

* * *

When Hilde thought of Vitus Weiss, she thought of dead dog's eyes, and when she thought of dead dog's eyes, she thought of the jester's eyes. Every Sunday she had dinner in Bärbel Körer's restaurant, and last week she had seen old Vitus sitting alone at a table. The restaurant was busy, and since she too was alone, she asked him if he would mind if she sat with him. He neither heard nor reacted to Hilde's question, since he was sound asleep. He leaned back on a wooden bench that was against the wall. With his head tilted back, eyes closed and arms folded across his chest, it seemed as if he were listening to music. Behind his white moustache and beard curled a satisfied smile. In front of him, on the tabletop, sat an empty glass.

Hilde looked around. She saw well-known faces everywhere. On Sunday afternoon big families took seats at the large tables in the middle of the dining room, smaller groups sat at the sides by the windows and individuals had places on the long bench or on the wooden chairs on the side near the kitchen.

Bärbel came up and welcomed her, and Hilde asked her for a glass of wine. Then she looked at the sleeping man again.

You killed the dog, she thought. *It was a long time ago, but I didn't forget. You ran right over it. That was the first time I realized how many soft, squishy organs a living creature can hide under his skin. They came out from all sides. It was Grübler, the black dog that always looked worried about something. Grübler, the old dog of Hans Schwarzburg the winegrower. Everyone in town was so fond of that animal. You pulled him from under the front wheel of your car just as I came walking up. My father had sent me to Schwarzburg to buy a good bottle of Karster Glut. I remember it so well. Just as well as I remember everything about the jester. You were so scared! You saw me look at the dead dog, who no longer looked worried. He had big, lackluster eyes, but the whites were not visible. The irises were almost black as the pupils. The jester I ran into had the same eyes.*

"We don't tell anyone about this," you said, bending halfway over and leaning toward me with your hands on your knees. *Your head was the height as mine now. I was a little girl. Eight years old. A year after my encounter with the jester, I had been allowed to go outside alone again. "It is no use to tell anyone I ran over Grübler. He is dead and will remain dead. You understand? Now we*

both have a secret, you and I. Grübler just went away and will never come back again."

You put the dog on the back seat of the car, on an old blanket, and said that it would be raining soon and that the water would wash away the bloodstains on the road.

Bärbel Körner brought the glass of wine. Smiling, the two women exchanged a look of mutual understanding and talked to each other in a whisper.

"What would you like to eat, Doctor?"

"Something tasty," said Hilde. She picked up the menu and let her index finger glide up and down the text. "Here."

Bärbel nodded and said, close by her ear, "We'll take care of that, Doctor. In the mean time don't expect any interesting conversation from your partner."

She walked to the kitchen door. Hilde took a sip from her glass.

Karster Glut, she thought, as she looked at the old man again. *The same wine I had been sent to get then. Only now Hans Schwarzburg is no longer here, and his son has taken over the business. You were a jack of all trades, Vitus. You worked for everybody. For my father, you brought medicine to patients who were not able to come and get it themselves. For Schwarzburg, you worked on the hillside vineyards, and you were always present for the vintage. You could do so many things. Garden, repair tools, repair fences. And knock down and kill the winegrower's dog and saddle me with a secret. Maybe you couldn't help it that the dog died. Maybe it had run out from the vines and onto the road. You would remain the nice, good-natured Vitus Weiss and not be pointed out as the man who had killed the dog.*

The eyes of the dog, the eyes of the jester. Grübler was the dearest dog in all of Karst, and you were the nicest, most helpful jack-of-all-trades in the world. So nice, that you didn't have the guts to tell Hans Schwarzburg what had happened, that you had killed his dog.

She took another sip from her wine. She began to think of ways to explain the events of the past few days. *It is the wine. The sourish bouquet hides a venom that affects us all. The roots suck it up and transport it to the grapes that Karster Glut slowly makes into the wine he gives us to make us crazy. Everyone has his own hallucinations, and they are so strange that no one dares to talk about them. We all experience something that is impossible, for the venom, the poison, has spread through our bodies.*

From the moment that Vitus Weiss awoke, and she looked into his blue eyes, she seemed to see black, dead dog's eyes, and it occurred to her now that she could very well use his help.

She didn't dare tell her stories to Burgomaster Lins or the local police. They would take her for a fool—or worse! Besides, Rainer Miethe had reminded her of her oath of secrecy. She needed someone who could make inquiries and report back to her and tell her if his experiences were similar to hers. The old man could get badly frightened: Frightened the way she had been when she saw the dead dog. The old man was in her debt, she calculated.

"Doctor Steiner," laughed Vitus. "Excuse my terrible manners! I sit here sleeping, while such a lovely young lady sits here at my table. How do you do?"

"Couldn't be better," she lied. "Everything is running like clockwork since I came home. I presume you're doing well, too, for I haven't seen you in my consulting room yet."

He pointed at his glass.

"I have my own medicine. Much fresh air, a schnapps in due course, and you need only meet the doctor on the street or in a cozy restaurant."

Bärbel brought the dinner, and Hilde asked her to refill the man's small glass. She began to eat and listened to him.

"I am seventy-two now, Doctor. Still rise every morning at six. They ask for my help everywhere. The older I get, the more work comes my way. People with the highest educations are not even capable of putting a new lock on the front door or repairing a leaking faucet. For all these and many other daily problems, Old Vitus has to find a solution. I even still do some work at the vintage; I like to watch what the winegrowers do with their harvest. I don't have to read the label anymore to know what I am drinking; the cork is barely out of the bottle, and I can already smell from where the wine comes and when the bottling has taken place."

"I don't know that much about that," said Hilde, "but I do know that my father always sent me to Hans Schwarzburg for some very special bottles of wine. They were not for sale below, in the shops of Karst, I believe."

He stroked his beard, and as they looked at each other, she wondered if he was thinking about the incident with the dog right now. "The big, powerful men get together to arrange these markets," he said. "Put an excellent vintage of wine aside in a corner of the cellar and sell the bottles sparingly to the notables, give one or two away every now and then. That makes for staunch friendships. Ah, it is all so long ago. Hans is dead, and his son Wilhelm has succeeded him. Your father passed away, and now you're our doctor. Everything changes, but still remains the same. There is the wine and the river; after you and I are long gone, there will still be wine, and the water of the Moselle will still run to the Rhine."

"You've got to help me," said Hilde abruptly. "There is something I need you to examine for me."

Vitus raised his white eyebrows. He had known Hilde very well as a child, but he had lost track of her when she began her studies. He had seen her walking about town many times since her return, but now she sat opposite him, and he could take a really good look at her for the first time. She had always had half-long, dark hair, and she still had a girlish face.

"You live alone, and you are very busy, Doctor. There must be a lot of things that need fixing at your house. It's for you to say."

"No, Mr. Weiss, this is about something else. You must promise me not to talk about it with anyone."

"You can count on that, Doctor."

"Have you ever heard of Rainer Miethe?"

He continued to stroke his beard with the palm of his hand and pushed up his moustache with his thumb and index finger. Bringing his hand down again, he slowly nodded his head.

"Certainly. His name is well known, but I have never seen him. You know, something odd must be going on in that big old house. We know he lives there, but we never even catch a glimpse of him. Among the storekeepers of Karst he is known as 'the unknown man who doesn't eat or drink.' No one knows who he is. He never comes into the village to even buy himself something as simple as a loaf of bread or a piece of meat. Do you know him personally, then?"

Hilde put down her fork and knife on her plate and wiped her mouth with her napkin.

"Yes. I have seen him. That is to say, I think I have seen him. It is difficult to explain. That is why I would like somebody to go up to the house and make up something that would allow them to enter. Then I would like to know what he heard, what he saw—and what kind of experiences he had there."

"Compare notes, eh?" said Vitus. "To see if the experiences of the visitor are the same as your own. You want that visitor to be me, is that correct?"

"Yes, you are the only one I would dare to ask something like this."

She looked him straight in the eye. Blue eyes. Black eyes. Dog's eyes. Jester's eyes. Then she lowered her own eyes, picked up her fork and knife again, and continued her meal.

"I am the one, I can help you, Doctor. To be honest with you, I'm rather curious myself. In front of the house is a big lawn, no bushes, no trees: just lawn. I could ask Mr. Miethe if I could have his permission to work some magic by turning his lawn into a park. Or maybe there is some painting to be done, or some other odd jobs. You know, Doctor, I have really wanted to go there for quite some time already. What do you know about this man? What shall I look for when I go to take a look at his place?"

"I don't want to say anything about that yet. After you have returned from your mission, I want to know how everything went. Depending on what you tell me, I can either enlighten you about several things, or perhaps I shall hold my tongue instead."

"That sounds rather vague, but—all right, I will go. And afterwards, I will call to make an appointment with you."

Hilde changed the subject of the conversation. She liked to sit here, among her fellow villagers, among her people. When she and Vitus fell silent for a bit, she listened to the voices of the other guests, and every now and then she turned around to look at all those familiar faces.

She finished her meal, and Bärbel Körner came to clear the table.

"Don't you think you should be a bit concerned about my health?" asked the old man, pointing to his empty glass.

"A schnapps for Mr. Weiss, Bärbel. And pour me one as well."

The restaurant keeper smiled. "I've never seen you drink this before, Doctor."

Hilde began to smile also. *I also never had the feeling that I was going mad,* she thought. *Fortunately, I am still able to control myself. It would not take much more for me to ask you to put the entire bottle on the table.*

The glasses were brought, and Bärbel also set a little bowl of cherry liqueur chocolates on the table. Vitus enjoyed them thoroughly, but Hilde did not even want to look at them. They reminded her of jester's eyeballs. She hoped the old man would dispatch them quickly.

* * *

That Tuesday the weather was bleak. It was October, the month of the harvest. The grapes had ripened, and the sun hid behind a gray layer of autumn clouds.

Vitus Weiss forecast a cold, white winter. He had lit the open hearth in his house and sat down close to the fire on a wooden chair with a straight back. Opposite him sat Doctor Hilde Steiner, who had driven over to see him.

"I say, the weather has changed quickly hasn't it, Doctor? Sunday was a glorious day," he said. "I walked to Bärbel Körner without even wearing my coat. Our hands will get cold soon enough, though, during the harvest. Hopefully it won't start raining, for then it will get extremely slippery on the hillsides."

He had poured coffee into two cups and put down a sugar bowl. He pointed at the spoon standing upright in the sugar.

"That's for spooning and stirring," he grinned. "A man alone isn't too fussy."

The house he lived in was old, but he had always maintained it well. The outer walls were white, and on the front wall he had made a painting of himself as a young grape harvester. He had made all the wooden furniture inside.

"The mystery around Rainer Miethe is solved, Doctor," he said. "Now I understand why we have never seen him in Karst before. He seems to be a rich man and spends most of his time on his luxurious yacht. His home port is in Monaco, where he also owns a home. This big house here is scarcely used. All the rooms are empty."

Hilde sat bolt upright in her chair.

"Empty? What on earth do you mean, empty? Didn't you see the collection of old automobiles? Weren't there any antiques? Didn't you see all those books, the medical apparatus and musical instruments, the tools? Are you sure you have been inside?"

"I don't know what you are talking about, Doctor. Yes, there were plenty of tools around, because Georg Wust is busy restoring the whole place—and believe me, he doesn't need a handyman! He does everything by himself. The electrical wiring is done, and he has installed heavy wooden doors everywhere. Now he is busy replanking all the floors with parquet. Must have cost Mr. Miethe a fortune!"

Hilde raised her hand.

"Now, wait a minute! You went up there, stood at the door and—"

"Yes, and I must say I was surprised when the door opened and a small, extremely fat man was standing in front of me. He introduced himself as Georg Wust and asked what he could do for me. I came right to the point. I was asked in, and it was immediately obvious what a truly skilled workman he is, and that he doesn't need the help of an old day laborer. He went nimbly from room to empty room, taking the stairs so quickly that I couldn't keep up with him, and everywhere lay tools that I would love to own myself. It was almost as if he was trying to make me jealous, the way all his equipment was strewn about. The best of the best. Somewhere in the house he has a bed, and now that he has electricity, he can make use of the fridge. He won't have to waste time shopping.

I'm sure his food supplies will carry him through the winter."

"I hope you didn't tell him that I had sent you?"

"No, of course not. But honestly, Doctor, I still don't know what it was exactly that you wanted to know. What were you talking about a moment ago? Automobiles and antiques? Trust me, Doctor, that house is so empty, that the echo of your own voice gives you a fright as soon as you start talking."

Hilde took a sip from her coffee to give herself time to think. Then she finally said, "Well, there are some very strange rumors. You told me about his nickname, given to him by the storekeepers of Karst. I have heard other things, too. There should have been a sick person in the house."

"Georg Wust is the only one staying there. He is way too fat, but I noticed myself that it doesn't seem to affect him. But didn't you tell me you thought you had seen Rainer Miethe?"

"Never mind that. It must have been a misunderstanding. However, Mr. Weiss, I thank you very much for your help. As a doctor, I prefer the certain to the uncertain, and now I know there is nothing to worry about."

They went on talking about other things; inevitably they began to reminiscence.

"I still think about Grübler, the black dog," she said, looking him straight in the eyes.

He nodded and did not seem at all surprised by this remark.

"Grübler. . . . Yes. He was old, very old. He liked to lie in front of Schwarzburg's house and warm his bones when the sun was shining. He had a lot of trouble walking, but when he suddenly appeared on the road like that, so unexpected, so fast—"

"Not fast enough to avoid the front wheel of your car."

"Maybe he did it on purpose. Although I think I know enough about animals to be pretty sure that dogs don't commit suicide."

"That's how our secret came into being."

"What secret?"

"I saw it, didn't I? You put Grübler on the back seat of your car and told me we should not talk about it, ever, to anyone."

"Now that you mention it, yes, you are absolutely right! I never thought about it again. I lifted up the dog, with his insides hanging out, and took care that you saw nothing more. That wasn't a very nice thing at all, especially not for a little girl to see. I figured that if the secret itself were more important to you than the dog, you would not talk about it, and maybe you would forget about the entire thing sooner or later. Do you know what I did next? I drove back to Hans Schwarzburg and thought up a good story along the way. When I got there we buried Grübler together. He knew I had been badly shaken, and when I left he gave me a beautiful bottle of

Karster Glut, the same kind you had gotten for your father."

Hilde was silent as she realized she had worried about a problem for years that didn't even exist. But the knowledge gave her no relief. The dog's eyes might be closed for ever, but the eyes of the jester were wide open, and looking deep into her mind.

* * *

Andreas Pallasch had not been the first to encounter the jester, nor would he be the last. When Josef Reimer had brought Pallasch to the doctor, the police officer had remarked to Hilde Steiner that strange things were happening all around Karst.

"My jurisdiction lies outside of Karst, but I think I have heard enough. Like the man who almost drowned, and the woman who was jammed in the rocks. The statements they made to the police were at the very least peculiar. 'I was walking through the mountains and all of a sudden I fell into the water. I am very well aware of the fact that the distance between the mountain and the river is a far cry, and that there are houses in between. But I know very well what happened to me, don't I?'"

This man, though, had taken Hilde into his confidence and told her quite a different story.

"I was walking along and suddenly stood eye to eye with a creature that looked human, but different somehow. He wore a jester's suit, with a fool's cap and jingling bells. His face—don't get me started talking about what his face looked like! You are the only one I dare tell this to, Doctor. Everybody else would probably just laugh at me. The creature lifted me up, held me above his head, and then threw me, in a grand arc, over a meadow, over roads and houses, and into the Moselle. That's what happened. I can't explain it, and I can hardly believe it myself. But that's what happened!"

The tourist who had been jammed between huge boulders insisted that she did not have the faintest idea how she had gotten herself into that situation. The emergency crew that freed her thought it would be wise to get her examined by a doctor, and so she had landed in Hilde's surgery.

She also took the doctor into her confidence.

"I was sitting there, with my back against one of those stones, resting and enjoying the panorama. A man appeared. Dancing, hopping, spinning round, turning somersaults. He had coal black eyes, and his skin seemed to be made of old, torn leather. It was a jester! He wore a bi-colored suit and a fool's cap with bells. I remained sitting there, rigid with fear. I wasn't even able to lift my arms to put my hands in front of my face so that I wouldn't have to look at that horrible figure. He lifted up a stone that was as big and heavy as the one I was leaning against. The weight of the rock didn't slow him down at all; he kept hopping and jumping. He stopped right in front of me and put down the stone. I managed to stand up, but before I could slip away, he pushed the stone forward against me until almost all the air was pressed out of my lungs. He climbed on top of the stone in front of me, Doctor, took my face in his hands and licked me with his long, dry tongue from my neck up to my cheek. Then, all of a sudden, he was gone. I cried until the police finally arrived and freed me. I tell you all this in confidence. It actually happened, but who would believe me?"

Andreas Pallasch was the first patient she saw who was actually wounded. His torn overalls were red with blood, his body covered with little wounds. Following him, more and more people came to visit her with injuries and told her stories that were very similar the ones she had already heard from the truck driver, the man thrown into the river and the lady trapped by the rocks. The police came around to have a talk with her, but she remained silent about the jester and agreed that she found this sequence of accidents highly bizarre, too.

Hans-Jürgen Lins, the burgomaster of Karst, had invited her for a dinner in the restaurant of Bärbel Körner and had expressed his concern about the large number of accidents taking place inside the local boundaries of Karst.

"Everyone is starting to worry," he said. "What is happening here is not only headline news for the *Karster Zeitung*, but for the national press as well. It's no longer a coincidence, when there are so many accidents near

Karst, and from Trier to Koblenz, along the same road, there have been none—everything is fine. Furthermore, Doctor, all these people make rambling, inane statements. It just does not make sense. Cars get pushed off the road, people fall in wells, barns collapse just like that, but no one is able to say anything sensible about it. How many people would have been stone dead already, if not for stupid luck and unplanned rescue? A wall comes down, a victim is covered with stones, but his head remains undamaged; on the bottom of a well someone lies moaning with pain because his hands and knees are grazed, when actually he shouldn't have even survived the fall."

"I know. I treated the victims."

"I had the police visit everyone involved one more time, to have a talk with them. We didn't learn much, but two people mentioned the same, odd incidental matter."

"Now you've made me curious."

"They said they felt as if they were in a dream state. They vaguely remember an odd figure, a jester, with bells on his fool's cap and shoes!"

Hilde gave a start. She felt the blood rush to her head and was overcome with panic. She opened her mouth to gasp for air. The message from Rainer Miethe was clear: Will you come to me now, Hilde Steiner, or must there be deaths first?

The burgomaster misunderstood her reaction and hastened to say, "You, as a doctor, see it another way.

You don't believe in supernatural powers. But yesterday a third victim opened his mouth: Andreas Pallasch. He also mentioned a jester with jingling bells."

When Hilde still remained silent, he raised his glass of wine to her and said, "Maybe there is something wrong with our wine? Please, ask your patients, Doctor. Let us know if you hear any stories like these, okay?"

* * *

And then the day came when Hilde finally decided to give herself up to the will of Rainer Miethe.

It was a cold Wednesday in November. After the consulting hour, she went upstairs. In the living room, at the dining table, sat the jester. The skin of his face was dark, lined and leathery like that of a gorilla. With his fingers he plucked crumbly pieces of cake from a dish that sat on the tablecloth. With slow movements he put them in his mouth. The coal black eyes were moist. The bells on his cap jingled softly when he slowly raised his head. His thick lips made smacking sounds.

Hilde's strong character and her experience had probably saved her from a nervous breakdown up to now. Every now and then she had taken a tranquilizer and used the time to think about the events. But now, finding the jester sitting at her table, in her chair, she realized that she could lose control at any moment. Maybe she would feel better if she screamed hysterically for a few minutes. Maybe she should pick up one of those nice, sharp knives sitting on the table beside the cake and stab the point of it in one of those big, moist eyes, to find out if the jester was a creature of flesh and blood or a mere phantom.

She was stood in the doorway, fighting the encroaching feeling of panic. Here she stood, face to face with the tormentor from her girlhood, who had come back to make life difficult for her again.

One more time the jester plucked a piece from the cake and brought it to his thick lips.

The right to steal, she thought. *The jester breaks into houses and takes what he wants.*

She had great difficulty bridging the short distance between the doorway and the table. Her legs hurt her, as if the veins under her skin had contracted. She grabbed hold of the armrest of a chair and leaned a bit closer to him. "Eat and get lost!" she said.

A gasp of breath from the jester brought the scent of decay to her nostrils; she began to fill sick and dizzy. Slowly she pushed the chair back and sat down opposite the creature.

"Do you have a voice? Can you speak?"

The little parts of his leather jerkin creaked when he leaned backward and crossed his arms. He held his head on such an angle that the left protuberance of his fool's cap touched his shoulder. He remained sitting this way this way, smiling. It was quiet in the room. Hilde didn't want to say another word. Tears were running down her cheeks.

Suddenly the jester began to move. He spread his arms and shoved back the chair, stretched his legs and turned a backward somersault through the air.

The chair was overturned. The jester landed on his feet, turned another somersault and then stood with his back against the wall beside a cupboard. It was the darkest part of the room, and it seemed to Hilde that he began to fade away and slowly grow into one with the busy design of the wallpaper. But she could still see the horns of his fool's cap move and hear the bells ring.

She looked at the cake. She had bought it herself this morning and put it on the table, but she hadn't eaten any of it. One half of the cake was gone, and the dish was full of crumbs.

"If you are real," she said, continuing to stare at the cake, "you actually have made use of the jester's right to steal. You have cake in your stomach. But if you are a phantasm, a dream creature, then something else has happened. I have eaten the cake myself, or what I see on the dish is a false projection."

She moved her fingers along the side of the dish where the cake was missing. She felt only crumbs.

"Did I eat it myself?" she asked herself aloud. "No! I haven't had breakfast for days! I eat cake in the afternoon, and only at night do I manage to have a normal meal. Even so, I should vomit to see if there is cake in my stomach. I don't even need a emetic for that, I—"

She looked up and saw that the jester had come loose from the wall and had taken a step forward. Her stomach tightened and pumped fluid up through her gullet. She started to cough. Through her tears she saw the creature approach, and quickly straightened her back and held her hands, fingers spread, defensively in front of her face. Her body stiffened as she felt the hands of the jester under her armpits. He lifted her up, above his head, the same way the jester in her childhood had done. Jumping from foot to foot, he turned around and around while Hilde held her breath and kept her eyes tightly shut. When he finally returned her to the ground, she opened her eyes and saw him standing right next to her, gesturing with both hands at the telephone. Two seconds later it began to ring. The copper bells of the jester jingled as he nodded to her. She picked up the receiver.

"Yes?"

As she was listened to someone from the local police, she watched the jester dance backward and vanish from sight, through the closed door of a cupboard.

"I'll be right there," she said and put the receiver back on the phone.

There was a calm, resigned expression on her face as she picked up her car keys and went downstairs. She took her doctor's bag and put on her coat. Outside, in the main street of Karst, she walked to her car, opened the door and got in. As she pulled away, she saw in her rear-view mirror that the jester was following her. He jumped from one side of the street to the other and turned forward somersaults. She turned and took a road at right angles to the main street, driving up to the left along the vines. At a point where the road curved was a small parking place with a view of the river valley. There were two police cars there, and she saw a few policemen, their hands behind their backs, standing there talking. They had been waiting for her; there was nothing more they could do for the old man who sat on the bench with his hands in his lap.

It was Vitus Weiss. A soft breeze stroked his white hair and white beard. His mouth was wide open as were his eyes.

"We think it was a heart attack," Hilde heard an officer say. "It looks as if he was frightened to death."

She walked up to the bench, and the officer accompanied her. She looked behind her, to see if the jester had followed her up here, but she couldn't spot him. Then she looked at the old man. He wore a worn coat and strong leather boots. Fear was written in his wide, dilated eyes.

"Have you seen what he holds in his hand?" asked the policeman.

Hilde bent down and brought her face close to the dead man's left hand. Between thumb and index finger he held a rosary, but instead of beads, it consisted of little copper bells.

He is right-handed, it flashed through her mind. *I am sure he is right-handed. So often I have seen him at work, and he always kept his tools in his right hand. With that hand he took up his schnapps, recently.*

While she began to examine Vitus, the officer, standing next to her, said, "Hermann Kreher, an employee of Wilhelm Schwarzburg, was driving past and saw Vitus just sitting here. He stopped and called to Vitus to ask if he wanted a lift to Karst. When he didn't react, Kreher got out. What he told us next sounds rather odd. He said there was a dog lying under the bench, a big, black dog. The animal began to growl when he came nearer and showed his teeth, and then scrambled up and disappeared at a run up the hill, between the vines."

Hilde looked at the officer. All that time she hadn't spoken a word, but now she said, in a soft voice, "Whose dog could that be?"

The officer shrugged his shoulders.

"No idea. My colleague, standing there, is quite some years older than I am. He knows Karst like the back of his hand. Only after some long thinking could he remember the last time a big, black dog lived in Karst. He knows all the dogs who live here now—the Alsatians of Max Flach and the Frevert family, Franz Deyle's brown mongrel, the hounds of Siegfried Hildebrandt. The last black one should have been Grübler, the favorite dog of William Schwarzburg's father Hans. As soon as we are ready here, Doctor, we are going on the hunt for that mysterious dog that crawled out from under this bench."

* * *

A quarter of an hour later Hilde sat in her Volkswagen again. Before she started, she opened her doctor's bag. She plucked two elastic bands from a little cardboard box containing medicine. Looking in her mirror, she plaited her hair into pigtails left and right from her face, and wound the elastics round it. She examined the result and was satisfied. When she was still a girl, she had looked like that so often. She wiped the lipstick from her mouth with the sleeve of her coat. After having smiled at herself in the mirror, she started the engine and drove away. Driving calmly, she left the spot where Vitus Weiss had died from a heart attack. and with a high, shrill little voice she began to sing children's songs she remembered from her youth.

The jester ran along beside the car, dancing and jumping, and he was followed by a big, black dog. She looked aside, saw the big, black dog's eyes and began to sing louder.

That is the way she drove to Miethe's house. She stopped in front of the iron fence and looked at the lawn, the driveway and the big, gloomy building. In the middle of the lawn, Georg Wust was busy burning something. When she had observed it well for a while, she noticed that it was a big wooden cogwheel. He had a tin of kerosene in his hands, and every now and then he splashed some of the contents on the burning wood. The gate was closed, but the dog and the jester had managed to reach the driveway and now approached the fire. Georg gave the kerosene to the jester and walked up to Hilde. He walked right through the fence.

Still singing, Hilde opened the side window. Only when the little, fat man stood right in front of her did she fall silent and give him a friendly smile.

"When will you come, Doctor?" asked Wust.

"As soon as possible," she answered. "I have a lot to arrange; I can't leave my practice just like that. There has to be a successor, and of course I'll have to explain to a lot of people why I'm leaving my house in Karst and going to work for Rainer Miethe."

"Your own, big, private clinic," laughed Wust. "Everyone will understand that you couldn't let a chance like that go by."

Hilde started another children's song, and to her great surprise the fat man sang along. He raised his hands and began to dance. When he threatened to drown her voice, she began to sing louder and louder, until finally she was screaming. Wildly she shook her head so that the pigtails at both sides of her head flung into her eyes. In the flames of the burning logs, she thought she saw the faces of Franciscus and Paulus. Now Wust picked up the heavy, burning cogwheel and threw it up into the air. When it came down again, he kicked it with his pointed shoe, and the wood flew apart in sparks. The black dog barked at it and attacked the rain of fire.

"See you later!" Hilde suddenly cried, and drove away.

The little, fat man ran next to her for a while. The speedometer climbed to fifty miles and hour, and still he kept pace with her.

The side window of the car was still open.

"Maybe I will find a doll from out of my youth in the attic!" she shouted at him.

"Who knows!" he shouted back. "What do you want to do with it?"

"Lift it up! Hold it high above my head and dance!"

"Of course! The doll will be frightened!"

He finally came to a stop. Hilde slowed down and continued into Karst. She plucked the elastic bands from her hair and tried to order her thoughts. Rainer Miethe, her tormentor, had showed her his patience was wearing thin. She'd had patients who had narrowly escaped from death. Now Vitus Weiss was no longer here, and the rosary of bells in his hand and the appearance of the black dog had told her that Miethe was responsible.

She drove into the main street of Karst. She would go, in a little while, at home, into the attic to search for a doll. She hoped she would find a doll with big, black eyes. With jester's eyes. With the dark, dead eyes of the dog.

 8 -Recollections of Otto Faun

"It's either us or him," Franciscus said to me. "If given the opportunity to murder Rainer Miethe, trust me, I will not hesitate for a single moment."

We paid no attention at all to Walter Fabry, who was sitting between us. We had sold Fabry's jeep and bought a van, the front seat of which the three of us now sat upon as we plowed our way slowly through the snow. So much snow had fallen that we could barely see where the road ended and the cliff began. Franciscus followed the road by driving in the tracks of cars that had passed through before us. He had the windshield wipers going at their fastest speed to keep brushing the thick snowflakes off the glass before they could freeze and form a solid white layer that would certainly stop our progress.

"We've got a rifle in the back," I said, "that already has our friend Fabry's fingerprints on it. Shoot Miethe right in the head, but make sure you wear gloves. That way, the blame will be on our friend here."

Koos Verkaik

"Exactly. Those crushed feet of yours will eventually heal by themselves, just as my wounds did, but a bullet through the skull will destroy his brain and put an end to his immortality. Even our bodies are not capable of recovering from such a grave wound."

"It's worth a try," I said. "He has caused us quite enough trouble, not to mention all the things he has done to others. He has killed so often and so mercilessly, the number of his victims is countless. It's strange to think about it, but no one will ever be charged or prosecuted for the crimes he has committed over the last two hundred years.

"And besides, who would ever believe such ridiculous charges, even if we did tell anyone? All the cruelty and punishment I remember so well cannot even be proven. Do you remember how I designed a wooden machine for him, on the banks of a river in France, and how we were chained and shackled together at the ankles? Do you also recall how we were beaten, Francis? Beaten until the blood ran, day after day. Our wounds, of course, healed. Not even a tiny scar was left on our skin, but around us we saw so many others die."

Francis was already driving at a snail's pace, but he slowed even more now, until the van was almost at a complete stop.

"What's up?"

"Strange that you should mention that now; just before I came to Europe from New York, I went into a trance and saw those days. There was a woman present at the worksite who should not have been there. I even remember her name—Hilde. There was a big, wooden cogwheel, which you and I had built from thick tree trunks. This woman looked into my mind, and I suspect she knows quite a lot about us now. I can even recall what she looked like. She looked remarkably like Maria Delaruelle, although not quite as pretty. The same color hair, the same figure."

Walter Fabry looked from one man to the other.

"I need to be sedated," he whimpered in a soft vice. "I cannot bear this pain much longer. A doctor has to take a look at my foot, you must take me to a hospital!"

"Miethe has told Fabry about Maria Delaruelle," I said, ignoring the wounded man's pleas. "One of us, Francis, should know her whereabouts. I have never seen her again, in trances or anywhere else, so you are the only one who knows anything about this. Miethe wants something from you, and more than likely, it is information about Maria that he is after!"

We began to drive faster again, or at least as fast as the weather would permit. We plodded along through the snow and hoped that it would not be too long before we reached Koblenz, from where we would travel on to Trier. Fabry had mentioned a meeting place where Miethe expected him to arrive—with me as his prisoner. We were going to surprise Miethe, and, as it appeared right now, Francis would kill him as soon as he saw him or at his next best chance!

"Indeed, Paul, I have met Maria several times over the years" he admitted, "and as crazy as it sounds, I have been in love with her for centuries! As for you, I would not believe you if you told me that she didn't mean a thing to you. I don't have to tell you how lonely we, the "chosen," the "immortals," can feel. I know you are aware of the empty feeling in your heart. That is why Maria and I have tried to look out for each other whenever possible. We looked for and found each other! I have met her in Paris, London and small villages along the Italian coast.

"She has always led a life of carefree luxury, having her fun with all the richest men on earth. She has been married many, many times, having naturally outlived all her husbands, who one for one left her with considerable wealth. The last time we met was in New York. We both knew that Rainer Miethe was hunting us at the time, so I moved from place to place on a regular basis, but didn't dare invite her to any of my homes. I owned apartments in the Bronx, Brooklyn and Greenwich Village, and at the time we found each other again, I was living in Manhattan."

He was silent for a while and concentrated on the white road.

"There is more, my friend." he said. "I won't deny that Maria and I had an affair. Although sometimes decades passed when we did not see each other, we have always remained compelled and attracted towards one another. As far as this tangled web of our three hearts is concerned, I have certainly been the most fortunate.

"Once, not too long ago, she and I were hiding in a hotel in Greenwich Village, after Maria had just had an affair with some millionaire. He had died suddenly from a stroke while they were on his yacht, moored in the harbor at Monaco, and according to his will she was his only heir. She came to me to get herself together and to make use of my considerable connections to help her invest her new capital wisely. We had such a wonderful time! I know the Village like the back of my hand, and I took her out for dinner every night. We roamed the streets and alleys, and I was so proud to be recognized by people we passed as we walked the streets of New York. Here I was, the famous composer, with one of the world's most beautiful women at his side. I forgot to be careful though, Paul. I forgot there were men like our friend Fabry here, a little man with no life at all, who sit around whining about their feet.

"One night, around midnight, I went to buy a bottle of wine at a liquor store that was open late. When I returned, Maria had disappeared. The door of the hotel room had been kicked in, and it was evident from the overturned furniture that there had been quite a fight. All her clothing, trinkets and jewelry were on the table, and her make-up and perfume were still on the glass above the bathroom sink. I knew immediately what this meant, Paul: Miethe's men had kidnapped her. Maybe it is Miethe who knows more about her present circumstances than either you or I!

"I took flight; I left America on a tour through Europe, to avoid suspicion and to try and stay ahead of him.

"But Miethe's men tracked me down. What happened after that, you already know. Francis Beck is dead. He came to a fiery end in Holland.

"It was not easy to find you, my friend. When you are recovered and feeling like your old self again, I will explain how I managed to find you. But I doubted whether or not I was even doing the right thing. Would you be the man I was looking for once I finally found you? Would you be the same man who had been my old comrade?

"The gift Alexander gave us so long ago has begun to ripen and ferment within our bodies. We possess powers that other mortals cannot even imagine. You were no longer conscious of whom you were, and it caused me quite a lot of trouble and took a lot of hard work to find a sign of life from you. Miethe is much better at that trick than I am. He knows how to hide himself, how to protect himself—just as I hope you will be able to do again soon. Right now, you are a danger to yourself and to me. When Rainer tries, he will find you.

"While you were living in Rotterdam, you were in fact, a switched-off transmitter. It was only when I was finally in your neighborhood that I received any kind of impulses from you. Now, slowly but surely, you are beginning to become yourself again and are restoring the powers you once wielded so artfully. You are indeed a transmitter, Paul, a transmitter whose signal is getting stronger by the minute, and I hope you learn how to handle your power again as quickly as possible.

"Pay attention, Paul, pay attention."

I stared out of the window in front of us and watched how Francis kept the van in the tire tracks of a Volvo in front of us. Suddenly his voice came to me, although he had not spoken a word. I heard him not with my ears, but with my mind.

"Please don't be angry with me. I know that you are jealous of me, but there is absolutely nothing I can do to change that now. Yes, Maria and I have often made love. I know of course that you still love her—who could blame you for that? What you need now, though, is rest. I have a feeling that you will soon be your old self again.

"Tell me Paul, can you communicate with me, as I am doing with you right now?"

I fixed my mind and formed images instead of words. It was clear that Francis and I were seeing the same thing, for he heaved a deep sigh, and said aloud, "Oh, yes! She is beautiful, Paul, she really is beautiful."

"If what you say is true," I remarked, "then Miethe should be able to find us by catching my vibrations. I have put you in danger, correct?"

Koos Verkaik

"It is very possible."

"But soon I will be able to, uh, remain invisible to his radar?"

"Yes, you could describe it that way, I suppose. This is good, Paul, very good—you are beginning to remember. A mysterious process deep, deep inside of you has come back to life. I can see it happening very clearly.

"When I first met you in Holland, I couldn't possibly read your mind. Now, though, I am in such close contact with you that I will always be able to find my way back to you should you slip away again."

"Maybe it would be better if we split up," I suggested. "You go on ahead with Fabry and try to get hold of Miethe while I will hide out somewhere until my feet are healed. What do you think?"

I suddenly had a strange feeling, and leaning forward, looked at my old friend.

"Wait a minute. I see it all very clearly now. I'm nothing but a lure!" I cried. "Isn't that right? You want to drive up to the place where Miethe and Fabry are supposed to meet, knowing that Miethe expects only Fabry and me to show up. You are planning to hide somewhere nearby and wait for your chance to aim a rifle at his head."

Franciscus smiled.

"You guessed it, Paul, or did you fish that information out of my head? You're improving quickly! And be honest: isn't this the best solution? Miethe is coming to get you, but I will prepare a surprise of my own."

It began to snow even harder now, and all we could see of the Volvo were its taillights. Fabry's head rested on my shoulder, and he was moaning in pain as he slept. I closed my eyes. If Francis could see everything I did, then Maria danced for him as she had done in front of the gates of Kasper von Karst's castle.

"Can you communicate with everyone this way?" I asked after a while. "Can you read Fabry's thoughts?"

"Sometimes I have spontaneous contact with people" he replied. "I cannot penetrate Fabry's mind and read his thoughts, but I can make him jump right out of his skin! I can make him see all kinds of things."

"Like you did during your concerts. When you showed the audience things that were not really there."

"Exactly—images, pictures. We have discussed this so many times, haven't we? You were always so busy with your experiments. Don't you remember why you went to Rome time after time?"

"Cats," I said. "There are so many stray cats there. The ruins of the old Roman Empire, the fragments of a great culture, and in between, all those damn cats! I know I went there often, but why, Francis?"

"You've always had a special bond with those animals. You even praised the ancient Egyptians for their love of cats, and you were convinced that the priests, like you, were able to perceive the strong images the animals sent to them. That is why you went to Rome: to wait, patiently, at a quiet spot and catch the images they sent."

"It's true," I said. "You and Miethe have never had that experience, but I have seen their wildest fantasies, the riot of colors that emanates from their souls. The magic light shining in their eyes—I am able to look into it, I can even look behind it and sink deep into their wonderful cat world."

"You thought you were back to normal," laughed Francis, "but now you see that there are still many things that you are not yet fully aware of. I know the process well, for I have been in much the same situation as you find yourself now. You're getting into your stride very well, Paul, and soon you will possess again all the powers that you ever had, and then, well . . . Rest now. Aren't you sleepy?"

"I don't' feel sleepy or hungry."

We sat silently and listened to the deep drone of the diesel motor. Francis began to tap his left hand on the steering wheel as he peered in front of him. The rhythm of his fingers was synchronized with the humming of the engine and the static, thumping movement of the windshield wipers. He was busy shaping images.

Fabry abruptly awoke and sat bolt upright.

Long, hairy claws suddenly grabbed hold of the wipers and brought them to a halt as a giant spider, as big as our van, crept down over the windshield and ran ahead of us through the snow. Fabry started to scream and thrash about wildly. Francis was having a lot of trouble keeping the van in the tracks of the Volvo now, and as we came to a bend in the road, I felt the van slip away.

Using my will, I caused a bird, a very big bird, to come swooping down from the steel gray sky. It spread its wings, and, with its strong talons, grabbed the spider and lifted it from the road surface. The long legs of the spider moved in a spastic motion from side to side as the bird flew higher and higher into the mountain sky. A few brief seconds later, both animals had vanished from sight.

"Congratulations," said Francis. "That's more like it!"

"Wha—wha—what is this?" stammered Fabry. "How—how could you—?"

He took a deep breath and pushed hard on his chest with both hands.

"You ain't seen nothing yet," said Francis. "Much, much stranger things than this can happen. You remember that, Fabry. If you lie to us about the plans with Miethe, if you dare lead us into a trap, you will see something guaranteed to give you a heart attack. Remember, Fabry: We are very special people, with very special gifts. We can be nice, or we can frighten you to death."

* * *

We had driven well past Trier and were lost on the small roads in the woods of the Hunsrück Mountains. It became obvious that Fabry must have remained in Bavaria for many years, for he was no longer sure exactly how to reach the place where he was supposed to meet Miethe. Finally though, on the way to Saarburg, he recognized the name of a little village. We entered a small, narrow valley with perhaps only a dozen houses in it.

"Above us are the ruins," said Fabry. "That is where Miethe and I are supposed to meet; my instructions are to be there tomorrow—with Paul. Perhaps he's already there. I don't think you can get the van up there using this road; it is very steep, and there is way too much snow. It will take you about fifteen minutes if you walk, Francis. You must leave me here though. I cannot move another inch. Or you can also drive around to the other side. I think I can still find the way. The slope of the hill will become more gradual, and you will be able to reach the ruins from there."

"For the time being we will stay right here," decided Francis. "I saw a place to eat nearby, and we can probably spend the night there as well. I'll go out there first and check it out it by myself."

The three of us got out of the front seat of the van. Francis pushed Walter into the back. I climbed back into the front seat; Francis got the rifle and put it into my hands.

"Fingerprints! Franciscus, watch the fingerprints!" I said. "After you shoot Miethe, you can't very well put the blame on Fabry if your prints are all over the damn gun!"

"A fat lot I care," responded Francis. "Keep an eye on him, and keep the rifle aimed at him. Now that we know where we have to be, we really don't need him any longer. He should be glad that I haven't already killed him. All I need him for now is to convince Miethe that everything is all right. You know, Paul, I'm feeling rather nervous."

The door of the van was still open, and Francis climbed back inside and closed the door. He pointed a finger at Fabry and said, "No crap now, you hear? Is there anything that you are supposed to do now? Do you have to call Miethe? Are there any particular arrangements?"

Fabry made a face that reflected his pain and, lifting his leg, rubbed his wounded foot. He did not answer, and Franciscus, becoming impatient, began drumming his fingers on the back of the seat. I watched as dozens of spiders the size of my fist crawled across the floor of the van and scurried around Fabry's wounded feet. The terrified man sat at attention and pushed himself back until he was pressed up against the back doors. He frantically tried to brush the spiders off, but he could not stop the monstrous arachnids from climbing up his legs, stomach and chest until they reached his face. More and more of them appeared, and he began to scream. A dozen or so of them had crawled along his chin up to his mouth, and when he closed his lips their legs became stuck between them. Fabry spat violently, shook his head from side to side and, using both hands, tried to rid himself of the mass of spiders covering his body.

"Stop!" he shouted. "Please, make them disappear!"

"Is there anything else I should know?" urged Francis.

"No! No! I don't have to make a call, I don't have to make contact. He will be at the ruins tomorrow, that is all."

The spiders crawled over his face and crept through his hair as he beat his fists on his head.

Francis stopped his drumming, and the spiders disappeared instantly.

"He's not lying," he said. "I'm sure of that! I'll be back as soon as possible, Paul."

He got out of the van. The snowflakes were beginning to stick to the windows, and it began to get dim inside the van. The journey had taken us two days because first we had to find a buyer for the jeep and then had to pick up the van. We had spent the night in a small hotel, Francis and I staying wide awake while Walter slept. We had treated and bandaged his foot and made him relatively comfortable.

The door I was sitting next to opened suddenly and I jumped, startled. I quickly pushed to my left and pointed the rifle to my right. It was Francis Beck, standing there smiling at me. In his hands he held a little kitten. The animal had light colored fur with indistinct markings on its back, and its tail was long and thick.

"A stray, I think," said my friend. "It was searching for food in the snow. Take it, Paul. Fix your mind on this little one. It will lessen the chance that Miethe will locate you. Wait, I will make it easier for you."

He closed the front door and a moment later opened the sliding side door of the van. He took a piece of rope and tied Fabry's hands behind his back.

"Now you don't have to pay that much attention to him. I'm off, and will return only when I know for sure if we can stay here or if we have to find accommodations elsewhere."

"Maybe it's better to drive a few miles further," I suggested, holding the little cat on my lap with one hand, and the rifle in the other.

"Maybe. But tomorrow morning I will be at the ruins bright and early, so that I may explore the place and see what we have to do to take Miethe by surprise. That's why I prefer staying at close quarters. See you later, Paul."

"See you," I said.

I took a roast beef sandwich on a roll from the glove compartment. We had bought some sandwiches down the road for Fabry, and this one was left over. I began to feed little pieces of beef to the cat. When there was nothing left of the beef, it began to lick the butter from the roll. Slowly, I stroked the fur, from head to tail, and the animal relaxed and lay down. I stroked the kitten in a steady rhythm and looked at Fabry, without actually

Koos Verkaik

seeing him. In my mind's eye, multicolored images began to appear; I entered completely into the cat's world. The sensation gave me a feeling of intense happiness and warmth. We had connected with each other, and I knew that the cat, whose soft purring vibrated in my finger under its chin, was happy to share its feelings with me.

I sat like that for two hours, until Francis returned.

He got into the van next to me and, after jarring me loose from the endless, infinite depths of cat-thoughts, he said, "I don't think everything is well with Miethe. He is not in the area, I'm convinced of that. In the old days, he would have been on the look-out and certainly would have had some unpleasant surprises in store. I kept an eye on our van and expected him to approach through the snow and use his magical powers to lure you out. After a while, I went up the hillside. It's a hard climb indeed. It was already dark when I arrived at the ruins. It is an ideal spot to meet with Fabry.

"You know, Paul, you're almost in the same condition as me now; you are no longer able to sleep, and you don't feel hungry. A few glasses of water are quite enough for us. Our normal digestion is completely removed from our continued existence. But now, after such a long time, after so many, many years have passed, I would like to have dinner with you, my old friend. A good meal and a nice bottle of wine. What do you say?"

"I would be delighted," I said.

* * *

I opened the door, swung my legs out and slowly put my feet down on the ground. They immediately sank in the snow, and a horrible pain racked my body. It made me sick, but at least I was able to remain standing.

"Do you think you can walk?"

"Yes. Do you remember how you were when you entered my shop in Rotterdam? You were much worse off."

With a tight-lipped face I began to shuffle my feet through the snow holding the little cat in my arms. Francis untied Walter and supported him as they followed me.

We were the only guests in the dining room.

We were men without plans, sitting in easy chairs by the fireplace, waiting for dinner to be served. Tomorrow we would see what would happen. Nobody bothered us. No questions, no conversations. We paied for our drinks, food and shelter, and it was obvious that our money was of much greater importance than our appearance. Francis and I spoke using a northern accent, and the man who served us must have thought we came from Hamburg or Bremen. Fabry didn't say a word, for Francis had made a vicious-looking serpent visible to him, and only him, in front of the fire, and it hissed threateningly whenever the man moved. The cat lay in my lap as we drank Asbach Uralt, and we felt our spirits lighten.

"It has been a long time since I tasted good, strong liquor," said Francis.

Koos Verkaik

He sprawled in his chair.

Miethe must have taken the bad weather into account and figured that Fabry would have to arrange some things before he could come to meet him. The meeting was set for tomorrow, and it looked like we could enjoy a quiet evening and perhaps a peaceful night.

"I'm going to call him Otto," I said.

"Who?" asked Francis.

"The cat. I'm going to name him after Otto Faun."

He looked at me in surprise.

"Otto Faun had something to do with cats, I recall. You and I had lost sight of each other once again, and I had traveled to Spain, to warm myself in the hot sun. In Barcelona, I met a man whose situation was very similar to ours. He was an adventurer, who had received the elixir of life by coincidence. He had witnessed an armed robbery while walking in the street. A pharmacist had been robbed and stabbed, and Otto ran to his rescue. He drove off the attackers, but it was too late for the pharmacist. Using his last ounce of strength, he pulled a small vial off a leather cord that he wore around his neck, and gave it to Otto. With his final words he told Otto to take the contents of the vial. Now, Otto Faun was a poor devil. He owned absolutely nothing and he told me he wouldn't have cared what it contained, even if it was poison."

"You met another immortal!" cried Francis. "You never told me that. I have always assumed that they were out there, that they did exist, but outside of our small circle, I have never met any others. Tell me more."

He asked the owner of the restaurant, who had walked right through the serpent to throw wood on the fire, to refill their glasses and wait a while with the food.

"Yes, Otto Faun became immortal," I said, after the man had gone. "I met him at the end of the sixteenth century. Spain wasn't exactly a safe place for a freethinker like Faun. He wanted to visit a relative in Valencia and asked me to join him on his journey along the coast. So I did, and later we decided to continue traveling together and headed for the Netherlands. For months we were together. I learned many things then that I forgot later, but am now beginning to remember again. Just as Miethe used the magic from the books of Alexander, so Otto Faun had his methods, and he was good enough to teach them to me. His practice had to do with cats. You went out of your to way to catch the animal for me. It seems to me, that right now, you know more about me than I do myself!"

"Not exactly. That is, I know that you can do some things with animals and that you always rather liked cats. This Otto Faun: do you think he's still alive?"

I shook my head.

"The dice were loaded against him. At the horse fair in Valkenburg, in South Holland, he wanted to buy himself a mount. He had set his eyes on a big, and extremely wild, black stallion. Someone told him the animal was unpredictable and could never be tamed. The horse happened to be the trader's eye-catcher, and the way it behaved drew onlookers, whose interest in the other animals might then be stimulated. The fact was, the trader didn't really want to get rid of his show animal at all, but Faun bid such a good price for it that he finally came around in the end. Faun immediately approached the horse from behind, the first thing a horseman learns not to do, and one, good hard kick from the animal resulted in disaster. The hoof went right through his head. From that time on I knew that people like ourselves must be very careful, just as mortals must. Accidents can happen that even we will not live to talk about."

We went on talking for a long time, and then for the first time in many, many years Francis Beck ate a meal. He enjoyed it greatly, and said over and over again how good it would be if only he could sleep the whole night through afterwards, but he knew he wouldn't and neither would I. Later, when we went upstairs to our rooms, he supported the weight of the crippled Fabry, while I painfully pulled myself up along the banister on my crushed feet, which hurt me terribly. There were two bedrooms for us, but we only used one of them. Fabry lay down on a bed, and we pulled chairs up to the end and sat silently. Francis softly tapped out a rhythm with his fingers on the side of his chair, and I stroked Otto's head and back and sank into a calm, peaceful world.

"Try to remember about Faun," said Francis, unexpectedly breaking the silence. "It just came to me that you have mentioned him before. He had special gifts, and had read books that don't even exist anymore, or were locked away behind the doors of libraries that no one is allowed to enter. When I picked the cat up from the snow, I knew immediately that you would be able to do something with it."

"Otto Faun knew the art of change," I said. "But his methods were different from those of Alexander and Rainer Miethe. He understood nothing at all of the changing of metals or of the elixir he had taken. He worked with life, with living matter itself, and he taught me how to do so, also. But let me rest now, Francis. I want to become completely absorbed in the cat's happiness and forget everything around me. Hopefully it will make the pain in my feet a bit more bearable."

* * *

The night before, we had enjoyed the hearth of the open fire at the inn. Now we found ourselves in the freezing cold and snow, and we made use of our powers to minimize the influence of the weather on the human body. We had left in the van early that morning. The road leading up to the ruins was far too slippery and dangerous to drive on, so we drove down through the valley until we came to a highway that Fabry said we could also use to reach our destination. Francis parked the van and sprang into action. He dragged Fabry along until they were right in front of the ruins, and pushed him down in the snow. He pointed at the ancient walls and towers behind us and said, "Hurry now, Paul. I want you to try to climb up to one of the towers and just watch what happens. I'm feeling strong. I feel rested. Soon it will be light, and hopefully Miethe will show up. Don't you interfere in the fight though!"

I had gotten out and followed him on unsteady feet. He took hold of my shoulders firmly and pulled me against him.

"If I don't manage to eliminate him, I will have to count on you. You will receive impulses from me shortly, and you'll know exactly what to do. See you soon."

"See you soon," I said, and turning, began to walk again. As I walked, the little bones in my feet creaked inside my shoes. "We'll survive. We always have."

I walked through empty, roofless chambers, where memories had vanished along with the crumbling stones. Otto, who had been tucked under my coat and pressed to my chest, crept across my shoulders and on to my back when I began to climb the wooden stairs of the tower. It was a steep, winding staircase that was relatively new, probably not even ten years old. Arriving on top, I looked out on a cold, white world. To the left and right of me were pine woods, down behind which the mountain sloped steeply. In front of and behind me were snow-covered fields, and I could see farms and the houses of villages that dotted the landscape.

Francis waved at me. He had entrenched himself behind the remnants of an outer wall, not far from Fabry, and from where it would not be too difficult for him to hit someone with a well-aimed bullet.

I had to lean over the parapet to overlook the whole scene, but I knew I was a sitting duck up there. So I climbed down to the floor below, from where I could sit on my knees and still see outside. Otto crept back down to my chest, and I opened my coat a bit so I could stroke his head. Outside, something had changed. It had stopped snowing. Walter Fabry sat hunched up in front of the ruins, and the snow around him began gradually to fade away. The snow drew back, like the tides at the beach, and bared an island upon which Fabry sat. The ground was covered with grass and flowers. The sun appeared in the gray sky and sent down a beam of spring light.

As I stroked the cat, I knew I was transmitting few or no impulses. The cat led me through its world of instincts and passions as our spirits traveled side by side, yet I remained susceptible and open to vibrations from the outside, for I knew Francis needed me and would try to get in touch with me.

"You're doing fine, Paul," it came to me. "Keep your thoughts with the cat, and try to follow my instructions. Stay alert and pay attention! I want you to try to project yourself. Make a decoy of your exact likeness, and take a place right beside Fabry. We must work together now. Make use of your powers. I know you can do it."

I felt odd as I gazed upon the oasis in the middle of the white wilderness. Francis led me, and I opened myself up to his spirit, while my subconsciousness continued to be preoccupied with what went on in the mind of the cat.

I found myself in two worlds at the same time.

There was someone sitting next to Fabry; I recognized—myself. I sat there, upright with my legs outstretched. My feet lay in an unnatural pose and seemed to be broken. I looked defenseless, with my head down and my arms crossed.

"I feel a strong power coming near," signaled Francis. "He is somewhere around here, Paul. He is coming. Just a little while longer, and we'll know what we're up against."

The little cat was sleeping, and I had sunk halfway down into its dreams. My mind's eye saw the splendor of its imaginative power, as I continued to stare down from the castle's ruined walls. I saw a figure loom up in the distance and was quite startled to discover it was Maria Delaruelle. Slowly, she came up to Walter Fabry and the likeness of myself sitting in the grass. The snow disappeared wherever she stepped, so that behind her a narrow path was cut.

"Hide yourself in the cat!" warned Francis. "Stay invisible to Miethe. I will support your projection next to

Fabry. Don't let yourself be dragged along by your emotions. What you see is not real!"

I began to sob softly, but no tears ran down my cheeks; I could not actually cry. Maria wore a cape, and her long hair flowed in waves over her shoulders. Beautiful, proud and majestic, she now walked here before me. She was still as pretty as on the day we first met her, when she had joined our small traveling party. I began to feel weak and warm, like the melting snow under her feet. She stopped directly in front of what she assumed to be two men sitting on the grass and stood still, leaning a bit forward towards them. Searchingly, she looked from one to the other. She put a finger under Fabry's chin. I tried to see her through the eyes of my projection, without success. My image sat there like a puppet—silent and motionless. Fabry began to make some kind of gesture, and Maria took a step aside to have a better look at him. She raised both her hands, began to scream and then slowly faded away. When she was no more than a shadow, she began to float away, with her half-transparent feet above the ground. In a few short seconds she had entirely disappeared. Fabry attempted to rise to his feet, but winced with pain when he put his weight on his injured foot and plumped back on the ground.

Miethe had sent out an image of Maria to be a scout and to size up the situation. If he only had to deal with normal mortals, like Fabry, a projection of a randomly chosen figure would have been able to arrange anything he desired. Miethe and Francis were able to charge their transmitted thoughts with physical energy, and such a transformation could hit home fiercely—the figure that looked like Maria Delaruelle could have lifted up Fabry and flung him a hundred yards away.

Miethe undoubtedly knew by now that the Paul Brand sitting on the grass was not real. He was probably thinking that I had made my image to appear there while I lay in ambush for him close by. His spirit could not penetrate me because, thanks to the cat, I was totally unfindable. And Francis knew how to shield himself from him.

I wondered what his next move would be.

"Now his powers will be put to the test," signaled Francis. "Soon he'll have to show us what he's made of. If he's well informed about you by his spies, he will know that you have suppressed the past and that you have forgotten about all your gifts and powers. He'll think that you're going to be easy to catch, and he will be surprised to meet me on his way—Wait! Something is about to happen."

The sun, still hanging low above the mountain, brightened as the sky became less gray. In front of me, not far away from the place where Maria had first appeared, a huge army materialized. It was a motley crew, made up of peasants armed with clubs, archers, musketeers, gladiators and lancers. There were soldiers in uniforms from many different periods of history, and the army was commanded by more than a hundred men, all of whom looked like Rainer Miethe. I watched as some of the Miethe strutted about like a men in their primes, their upper bodies bare and long, curly hair reaching to their shoulders and chests. Other Miethes were older and wore long habits and robes.

"It's the old trick of multiplication!" thought Francis. "Look, Paul, look! He is still so very strong. He is relatively safe in the crowd. He has duplicated himself so many times that it is impossible for me to figure out who the real Miethe is. I need a machine gun, not than a rifle!"

"Maybe he isn't really there himself at all," I suggested. "Or maybe all the Miethes are projections, and he is hiding behind one of the soldiers."

"Exactly! I have to think now. Remain hidden in the cat!"

The roaring army neared quickly, marching with rapid strides, their voices echoing off the crumbling walls of the old castle as they surrounded the two figures sitting on the grass. From my elevated hiding place I could see everything very well, but had to take care not to get too spiritually involved, and do exactly as Francis had advised.

Again Walter Fabry tried to rise to his feet. He started to topple, falling backwards, but grabbed hold of the habit of one of the illusionary Miethes and pulled himself up, where he remained standing on one foot. It was an elder Rainer Miethe whom he looked in the eyes now, full of fear. I heard him shout, "I cannot help it! It is Francis!"

He never got a chance to explain himself, for Miethe's hands had closed tightly around his neck and throat and he was lifted, kicking and flailing wildly. When he hit the ground again, he was already dead. Thankfully, he never got a chance to utter my name!

"He could be the real one," was the next thought to reach me from Francis. "I have to try—"

I saw him appear from behind the wall and aim his weapon. A shot rang out, and a bullet went right through Miethe and glanced off the tower.

"The wrong one," I signaled to Francis, "but I see no one giving orders."

"He need not even open his mouth to do that," he signaled back. "All he has to do is think. But wait, I have another surprise in store for him."

The peasants and soldiers swarmed to every side. They went to the outer wall behind which Francis stood, climbed the defensive walls of the castle, peered through the loopholes and made their way up the stairs in the tower. They swarmed straight up the walls, like some sort of phantom insects. They stood on each other's backs, floated up along the stones and then slipped between the battlements. I could hear them shuffling right above me. As they closed in on me from two sides, I remained sitting completely motionless, save for the slight movement of my fingers through the cat's fur.

A peasant walked right through me as two soldiers descended from above me with sabers in their hands. At the same moment, other warriors came from below, armed with axes and rifles. The room was filled with them now, walking right through each other and then, as they got too near the walls, falling from the windows.

I looked outside again. The lifeless body of Fabry still lay on the green spot, but my own image had disappeared. I tried to count the number of Miethes that were gathered around the castle but had to give up because they kept disappearing and re-appearing at totally random places and intervals.

"Did he discover your hiding place?" Franciscus transmitted to me.

"No. They couldn't find me."

"But they did find me, because I foolishly let Maria appear, the same way he did."

Suddenly, I saw her next to Fabry, naked, and dancing as only she knew how. Her feet seemed to hardly touch the grass! A man stood not far from her and watched her, his eyes filled with lust and surprise—it was a young Miethe. Another shot rang out. Francis, surrounded by soldiers, had climbed upon the wall and fired his rifle a second time. The young Miethe turned towards him, waved, and then went to Maria. He was at her side in two steps, and as he embraced her, they began to fade away.

Behind Francis, someone had climbed on top of the old wall, which was a good four feet thick. It was Rainer Miethe, much older now, and there appeared to be a strange haze in front of his face.

"Turn around, turn around!" I mentally beseeched my comrade.

Francis was about to comply with my entreaty, but moved too slowly and never got the opportunity. Miethe clenched his fists and, raising them high above his head, slammed them down on the neck of my friend with incredible force. Odd figures, small fragments of Francis's brilliant imagination, sprang up into the air. I saw a whirling of dragons, unicorns, serpents and scorpions. But they all disappeared when he fell.

I closed my eyes. What Otto was showing me was far more beautiful and peaceful than the drama unfolding before me. This little "Prince of Predators" ensconced himself in warm thoughts and selflessly shared his euphoria with me.

After what seemed an eternity, I looked up again. The world was white, and snow was again falling from a gray sky. The open, green spot had disappeared, as had the bodies of both Fabry and Francis. The army of peasants and soldiers had vanished into thin air, along with the countless projections of Miethe.

I am on my own now, I thought to myself. Francis has been taken from me—again —and Miethe will get to practice another of his talents that he has become so expert at over the years: the discrete disposal of Francis's body.

I shuffled slowly to the winding stairs and began to slide down on my back so as not to injure my battered feet any further. Otto, safe and warm under my coat, slept quietly throughout my downwards journey.

Outside I crept to the van, which still stood by the roadside where Francis had parked it. Driving was going to present a whole new problem for me now, because although I knew I had enough strength in my feet to depress the gas pedal, I did not have enough for the clutch. Fortunately, the doors were unlocked, and Francis had left the key in the ignition. I climbed inside and wished that I could remain sitting there until my feet were entirely healed; but, unlike myself, the cat must have something to eat and drink in order to survive. I looked in the glove compartment, where I had found something earlier for him. There was one last roll, wrapped in plastic, which I gladly gave him. He drank melted snow from my hand.

As soon as I feel a bit stronger, I thought, *I'll look for a long, thick stick I can use to push down the clutch. I have to get out of here in case Miethe decides to come back and have another look around.*

The problem was, where should I go?

Dejected, I stared blankly at the inside of the snow-covered windshield and stroked Otto's little head, as he carried me away once more on the stream of his gentle feline thoughts.

 # 9 -After the Dance

I felt at home in Trier, where I had lived, long ago, for about eighty years, and I was familiar with all the streets and squares there.

Leaving the van behind I walked, with Otto under my coat, towards the center of town. With my hands in my pockets, I strolled through the Olewiger Strasse, by the ancient Roman amphitheatre. I remembered how in the past, the stones, which were used as seats for an audience of twenty-five thousand people, were carted away and used to build churches. It gave me a good feeling inside to see things older than myself. I crossed the palace gardens and strolled through the narrow streets filled with shops, where I saw old Roman coins in the windows of little antique stores. I reached the Hauptmarket and looked through the Simonstrasse to the Porta Nigra, the sandstone gate that was built in the second century to protect the town, and not far from where I once had lived. There I found a small hotel and took a room.

After I put Otto on the bed and gave him food and water, I went back outside and roamed about Germany's oldest city until dark.

I heard music playing. Following the pleasant sounds, I entered a building where I knew I had been at least once before—but back then it had been used as a storage space for casks of wine and other merchandise. There I danced, like a figure doing the dance of death, to the music of a five-man band. I paid no attention to the people who were soon standing around me and staring.

I danced steps from the past, limp on one leg to give expression to the imperfection of existence, leaping up to show how high the corn must grow, backwards and forwards to show that life's adversity also brings prosperity. No one would have believed me if I had told them that only a few days ago my feet had been so horribly broken.

The people watching forgot their own dance and formed a tight circle around me. In the faces surrounding me, I saw the indices of familial histories and relationships to families I had known in Trier such a long time ago. The young folk present clapped for the dancer and laughed at the strange movements, but they also stood in awe of the strength of my high jumps. Sweat soaked my clothes and my breathing came faster and faster as I sank to a lower, baser level of spiritual awareness.

The band was mine now; they played only for me. The rhythm of my movement dictated the tunes they played. The thump of the drum was of more importance to my primitive dance than was the modern twang of the guitar. Sweat stung my eyes, and images of fantasy flashed before them. The onlookers became ancient Celts, and we danced and clapped our hands here on the holy ground of the Treveri tribe.

"He's raving mad!" I heard someone shout.

I thought, *You just laugh. I was here long before any of you were born, and when you are all dead and gone, I will still come back.*

My endurance must have surprised all who watched me. I performed a fertility dance that degenerated into a wild, warlike stamping. I darted to the left and then to the right and, screaming and roaring, the crowd gave way. My breath was shallow now, filling my lungs with air through my mouth and escaping again through my nose. I wanted to tire, to be on the verge of exhaustion and then lie down, relax, and open my mind to the images that I hoped Francis wanted to show me.

Out on the street again, nothing bothered me, not even the bitter the cold. I went back to my hotel room, where the cat still lay asleep on the bed. I shoved him aside and lay down on my back. My feet began to hurt as I lay there and stared at the ceiling. There was one lamp lit, and the room was silent. Slowly, I drifted off to a dreamlike world; if I had been able to, I surely would have fallen asleep. A physically exhausted body gives the mind room and freedom to transcend itself, and I was receptive to any impressions that my friend might send.

Images appeared in my mind's eye the way Franciscus had told me they would when we were in Holland, by the lakes in Rotterdam. They were hypnotic images that quickly changed. Faces and landscapes, order and chaos, sparkling colors, flashes of light, and street scenes—all came and went from my turbulent brain without the need for me to guide them. Relaxed, I waited for whatever would happen next.

I did not have to wait long, for I suddenly felt a force within me that was not my own—it had entered my mind from the outside. As I continued staring at the ceiling, Francis appeared. He, too, was lying on his back with his arms down, but unlike me, he had been tied down, with broad, leather straps, to a small bed. Behind him, I saw various pieces of odd-looking equipment, to which he was connected by wires that were attached to his forehead, chest and arms. The upper part of his body was bare.

The words "Are you there, Paul?" entered my mind so loud and so clearly that it seemed as if he were right beside me and speaking directly into my ear. "Are you really there at last?"

"Francis."

My lips formed his name in an almost inaudible whisper, but I knew my voice had reached him, because I saw him nod and smile.

"I danced until I almost dropped dead—it is good to be exhausted, it makes it easier for me to communicate with

you this way. Your picture is so clear, but why are you lying there like that?"

"It seems I am able to establish contact with you without much difficulty. I must be even more exhausted than you are. My physical state is not exactly great right now. I have given a lot of blood recently."

Shocked, I sat up straight. I got up from the bed and walked to the door to lock it.

"Where did you just go?" asked Francis, when I had lain back down on the bed again.

"To lock the door. I feel safer that way. Are you giving blood to Maria?"

I felt it—I knew she had to be around there somewhere!

He remained silent, and his image began to fade momentarily but then became clear again. Francis swallowed a couple of times. I didn't know how far away he was from me, but as he stared down at me from the ceiling I saw he was even thinner than before. He softly tapped a rhythm on his mattress, but the straps around his wrists hindered his movement, and he couldn't lift his fingers very far.

"I'm doing two things at once now, Paul. I am talking to you and trying to make sure that Miethe does not see or feel our images. And no, my blood is not for Maria. I am feeding Rainer Miethe."

A noise from the corridor startled me. I sat up and listened with apprehension to the sound of voices and footsteps outside my room, but thankfully my fear was unjustified—the sounds faded again as some hotel guests headed on past for their own rooms. I began to feel sick and was glad that I hadn't eaten anything all day. I sank back on the bed.

"Stay with me," warned Francis. "Soon I will be too tired to communicate with you this way. Miethe was looking terrible. He really has spent his last efforts on catching one of us. Walter Fabry was the umpteenth victim who had to pay with his life for the privilege of meeting Miethe. I am being kept alive for my blood. When I regained consciousness, after the blow to my neck, I was lying here, tied down and the first blood transfusion was in full swing."

I had many questions: where he was, how and if I could rescue him, if he had seen Maria, what Rainer's weak spots were. After giving it some thought, though, the thing I wanted to know most was about the transfusion.

"What about the blood? Do we immortals all have the same blood type? The Rh factor—"

"That's not the problem, Paul. The elixir seems to be the determining factor in the structure of our blood. Which means that you, I, Maria and Miethe all have almost identical blood types. Miethe has made a detailed study of his own blood and has all kinds of equipment here to do blood research. The problem is the condition of the blood. What flows through your veins and mine you could compare with a fine wine that has improved with

age. Maria and Rainer reacted differently to the elixir of life. Miethe's blood is thick, like maple syrup, and black!"

I saw a wry smile creep across his face.

"What I have, what I can give him, works miracles! He is getting better and stronger as we speak. His face was so old, so very wrinkled, that he created a haze to keep in front it of lest people look upon the horror he feels he has become. On the days he feels a little better, he changes his outward appearance with the power of his thoughts. Paul, he is incredibly egocentric; he thinks only about himself. I had some time to roam about the house that he is keeping me in. There are unbelievable riches piled up in every room. I am lying in a small room right next to a huge chamber filled with hospital equipment. Maria is next door to me, in a similar but smaller room. She and I have decided not to send images of her likeness to you because we feel that it would be extremely upsetting to you.

"Believe it or not, I am very happy to give blood to Rainer Miethe. The sooner I get him back on his feet, the sooner I can make Maria well again. I hope she will stay alive long enough for me to offer her my blood. But Miethe, the vampire, is not easy to satisfy, and everything is going slowly because of the structure of his own blood. He has help with his work now, a doctor. This doctor is a woman who looks very much like Maria. He has secured her help by virtually scaring her half to death with horrible specters from her youth. I'm telling you,

Koos Verkaik

Paul, he has plans for her that are certainly not in her best interests. Her death could clear the way for Maria, provide her with a new identity: A well-respected doctor with a valid passport. But first she has to help get Miethe well again. Then she has to assist him with the care and nursing of Maria and in appreciation of all her good services—"

"Good heavens!"

"I had the opportunity to penetrate deep into Miethe's mind soon after I was brought here. I was lying in my bed in his private hospital, and he was lying in the bed next to me. He had allowed himself to relax so that the good doctor could do her work. He tried to repel me when he realized that I was concentrating on his thoughts, but at the time it was of much greater importance for him to stay calm so that the doctor had no trouble with the transfusion. He obviously thought he could permit himself this indifference, for I am completely in his power. I know that he has many more men working for him than Walter Fabry and the guy who tried to kill me in Rotterdam. All these men have only one task now."

"To find me."

"Correct. Rainer Miethe knows exactly what he wants. One of us will be kept here with him as a blood donor, and the other will literally be sold to science. He has contacted a number of scientists, and told them about the existence of an immortal human being. They will give him a fortune to turn over such a person to them. Miethe will make them pay dearly, and he will, of course, be given all the results of their research."

"No doubt I am the experimental rabbit," I said. "You have already proved that you are valuable to him with your blood, and he will want to keep you close at hand."

"He is starting to speed things up. He wants to have you under his complete control as soon as possible, so you must remain hidden from his sphere of influence. He is aware of the fact that you and I can get in touch with each other just about whenever we want. He knows that I will inform you about where he is living, about the doctor and about anything else you should wish to know."

"Keep talking, Francis, while I can still follow you clearly."

"Now, tell me Paul, how are you doing? Are you back to your old self again? Can you do all the things you used to do in the past?"

"Don't worry about me," I said. "I understand now why I suppressed everything. Nothing can be found in an empty mind. By pushing the past out of my mind, I could live freely, and Miethe could not locate me. But now that you know that I can shield myself again, tell me Francis, where can I find you?"

"Wait a minute, Paul. Slow down a bit. We can't be too hasty, my friend. I just told you that Miethe will know that I am informing you about everything."

"So?"

"He knows that you will show up here sooner or later, and is prepared for that. All his men have to do is be patient and wait for you."

"Yes, yes, this all sounds very logical, but the fact remains that he has Maria, and he has you. I am the only one still at large, so stop beating around the bush, and tell me where you are."

"Miethe has built a new house on the site where the castle of Count Kaspar von Karst once stood, outside the village of Karst. From the village you have to go uphill. The woman who is in his power is the village doctor, Hilde Steiner. She has disposed of her practice and has told people that she will probably start a clinic in the house of Miethe. Miethe's plans are all very well thought out. She assists Miethe in any way she can; and as soon as he doesn't need her any more, Maria will be given a new identity and will be the proud bearer of the doctor's name."

"Karst," I thought. The name echoed through my head. "Miethe is back on the spot where he committed his first murder."

"You must have forgotten about Alexander."

"Yes, of course. Alexander was his first victim."

"After the count, there were many others. And I'm sure that Doctor Steiner will not be the last. I can do nothing more, Paul. All I can do is give blood, replenish the source and then give again—and again and again.

272 | P a g e

Until, one day, I have nothing more to give. What can you do?"

I reacted immediately.

"You gave me the cat, remember? And I told you about Otto Faun."

"Yes. So?"

"I traveled with him from Barcelona to Valencia, and after that we journeyed to the Netherlands."

"So you told me, yes. You went to visit one of his relatives."

"Uh, by the way, can you handle this, Francis, staying in contact with me for such a long time? Doesn't it tire you too much? I can see you very clearly now, lying with your back against the ceiling, looking down at me."

He smiled. "Yes," he said, and I was happy about it.

"Neither one of us needs to sleep anymore, Paul. As far as I'm concerned, we can keep on communicating with each other the whole night long. No, it doesn't make me tired. It makes me forget the circumstances here a bit; maybe I can even regain some more energy, so that—"

"So that tomorrow you will able to give more blood."

I quickly passed on to other thoughts, for I didn't want him to know that I was seeing him as he really was at the moment. I knew that he thought I would be frightened by the vision of him being held prisoner and being milked for his blood, so I shook fiercely to try and clear it and sank my teeth into my thumb.

"Your story. I know that it's important too. My memory also fails me from time to time. However, when I saw the little cat sit in the snow, I knew you would be able to do something with it, and I'm not talking about simply diving into the animal's dream-world to escape."

I heaved a sigh, put my arm down, and touched Otto's fur with my fingertips. He came closer, and I was tempted to let myself sink safely into his mind. I let go of him and folded my hands under my head. Lying there, staring at the ceiling, a new image appeared next to Francis: I was back in Spain, traveling with Otto Faun.

"Otto Faun practiced the art of transformation, Francis. He made no magic potions, there was no changing of metals. He was no alchemist, but he had taken the elixir of life."

"From the pharmacist."

"Quite right. I know that Faun was much older than I, at least a hundred years or more, and he had made good use of his time. He had learned early on that the elixir would be a major influence upon his body and cause all sorts of changes within him. You know what I mean, and I am glad that I understand it myself again also. We learn to understand things that other people will never understand at all—formulas, enchantments, curses, communicating over long distances as we are doing right now, evoking specters, even working wonders. Otto Faun explored the books of long forgotten magicians and studied tirelessly for years at a stretch."

"Yes. Go on. I want to lay here quietly, without thinking about the fact that I am not free leave when I wish. Show me as much of your journeys with Otto Faun as is possible, so I can determine what is so important about his methods."

Francis and I watched Otto and myself entering Valencia.

We wandered through the winding streets, amused at the sight of a man kicking a pig, and laughing at another fellow sliding over the muck-covered pavement as he tried to run away with some stolen goods. We came into a poorer quarter of the town, where a relative of Otto's named Diego lived.

"Otto called him uncle, although he apparently was not actually related; he was the uncle of a woman Otto had lived with but never married. This man owned a piece of land outside of town where he grew fruit and bred cattle. He had been forced to give up his land and leave all his possessions behind after being accused of sorcery. The rich farmer had become a poor town dweller. Diego's niece, Otto's common-law wife, was dead and gone a long time, but he had never forgotten Otto, and had sent him a message. Diego wanted to reclaim his property, but most of all he wanted his pride back. So, Francis, I got to see how Otto Faun worked."

"Now it's getting interesting! What he could do, you can do also—like changing the cat."

"Oh yes! The word *werewolf* simply means man-wolf, a man changing into a wolf. Otto didn't know how to do that, but he knew very well that something like that had to be possible. He had read all about it, but he preferred to start with animals instead of humans; exactly the opposite transformation, if you will. Many actions are needed to change an animal into a human monster. The time must be ripe, spells have to be pronounced, and certain ingredients are needed. But the most important factor is—"

"I know. You won't shock me. It is the blood of an immortal."

The ceiling became red. The blade of a knife disappeared deep into the forearm of Otto Faun. Blood fell in thick drops onto the neck of a black cat that lay stretched out on its belly on a stone.

"The result! Paul, what was the result?"

"The divine spark caught on. The human element took possession of the beast. A sharp-witted mind, with even sharper claws. The black cat became a—"

Together, we saw the monster, covered in cat fur, before us. It ran across the fields, on its hind legs, like a human, followed by the farmer. The cat tore Diego's enemies to pieces. It sank its sharp teeth into their necks and shook their bodies mercilessly. It embraced its victims with its front paws and simultaneously raked them with its hind legs, ripping apart the flesh of their bellies with its razorlike claws. Lively, intelligent eyes peered above the bloody grin of its mouth, revealing pointed teeth. Afterwards, the black monster walked next to Diego as he returned to his farm.

"The time must be ripe, you said. When can you get cracking, Paul?"

"I'll get to work on it soon. I have no idea how long it will take me, but I must succeed. The masters who wrote the books that Otto studied admitted that it's not easy. They discovered that everything that happens in this world is proportionally connected to the rest of this immense universe: the position of the stars, planets, sun and moon, even the radiation that reaches us from all areas of the sky. But what is big, is also little—what happens outside of us in endless space also happens inside of us. Otto Faun learned how to figure out when the time was ripe for something and he, in turn, taught me. And I learned fast, Francis. I concentrated on cats, because they have the most to say to me, but there are more possibilities. Turning a goat into a young man. Have you ever heard of that?"

"No."

"You need a lot for that. The scrapings from the inside of a church bell, a nasty extract of different plants and the presence of a virgin. You can also change billy goats into devilish creatures, but Otto turned his nose up at that. He didn't care for the tamer animals who are so easy to domesticate by man. He also didn't like to work with dogs or wolves. For the same reasons: too tame, too obliging. For him, it was the wild, fantastic nature of the cat that attracted him. I promise you that I will set to work as soon as possible. Now that I can rely on my own powers again and soon will be able to count on the help of Otto," I stroked the little cat under its chin, "I can dare to wage war against Miethe."

We stayed in contact for the rest of the night. We shared our images, and I knew that this spiritual communion was a great help to Francis. It was already morning when he told me that he felt a bit stronger and would take me on a short trip through Miethe's house; something I couldn't do by myself. I let myself float towards him and was able to take a better look into the small room where he was lying.

"Maria—" I started.

"No," he reacted immediately. "I don't want you to see her yet."

We floated through corridors and along staircases.

In a room looking very much like a convent cell with no furniture other than a bed and a low cupboard, I saw a woman sitting. It was Doctor Hilde Steiner, and she did indeed look like Maria. The same height, the same hair color, the same physical appearance. She had dark bags under her eyes and sat in the corner of the room with her legs pulled up and her arms around her knees. On the bare floor, right in front of her, a jester danced. The sound of the jingling of the bells on the fool's cap, sleeves and curled toes of the shoes reached my ears.

"She is afraid of this, she fears the apparition. There is a special bond between her and the jester," I observed.

"Remember Paul, she must also be set free from this horror. Good heavens, my friend, you get to free us all! The doctor, Maria and me!"

My projection was weightless. Francis I floated along and saw the riches Miethe had managed to accumulate over the course of time.

"Remember all you see. And as long as you are preoccupied with the transformation of the cat, you must stay in contact with me, so I can show you how to find your way around the house. I beg of you, Paul, get us out of this deathlike limbo!"

"I want to see Miethe!"

"He shields himself very well. No one is better at that than he. But let me try. Maybe you can catch a glimpse of the man who once called himself our friend but has so maliciously turned against us! Follow me."

I felt as if I were looking through frosted glass; it was an extremely odd feeling. I exerted myself to try and see better, but it cost me too much energy. In a large hall a vague, nervous figure paced up and down.

Bright red flames burned under flasks and pots. It was like looking through a thick mist into the past, into the underground workshop of the late, great Alexander.

"The fire never goes out," Franciscus said to me. "After he felt that he could learn no more from the old man, he took him out into the forest and murdered him. By that time, he must have had the ability and knowledge to make the elixir. Over the course of time though, he must have forgotten some of the procedures. But he is working now with redoubled energy, for my blood is doing him a lot of good and seems to be restoring his memory."

Francis showed me another room, this one filled with musical instruments. I recognized several violins that hung on the wall as ones that I had made so long ago.

I was tired and began to lose contact. Staring at the ceiling, I made a mental list of everything that I would need to successfully complete the transformation of my little cat.

The atmospheric conditions must be correct, as well as the time and place. I had to make sure that I could properly recite the incantations, beginning with "Here now a power is forged from matter and thought," and be able to repeat it until I was of the right temperament to perform all the necessary actions.

The opening of the vein, the flowing of the blood. The blood of an immortal for the baptism of the cat.

I had to fill its tiny body with my confidence and energy. With my psychic eye focused inward, I must have the resolve, power and self-confidence to allow my powers to complete the jump from myself to the cat. A part of me must be inside the cat—the part that is human, yet divine. I must embrace the animal's spirit.

We will become one, and so shall the monster grow.

* * *

By the time my plan was ready to be put into action it was already springtime. The snow had disappeared and the world was green again, basking in the warmth of the sun. I had fed the cat well, and the animal had grown big and strong. I had remained in contact with Francis through all those long winter weeks and was fully informed about everything that happened in Miethe's house.

Francis though, was weaker than ever.

It became more and more difficult to understand him. H had begun to act confused, and his projections were blurred. I learned that Miethe was feeling like a young god and that my friend Francis's blood was now mainly being used for Maria's treatment.

"I am a key link between Miethe and Maria," Francis told me. "Maria doesn't care for him at all, but she has been face to face with death, and she wants to live, just like the rest of us. My blood, given to her a bit at a time, makes her dependent on her host. Alexander's elixir brought us gold as well as eternal life, Paul. Red gold that runs through our veins. Every drop of it is worth a fortune."

He told me that Maria had been feeling pretty well. She kept herself busy by cataloging Miethe's possessions, assisting him in his laboratory and taking walks round the house. Several times I had begged Francis to show me images of her, but now he was too weak to grant my request.

Not wanting to upset him, I did not tell him that I was in Karst. I couldn't stand waiting around helplessly any longer while my friend grew weaker and weaker. He was probably on the verge of exhaustion, lying in his little room in Miethe's house. Miethe was far too powerful now for me to try to bring an end to this myself. My only chance was the cat, for Otto knew neither pain nor fear and could strike at precisely the right moment.

I had driven to Karst in a second-hand Volvo at a time of year when it was relatively quiet in the town. The first tourists of the season would not arrive for a few weeks yet, and there was still plenty of parking space to be had on the streets. Even the cafes and restaurants along the river had not yet put out their tables. I walked up the middle of the road, looking at the hillside vineyards that rose up behind the houses.

A strange feeling came over me; it was odd to be back here again. Long ago, before I was an immortal, I had been here with Francis, Miethe and Maria. I was born somewhere in the area, but was not sure in what year. Between 1410 and 1420? I didn't know, I had never known. It was information that I had never needed to survive.

Somewhere up there, behind the vines, Miethe had built his house on the remnants of the castle of Count Kaspar von Karst. Francis and Maria were so close, but if I was stupid enough to get too close to Miethe, he would catch me and never set me free again. It was useless to try an assault on the house, even with the best-trained army in the world, and Francis would be dead the moment that Miethe was forced to surrender. Only with magic could I even consider such an undertaking, and my own powers were not sufficient to succeed. The lessons I had learned from Otto Faun were just what I needed now; all the knowledge from the old manuscripts, now lost, moldy and forgotten, formed the basis of the power I was going to have to fall back on.

I was still looking up at the hillsides feeling oddly, for while I recognized so many buildings in old Trier and had found my way about there easily, everything in Karst was strange to me.

I was suddenly startled when a vehicle screeched to a standstill right in front of me. The creaking of the brakes followed the ticking of a diesel motor, and as I turned around, I realized that I had been in the middle of the road the whole time. The window opened on the driver's side of a big truck, and the look in the eye of the driver told me that this was not a fellow who gets angry about something as petty as a stranger who doesn't know enough to get out of the way of an oncoming truck. There was fear in his eyes. The door opened slowly and the man stepped out carefully. He was of impressive stature, at a rough estimate well over two hundred pounds. His face was round with red, flushed cheeks, and he wore blue overalls. He walked up to me without ever once taking his eyes off of mine. He had to stoop a bit to get his face even with mine, and I felt his breath in my face. His fingers trembled as he raised his hands, and with his thumbs he gently stroked my cheeks, rubbing his fingers back along my face towards my ears.

"You're human," he said. "Isn't that so? You're just a man standing in the road not paying any attention."

Suddenly he became very nervous and didn't know what to do with his hands. He put them at his sides, behind his back, and then finally in the pockets of his overalls.

"What else did you expect?" I asked.

"I could have run you right over."

"How right you are. It was indeed stupid of me to be here, but that does not make your remark any more clear to me. What was on your mind, my friend? Why didn't you just sound your horn?"

He looked as if he wanted to answer me, but instead he pressed his lips together. The color vanished from his face. He began to totter back and forth and seemed about to collapse, so I wrapped my arms around him and tried to keep him on his feet. His weight was too much for me though, and I had to ease him down, so that he sat on the street.

"Just a moment," he sighed. "I'm sure I'll feel better soon. Please, help me to get up again."

Wolf Tears

He stretched out his arms to me, and I took hold of his hands. I pulled with all my might, and as he rose to his feet, I said with a smile, "My name is Paul Brand. Pleased to meet you."

"Andreas Pallasch," he said, and he smiled too.

* * *

After he had parked his truck in front of the restaurant, Andreas invited me to join him for a drink.

"Bärbel," he said to the woman who welcomed us to her restaurant, "two glasses of Karster Glut, please. We both need it badly, I think."

He needed some time to get over the shock of almost killing me, but once he had, he found it pleasant to have a stranger sitting in front of him who would listen to him patiently. He talked in a subdued voice, and every now and then covered his mouth with his hand when he told me something he wanted no one else to hear. It was comical to see him act this way, for we were alone in the restaurant; the woman who served us was busy behind the bar and paid no attention to us.

He was not from Karst, but passed through daily as he drove along the Moselle, transporting bottles. He said he had led a quiet life until one day, when he had seen a beautiful woman step into a BMW and gone after her with the pedal to the metal. His path had been blocked by a jester, of all things, who, Andreas claimed, had dragged him out of the cab of his truck and then lifted the truck up and thrown it across the road.

"I am so glad to be able to tell this to an outsider," he said. "Here, in Karst, the madness is complete. Everyone believes what I say, but no one is actually listening. Do you understand what I mean? So much has happened. The people have resigned themselves to their fate. No one has an explanation for all the accidents that have happened around here. Imagine, jesters dancing on the road, complete with ringing bells. Terror reigns here. If you asked Bärbel—Bärbel Körner, the owner of this place—how many people have talked about jesters here, she would tell you that she'd lost count a long time ago. What happened to me, many other people have also experienced. So when I saw a man standing in the middle of the main road of Karst . . . I beg your pardon, but the way you look."

I was wearing a long raincoat and dirty shoes, had a five day's growth of beard, and my hair was uncombed.

I nodded in agreement.

"There stands another fool, you must have thought."

He made averting gestures with his hands.

"No, no, I wouldn't call you a fool, I'm the one who is to blame. My mind immediately went back to my experience with the jester. You know, I am so happy to be able to sit down and talk for a while, to take a break. Let's drink another glass of wine, Karster Glut, now, while the taste is still good. Because soon the scent of death will find its way into your nostrils."

I raised my eyebrows, sprawled in my chair and said nothing. After Bärbel had provided us with more wine, Andreas began to talk again in a soft, almost whispering tone of voice.

"Wilhelm Schwarzburg is dead," he said.

The color came back to his cheeks. He took a sip, smacked his lips and looked at me as if I understood perfectly what he was talking about. When I didn't react, he slowly shook his head.

"Of course, of course, you don't know who he was. Wilhelm Schwarzburg, the son of Hans. You are drinking his wine right now."

"Kartser Glut."

"Yes. I knew Wilhelm well; I have delivered bottles to him for years, and he shipped his wine in my truck. He had many good sales contracts and had managed to do better at the business than even his father, and he was very proud of it. He had often told me that his wine was for sale everywhere, that you could go into a wine shop in New York, Amsterdam, London or Ottawa and choose from the many different vintages of his best wines."

I wondered what would happen if I suddenly projected an image of a jester on a chair at one of the tables, or if I made the door swing open and let a group of jesters in. Looking at the man, I focused on his mind; I wanted him to feel more relaxed and tell me anything that might useful to me.

"The scent of death. You were talking about the scent of death."

"And about Wilhelm Schwarzburg," said Pallasch. "One Sunday afternoon, he went out alone for a walk in the woods. Somewhere along the way, he strayed off the path and down a hill between the trees, to a scenic overlook that only the inhabitants of the region can find. From there you can look into the valley of the Moselle and see the Hunsrück rise up right in front of you. It was a risky undertaking, for it had been cold and snowing and the slope was slippery.

"But he definitely reached the spot. His footprints ended at the wooden fence."

"And on the other side of the fence?"

"The depths of the valley."

"Did he slip? Did he fall?"

"No. Four yards above the spot where his last footprints were found in the snow, he was found hanging in a tree, his head stuck between a forked branch and his neck broken. I heard that he was already half-frozen when they found him."

"Strange," I remarked.

"Strange?" repeated Pallasch. He leaned back so brusquely that the back of his chair creaked. "That is putting it mildly! Haven't you heard anything at all of what is happening here in Karst? Don't you read the papers? Don't you know anything about the jesters and dead people?"

Bärbel Körner looked up. It was the first time Pallasch had raised his voice enough that she could hear what he said. Resolutely, she picked up a bottle of Karster Glut and brought it over to us. She pulled up a chair, sat down and filled our glasses. Now I tried concentrating on her mind and hoped that she would also be susceptible to my impulses and would feel free to talk about the strange things that had happened here. Pallasch brought her up to date about all that he had told me, and she confirmed his story about the apparitions of jesters, who seemed to have supernatural powers at their the disposal. Andreas continued with his tale about the death of the winegrower.

"Try to explain that! How did he get there, so high above the ground?"

"The imprints of his last steps were no deeper than any of his others," said Bärbel. "Otherwise, you might be able to say he had jumped up and thus gotten stuck in the tree. But on the other hand, who can jump that high? It was as if he had been lifted by an invisible hand and forcibly wedged between those forked branches.

"The local police eat here almost every day, and they have also told this story quite often. Vitus Weiss always sat right there." She pointed at the wooden bench near the kitchen door. "The old handyman came here to drink his Schnapps. He was found by one of Schwarzburg's men, Hermann Kreher, dead. And they say that it seemed as if something had frightened him so badly that his heart simply stopped beating. In his hand they found a rosary made of copper bells—little bells like jesters wear on their caps, sleeves and shoes."

"Everyone was quite surprised when Schwarzburg's wife abruptly sold all the family holdings," said Andreas. "The house, the bottling rooms, the cellars, the vineyards, everything! She had no children, and although she herself had been born and bred here, she wanted to leave Karst immediately. At one stroke of the pen, this sale made Rainer Miethe the richest and most powerful man in Karst."

I straightened my back.

"Rainer Miethe? That name rings a bell. Is it possible I read about him in the papers? Do you know him?"

"There are many stories told about him," said Bärbel. "That his great house is always empty, that he owns many houses elsewhere and that he has a yacht lying in the harbor of Monaco. The house is supposedly not empty at all, but contains the most fantastic art treasures. We never see a glimpse of him. He has never showed himself in Karst. Hilde Steiner, our doctor, sold the practice that had once belonged to her father and went to stay with him. Mr. Miethe is apparently very seriously ill, and she was hired to take care of him; in return she was to be allowed to use part of the house to start a clinic. And then, one day, in the dead of winter, that mysterious man appeared in Karst."

"He did not seem to be sick or in need of a doctor," said Andreas. "And if he was, our Doctor Steiner must have worked wonders in a very short time. He is an impressive man, tall, with long hair streaked with gray. I have seen him walking around town when I drive into Karst. It's strange, but I knew who he was on the spot without being told. I looked at him from inside my truck and immediately knew his name: Rainer Miethe."

"He finally made an appearance in town to conduct his business," I ventured.

"So it is," said Bärbel. "You don't sell a big, famous, family estate just like that. It is something that one should consider for a while. Maybe the offer was simply too attractive to refuse, and Mrs. Schwarzburg just took the money and ran. Burgomaster Hans-Jürgen Lins tried to put a stop to the entire deal."

"Who?"

"The burgomaster of Karst. He didn't know of Mr. Miethe, he had never met him," she continued. "He said that the local winegrowers should have the first chance to purchase the property, that experienced people should carry on the local traditions, and everyone agreed with him. It was difficult to know what to expect from a newcomer, and besides the local winegrowers could come up with a great deal of money too. They wanted to take over from the widow and operate it as a common property. Hans-Jürgen Lins fought for that end, for if Gisela Schwarzburg decided to sell to them, it would make him very powerful among the winegrowers, and he could assure the continued quality of Karster Glut."

She heaved a sigh and looked at me a bit queerly, as if to ask herself why she was suddenly telling all this to an outsider. I stared back at her with a neutral glance, but continued to transmit impulses to encourage her to unburden her soul.

"Lins is dead and gone now. And Rainer Miethe and Gisela Schwarzburg met to talk about the last details of the sale over dinner right here in this restaurant."

"How did the burgomaster of Karst die?" I asked.

"He drove his Mercedes into a rock wall in the mountains. The experts who examined the car wreck estimate he must have been going at least one hundred miles per hour! On a winding mountain road! I knew him well, and he was a very good, safe driver. His place at his regular table remains empty; no one will sit there out of respect for him, a man who loved order and calm, and saw to it that everything in Karst went the way it should."

I remained sitting there, talking to them for quite some time. Andreas Pallasch was the first one to get up. and as we shook hands he said, "It was so nice of you to come and sit with me for a while. I was scared earlier. Don't you ever stand in the middle of the road like that. And now I must hurry, for I have a load to deliver."

Bärbel asked me if I wanted something to eat, but I was not hungry. When it appeared that she had no intention of getting back to work again and kept on talking, I concentrated on the outer door. It opened, and a man walked in wearing a long, green coat and carrying a big leather suitcase. He stood still and with a polite bow he took off his little green hat.

"Ma'am," he said in a clear voice, "a glass of wine, please, for a traveling salesman who has something special to show you."

I wasn't sure if I owed her any money, but to be on the safe side I left some cash on the table. After all, she had been very generous and refilled out glasses of her own accord. She did not look at me when I walked past her and said goodbye. She was much too preoccupied with what she saw in the salesman's open suitcase. I had created some beautiful, hand-painted decorative plates to catch her eye and take her attention off of me. The moment I reached my car I made the salesman leave again. The price he asked for his merchandise was far too high, and besides, it wasn't really there!

"I'm sorry I kept you waiting so long," I said to my little feline friend, who was stretched out on the rear seat of my car. "This is no life for a tomcat. You need a home. But come, let's get out of here; I'll stop somewhere and get you something tasty to eat."

Purring softly, the little cat pressed his head against my elbow as I started the engine. backing into the road, I checked my rearview mirror and saw that a big passenger car had stopped to give me the right of way. The driver flashed his headlights. I raised my hand in acknowledgment and then quietly drove out of Karst. I would have liked to drive up to Miethe's house, but I did not dare. If he had the slightest idea that I was in the area, he would be all over me immediately.

Actually, I had intended to buy some things here that I needed for the transformation of the cat. I needed a box of matches to make a fire; a pan or a kettle; and a big, round glass jar in which I could magnetize water. But because of the interlude with Andreas Pallasch, I had already wasted too much time.

Following the road along the river, I thought of Francis again, my poor friend, who made blood and gave blood. The impulses that reached me from him were a lot less powerful now, and he could no longer show me pictures of his surroundings.

Earlier, we had discussed the past and talked about the skills we had acquired.

"You really could do everything," he recalled. "Cut wood, build musical instruments, design machines."

We thought back to the time we were bound to each other with a chain, our ankles shackled. Day and night we had worked on the wooden monster that would bring the immortal Miethe power and glory. I suppose the flowing river sparked my memory back to those days of enslavement.

Looking in the mirror, I noticed that the car that had stopped for me in Karst was behind me. It was a dark blue BMW with two men sitting in the front. I sped up, and the BMW followed suit.

"We've got trouble, Otto," I said to the cat, who sat beside me.

With my left hand firmly on the wheel, I grabbed the cat with my right and put him on the back seat.

"I'll take the first turn-off I see," I said aloud, "and if they turn too, I'll know for sure they're following me."

I was driving at fifty miles an hour when I finally saw a side road. Without giving a hint as to my actions, I went to the middle of the road, brusquely stepped on the brakes and took the bend. I immediately gave the car more gas and drove up along the vines.

The BMW followed.

Maybe this is how Hans-Jürgen Lins met his end also, I thought.

The man who sat next to the driver opened his side window, and I saw a hand appear, clutching a revolver. A shot rang out but missed its mark.

"A threat," I grinned. "Schwarzburg and Lins had to die, but I must stay alive; dead, I am useless to Miethe."

We had left the hillside vineyards now, and I was driving over a straight road through the borough of Eifel. I made monstrous creatures appear all around me that went after the car behind me with large leaps. I sent them in large groups that ran right through the BMW, caught hold of its doors, crawled over the windshield to the roof, and hung on the bumper until their skin was torn open and their syrupy monster blood covered the road. The noise they made was deafening. I saw in my mirror, though, that the car was still following me. An oncoming car prevented the driver of the BMW from passing me; a few moments later we reached a village and had to slow down. It was clear that these men had been well instructed by Miethe. If I sent a hundred thousand horrible monsters at them, they would go on chasing me. They were in his service, just as Walter Fabry had been, and I could only imagine how generously they would be rewarded when they handed me over to their boss.

We were coming to the end of town, and as civilization dropped away again, I sped up once more. In my mirror I saw one of the men using a telephone.

He's calling Miethe! The thought flashed through my mind, and I realized that if he told him where I was, Miethe would send the greatest horror he could imagine after me. Miethe could easily overpower me. I possessed only enough power to show someone like Bärbel Körner an imaginary traveling salesman. Miethe and Francis could have maintained an apparition for a much longer period and over a much greater distance.

I had no time to make myself untraceable by hiding myself in Otto's world, or anywhere else for that matter. I stepped on the brakes. The driver of the other car was passing me and braked also, the side of the BMW grazing the back of my Volvo. I kept my foot on the brake, and felt the strength of the other car's motor as we pushed each other with our cars. We went off the left side of the road together, over the uneven grassy shoulder, and came to a standstill on bare farmland. I got out quickly and sent fantasy creatures up to the BMW from all sides, hoping to strike terror into the two men and divert their attention from me.

The collision of their car against mine had frightened them out of their wits, and they had been shaken up badly when they hit the shoulder. I was better off, since I knew how to banish pain, and I jumped out of the Volvo, wrenched open the door on the driver's side of the BMW, and kicked the man as hard as I could. He looked at me with his mouth open and didn't lift a finger to defend himself. The man next to him tried to undo his safety belt and bent down to pick up his firearm from the floor with his other hand. I crawled over the legs of the driver and beat the other one about the face with my fist. He returned a blow, and the knuckles of his hand crunched against my cheekbone. The monsters, screaming with a horrible, unearthly sound, came close to his door. He turned his head to look at them, and I hit him so hard in the neck that he lost consciousness. Crawling back over the driver, I grabbed the phone, threw it onto the road, ran after it and crushed it into a thousand pieces with my foot. I ran back to the BMW, opened the passenger side door, leaned in and grabbed the gun.

I knew that I had to get out of there fast! No other cars had passed, and I didn't think that anyone had seen the accident. The Volvo was a little battered, but the motor was still running. I climbed in and drove off.

For three quarters of an hour I followed narrow, side roads, until I came to a place where I felt relatively safe. Then I put my humble possessions into a rucksack and, with Otto nestled between my sweater and my coat, I left the car there in the forest.

"It's going to happen tomorrow," I said to the cat. "Tomorrow you will be almost as tall as me."

I found a rural bus stop, and after waiting about fifteen minutes, I got a ride into a little town nearby, where I bought the things I needed. I found a used-car dealer, who sold me a reasonably priced Ford, and after having taken care of Otto's food, I drove along looking for a place where I could wait until it was time to start the metamorphosis.

It was not a difficult task in this wooded area, for I could park my car along a deserted path and remain there for some time unnoticed. It was starting to get dark; I would have to wait for morning to get started again. At dawn the time would be ripe for me to make use of the power of the sun, the planets and the stars, which now, out of sight in the blue sky, were in a favorable position to bring my work to a satisfactory conclusion.

Desperately I tried to get in contact with Francis one more time, but no pictures came through. With my eyes closed, I sat in the car and my fingers tapped a rhythm on the wheel.

"Francis . . . Francis . . ."

I saw his body, white, lean, bled dry. But I had formed that picture myself, and it was how I was imagining him, not an image he had sent to me. Finally, I gave up my efforts to reach him. There was a better way to pass the time.

"Otto, come." I said to the cat.

The cat climbed into my lap, and I stroked its head and chin. The purring rose, and I felt the vibration against my fingers. We made contact. Otto was happy to allow me into his mind. I opened the door, held Otto under his belly and picked him up. Carefully, I set him down on the ground, and he began to walk around the woods and along the edges of the fields. His hunting instinct awakened, he embarked on a thrilling chase, taking me with him through the darkness and showing me, through his eyes, the world of mice and beetles, of birds and rats.

We stood in front of dark holes looking for rodents and climbed tall trees in search of nests. Every now and then I had to leave him, to get back to myself, so that I could look around and see if I was still alone there. Then I would return to the cat, who waited patiently for me.

Just before dawn, Otto returned to the car, and I let him in.

"You needed that," I laughed. "Stealing through the night, with your little cat chin almost to the ground, muscles strained and eyes wide open. Climb onto my lap, go to sleep and amuse me with your dreams."

The sun was rising. Red light flamed up behind the trees. I made a jester appear, who climbed onto the hood of the car and sat there with his legs crossed. The bells on his fool's cap jingled softly whenever he moved his head.

I made the jester disappear again and waited for another hour before I started the engine and drove a couple hundred yards farther up the road. I backed the car into an opening in the forest and, with Otto in my arms, got out. I opened the trunk where I had put all the supplies I would need. I began to make preparations and to recite the incantations that would have to be repeated over and over.

"Here now a power is forged from matter and thought; here heavenly and earthly powers are concentrated; here knowledge, trust and wisdom come together. Here the divine comet strikes deep into the animal."

10 -The Bite of the Cat

We watched the world change. Almost nothing remained the same. In Rotterdam, Francis he had made us see a great cathedral rise up to the arch of heaven itself, like a flower, and then fall back on its foundations. The wooden machine at the river, which I had designed and helped build while enslaved, destroyed itself, and its splintered remains were dragged off by the eternally running water of the river.

We lived on and on and were witnesses to the omnipresent transitoriness of the centuries and of life itself.

Built up, broken down.

Raised up, fallen down.

We welcomed the dawn and continued on our way to new times. But the past lived on inside of us. My attack on Miethe's men had been a deed of unbridled aggression. As I lashed out in fury, I saw before me the pain of former centuries in many forms. I saw all the shapes of violence that men had thought up in order to rule and to oppress. There had been times that death grinned at people from every street corner, and stalking disease had surpassed even the punitive expeditions of emperors and kings.

Miethe's methods had never changed; he still behaved as he had when he beheaded the old man in the forest and skewered Count Kaspar von Karst to the tree with his own sword. It was about time that his world collapsed, just as the cathedral had fallen down and as the wooden structure had splashed into the river. Francis and I longed for rest and peace. We had learned to adapt ourselves to circumstances, but Miethe knew no restraint.

That was why I was so busy now in the forest.

"Here now a power is forged . . ."

I recited the incantations in the exact order.

I had a fire burning, and I melted different elements together in a pan. I added water that I had first magnetized with my own hands. It became a viscous liquid, which I dripped in a wide circle around the cat. I had put the animal into a deep sleep so that later it would not feel the small incision I had to make in its neck.

I repeated the incantations continuously. I was in a trance.

I raised my hands and felt my body filled with heavenly energy. The most important and most difficult ingredient to obtain now had to be added. I gently ran a sharp knife across my arm and let my blood fall into the open wound on the cat's neck.

"Here the divine comet strikes deep into the animal."

The cat began to grow until the tip of his nose and the end of his tail touched both sides of the circle I had made around it. His chest swelled up, and his spine stretched out. There was a creaking sound when the outer fangs grew faster then the flesh surrounding them. When Otto finally awakened and got up on all fours inside the circle, he still looked like a feline, but in the yellow eyes there glowed the divine spark—and the grin on his jaws had something unmistakably human about it.

I walked up to him, and he sat down on his hind legs. Impulsively, I knelt down and wrapped my arms around his neck. I embraced the monster that I had created with my own blood. The fur felt soft and warm and still had the scent of a cat.

When I rose to my feet again, Otto looked me straight in the eye and let out a deafening roar. He shook the dust from his fur, which now sparkled golden in the sun that had just climbed above the trees.

"Thank you, Otto Faun, for teaching me this," I said aloud. "A bit of my own immortality has been passed to this cat, my spirit is connected to his. I can hide myself in the monster whenever I want, and Miethe will not notice my presence even if we stand right next to him. Just as your monster raised hell on the fields outside Valencia, so shall mine show his strength in the house of Rainer Miethe."

I cleared away all the things I had used to bring about the metamorphosis and locked them in the trunk of the car. I had Otto crawl onto the back seat and then got in myself. There was just enough room in the back for the monster, and I used a large blanket, which I had bought the day before, to cover his big body.

We drove away. The day was still young, and I decided to roam around and think for a while. I hoped that I would not get stopped by the police for any reason, since I still had the revolver which I had taken away from Miethe's thug stashed in the glove compartment. I also could not imagine how they would react if they looked under the blanket in the back seat!

My thoughts bridged many centuries. For a moment I felt like the young man who had feasted in the field in front of the castle of Count Kaspar von Karst. I saw the double tower before me and the gate through which he had led Maria inside.

I was on that same ground once again. It was obvious that there had recently been a fence there, for along the side of the road there were still deep holes in the ground, and on both sides of the driveway sat concrete posts on which the gates would have hung. It was a beautiful spring day, and the field in front of the house that now sat on the site of the original Karst castle had become a fairgrounds for the inhabitants of Karst, who had come up to the mountain in great numbers to meet the new owner of Wilhelm Schwarzburg's property. The best wine was brought out of the cellars, and no doubt Andreas

Pallasch had driven up and down quite a few times to get everything to the house. Wooden trestle tables bent under the weight of the bottles. Meat was being roasted, and tents had been put up where the guests could sit down to wine and dine.

My car stood at the side of the road, and Otto lay under his blanket on the back seat. I was sitting on the ground not far from there, playing a violin. When I had bought the instrument in Trier, I had noticed immediately that it was a rather old and special model. The construction was perfect, as if I had built it myself, and the wood that had been used gave it a full, warm sound.

I had partly retired my spirit to within the monster, and by the power of my thoughts I had changed my appearance so that I looked like an old man. I knew I had done well when Andreas Pallasch passed by without paying any special attention to me or my music and threw a coin in front of my feet on the grass. The man who was with him was short and fat and I immediately knew who he was. He called himself Georg Wust and was one of Miethe's projections. No doubt he was here to look for me.

It was impossible to enter the house undetected. There were small, barred windows and locked doors everywhere. Only the big, front door at the top of a flight of stairs was being opened every now and then to let guests in. Just as Kaspar von Karst had invited the nobility and clergy, Rainer Miethe received the notables of the village.

Every quarter of an hour, two people were given the opportunity to see the house. There were four men standing on the steps, undoubtedly armed, who asked anyone who tried to go inside for their invitation card. Fat, little Georg Wust also kept an eye on the door. The local winegrowers were allowed to enter, as were the new town doctor who now lived in the house of Hilde Steiner, the new burgomaster and the chief of police.

In one of the tents, an orchestra began to play so loudly that it drowned out the sound of my violin; I let the instrument rest on my knees and remained sitting silently, watching the people in the field. A man who had been in the house was walking in my direction accompanied by his wife. I focused my thoughts on him and learned that he was one of the winegrowers from Karst, but I could not figure out his name. All that came to me were a few vowels—an *a* and three *e*'s. Arm in arm, the couple got closer, until the woman made a gesture in my direction.

"That old man over there," she said. "Give him some money. He certainly cannot earn a single coin with the other musicians making noise like that."

The man stopped, put his hand in his pocket and produced a coin, which he turned between thumb and forefinger, as if he wanted to think for a while about whether or not to give it to me.

Karl, I thought. Karl Beeren.

A shudder went through me. I still had to get used to the idea that I possessed such special gifts that allowed the name of a complete stranger to come into my mind just like that. Compared with Francis Beck and Rainer Miethe, though, my talents didn't amount to anything. When Francis built the cathedral in Rotterdam by playing the piano, he was only displaying a small facet of his possibilities. With a friendly nod, I thanked the man.

"I saw you enter the house with your wife," I remarked. "Mr. Miethe only lets important guests in, so there's no chance for me to see what you have seen."

"It was very special," said his wife. "No, *special* is not the right word. *Impressive* better describes it. Never before have I seen so much wealth under one roof. One cannot even speculate as to Mr. Miethe's worth."

"He doesn't understand what you mean," said her husband. He turned to me and with wide gestures said, "Everything there is made of gold and silver, from the plates and the tableware to the faucets, from the littlest trinkets to the biggest ornaments. Priceless art hangs on all the walls, and there are hundreds of pieces of antique furniture. You can wander through libraries. And a music lover like yourself would not believe his eyes if he saw the chambers where he keeps his musical instruments. But by far, I found the most beautiful to be his collection of old automobiles! A huge cellar full of them! Maybe you will get to see something of it, for I heard the cellar will be opened presently to the public."

The orchestra stopped playing, I took up my violin to play again, and Karl and Christiane (for I knew her name, too) Beeren moved on. The part of my spirit that wasn't hidden in the monster concentrated on the tones of the strings, and slowly I began to sink into a lowered state of consciousness. It was time to create hypnotic images that I could make visible before my mind's eye and manipulate the way Francis had done. I was able to make forms and colors appear in faster and different ways and didn't need my violin to do so. I would rest and enjoy my magic now. I needed my strength, for the time was getting near when I would attempt to enter the house.

After an hour I looked up; coins lay all around me in the grass. As I picked them up, I noticed a sudden change had taken place on the lawn. The music had stopped, and voices had become hushed. The big door of the house was open now, and Georg Wust was walking backwards down the steps, bowing deeply the whole time.

Miethe suddenly appeared, with Maria at his side, but because I was sitting near the edge of the road, with the great lawn between us, they were only faintly discernible. I saw that Miethe's long, dark curls, that had made him look so much like Albrecht Dürer, were shorter now and silvery gray in color. He still had the same majestic strut of former times, and Maria's hand rested on his forearm. Together, they came down the flight of steps and mingled with the crowd. Happy voices were raised again, and once again the music began to play. Georg Wust walked in front of them, and I heard him say in a loud voice, "Rainer Miethe hopes you are all having a good time. Also, on behalf of his fiancée, Doctor Hilde Steiner, he wishes you all a pleasant day."

I sat up, and the hair on the back of my neck stood straight up. My eyes narrowed as I stared at the man and woman who walked with royal grace across the field. Every now and then they stopped, shook hands with somebody, had a brief conversation and then continued on their way.

He couldn't be Miethe. He would not be so stupid as to show himself in public this way while he still did not know where I was. With the revolver I had taken from his own man, I could shoot him right through the head, just as Francis had planned to do with Fabry's rifle.

The two figures I saw were definitely not Rainer Miethe and Hilde Steiner. She was Maria, not a projection but the real Maria Delaruelle, revitalized and made healthy by the blood of Francis. When she came nearer, I saw she had changed her looks a bit, in exactly the same way I had changed myself to look like an old man. Her hair was cut and her face was pretty, but not as beautiful as it would have been if it were really her own. Maria was Hilde, and except for myself, there was no one there who would think that the doctor was actually someone else. Miethe was obviously still safe inside the

Koos Verkaik

walls of his house and had sent a projection of himself. Together with Georg Wust he was looking, while he smiled, acted friendly and shook hands, for me. As they walked right past me, I began to play a melody I had never played before. He bent towards me and looked me straight in the eye.

"That sounds very nice, my good man," he said, his clear voice louder than the sound that my bow produced from the strings of my violin.

No, he hadn't recognized me. I looked at Maria. Now that she was so close to me, I was afraid my feelings would finally betray me.

"There is plenty of wine for you too, old man," Miethe said to me and then moved on. They walked once around the field but did not go back to the big door. Instead, they went to the side of the house, a number of the partygoers following. I rose to my feet, put the violin under my arm and crossed the lawn.

At the side of the house a door stood open. I noticed that there were bricks piled up on a spot where, once, there probably had been a big gate. I followed the other guests inside and saw a big garage door, where the cars that now stood in the cellar had been brought in. Together with the others, I went down a staircase. I looked around to see if Miethe and Maria were still there; I couldn't find them, but Georg Wust was present to give chapter and verse to anyone who wanted to know more about any of the automobiles.

Now I can finally chance it, I thought. I went outside and ran across the lawn to my car. I opened the back doors and lifted up the monster, keeping his big body covered by the blanket. Slowly and steadily, I walked back to the house. With every step I took, I felt my strength grow, and I knew I had the power to literally think myself away and become invisible. I was actually there, walking over the grass in the direction of the house, but no one noticed me, no one paid any attention to me at all. Every now and then I tried to see if I could receive any vibrations from the house. Through my eyelashes I peered at the barred windows and wondered if Miethe was standing up there watching me. I had to take the risk, I had no choice. At the door, I had to stop to let some people out who had come up the stairs. With Otto in my arms, I entered the cellar and walked up to Georg Wust, who was showing people around and now opened the door of an old Daimler.

"From 1950," he told them. "An extraordinary feat of craftsmanship like this you don't see anymore. A veritable castle on wheels, with a throne for the chauffeur. Quite a difference from this little, open Austin here, with a souped-up engine."

He attempted to close the door of the Daimler again, but I had pushed my knee against it. He raised his eyebrows and turned his head, but it was if he looked right through me. He moved on to the Austin, his audience following him. I put Otto on the back seat and

Koos Verkaik

sat myself down behind the wheel. There I remained sitting for the next few hours, staring outside over the long hood, until Georg Wust had walked the last of the guests to the door. I heard him draw the bolts and come downstairs again. When he walked past me, I noticed he was a changed man. His eyes were lackluster now; his arms hung down at his sides; and his soft, flabby belly moved up and down. Bending forward a bit, he gradually came to a complete stop. He wasn't even breathing anymore now. Miethe's concentration had been withdrawn from him, for he no longer needed his services. The light in the cellar was still on, and I saw that there were no surveillance cameras installed to watch over the collection of cars. Miethe was capable of seeing without cameras, or eyes for that matter, and could explore all the rooms of his house from top to bottom without ever leaving his bedroom. He had no use for electronic equipment.

Carefully, I removed the blanket from the monster and stroked Otto's head.

"There's another door there, Otto," I thought to the cat. I didn't use my voice, for I wanted to make as little noise as possible. "I wonder what I will see when I open it. Come! Let's go to it together. You are a part of me. My blood made you grow, and just like me, you don't need very much. No food, almost no liquid. Inside of you, deep down there, the hate and aggression are growing. You will go your own way pretty soon. Protect me against Miethe. Come! Let's go."

Silently, I opened the door of the Daimler. I got out and felt the smooth fur of the catlike monster brush along my leg. On soft paws and retracted claws, Otto went in front of me to the door. He curled his lips in a catlike grin, and I saw his big, sharp teeth. I held the revolver in my left hand and opened the door with my right. We came into a big, unfurnished hall with a stone floor.

If Doctor Steiner attempted to flee and managed to reach this hall, a big surprise awaited her here . She would be terror-stricken the moment she got to the stairs and looked down.

Miethes had used his power of thought to gather over a hundred different jesters here, but because it was not necessary for them to be alive right now, they existed as mere contours filled in with pastel tints. One quick psychic impulse from Miethe could bring the inanimate props to life immediately and turn them into three-dimensional beings. They would dance, jump, tumble, let their bells jingle, grab the doctor, lift her up, pass her along from one to the other in a hellish dance. Within the house, a fortress of tension had been built by Miethe, a magnetic web in which he caught, just like a spider, every vibration. His power reached to the farthest corners and niches. Nothing remained hidden for him. I was too clever for him, though. I had hidden my essence within the monster. The monster had the formidable qualities of the feline, and could come and go as he pleased without ever being seen or heard. Miethe knew nothing of the knowledge Otto Faun had given me.

As I silently stole past the motionless jesters, I thought about how in the course of time there had been many experiments with cats by men like Faun. Over the years, different breeds had received the elixir of life through the gift of human blood and had passed it on to new generations. I understood now why it was said that cats had nine lives! My cat was in the second phase of his existence; his third life would begin the moment I freed him from his monstrous condition and brought him back to his natural size and shape. He would never really be a normal cat again, for a bit of my immortality had now become his own. My blood, mixed with his own via the wound on his neck, saw to that.

Together we crept upstairs, where Miethe had changed everything into a dream world. Floors, ceilings and walls had vanished, and I found myself in a treacherous labyrinth of colors and spheres. My feet did not touch the ground, and a warm glow seemed to caress the skin on my face and hands. In the distance, I heard what could only be described as the monotonous beating of a drum.

I could go no further alone, and besides, if I did go any deeper into this madhouse without some assistance, I would probably never find my way back to the stairs. So I grasped the top of Otto's head with my free hand and let him lead me.

Suddenly, the colors around me became much more vivid. Red flames licked along the flanks of my monster and myself. Otto began to run, trying to avoid the high, scorching pillars of fire, and I had so much difficulty keeping up with him that I grabbed the loose skin on his neck and held on for dear life.

Without warning, Miethe materialized right in front of us and brought us to an abruptly halt. It was Miethe's idealized image, the way he wished to appear, the most beautiful Miethe he could possibly create. Young, strong and virile, he stood there, the long dark curls cascading over his broad shoulders and his eyes sparkling with the reflection of the flames that surrounded him.

I aimed my revolver and pulled the trigger. I shot him three times right through the head before I realized that the image was not real and that I had betrayed myself by using the weapon. Somewhere in the house the real Miethe had certainly heard the shots ring out. The fire went out and the projection disappeared.

I stood in the middle of a big room, where the walls were hidden from view by rows and rows of bookcases. The bullets I had fired had made holes in the back of an old book bound in leather. In a panic, I released my hold on Otto and ran for the door. Hearing footsteps coming from the direction where I thought the stairs were located, I turned and fled in the opposite direction.

Doors, chambers, another staircase, all were arranged in chaotic disorder. Sick with fear, I ran, stumbling and bumping into walls, all the while the sound of a jester's devilishly jingling bells coming from behind me.

I should never have shot; I should have known he would not show himself to me just like that.

Only when I finally stopped to catch my breath did it dawn on me that I was no longer walking with my feet in the void, and that Rainer Miethe was no longer wielding his mighty magical powers. The only thing that I was certain of was that the sound of the jester's bells was becoming louder and louder. There was no need to impress me with his sorcery any longer, or try to confuse my sense of direction by making the surroundings fade away in magical infernos.

I had been found out and just about caught.

Otto growled softly and, raising his head, looked up at a high door. I approached it slowly and opened it. I knew what I was doing, or at least I was pretty sure I knew, because Francis had shown me the chambers of the house, and I had recognized the door. With bated breath, I entered Miethe's laboratory, where he did his research and searched for the secret to the elixir of life. Pots, kettles, decanters and hermetically sealed jars hung above the fires.

I stood face to face with the man whom I had wanted to surprise by moving unseen, with my hand on the monster's head, through the labyrinth of spheres and color created by the power of his thoughts. He looked much older than me, but he radiated pure strength and gave me a defiant look. Not far from him stood Maria, leaning over a table and studying the contents of a book. She closed it now and stared at me in silence.

Behind me the monster I had created grew stiff, and the fool's bells became silent.

"Paul," said Maria and shook her head slowly.

A searing stab of pain shot from my shoulder to my hand. I spread my fingers, and the revolver flew through the air and landed with a thump on the table.

"This is good," said Miethe. "Now we are all here."

He came right up me, and I was no longer able to move. All I could do was speak, and I said in a flat tone, "The bullets that were meant to kill you have betrayed me. I should not have used the weapon so soon."

"You'd already come a long way, and I already knew of your presence," Miethe said to me. "It is a mystery to me how you managed to get so far."

Hunched up and motionless, Otto sat behind me. I don't think that Miethe had noticed him yet, because he did not transmit any impulses that Miethe could have received.

"The most important thing though, Paul, is that you are here, so that now you can be at my beck and call once again. I have such grand plans for you."

"You've already destroyed so many lives," I said. "You might as well take mine too."

"Oh no, no, my old friend, not yet! For the time being you are worth much more to me alive," he grinned. "There is liquid gold running through your veins!"

Back perfectly straight, arms crossed on his chest, he stood there looking at me, very well aware of and confident in his power. Once my friend, now my enemy, all he needed was his desire and imagination to make my eyes pop out of their sockets, or crush my beating heart within my chest. If he wanted to, he could squeeze the last breath of air from my lungs.

On the table, in a sealed decanter, a liquid substance began to emit sparks. Behind Maria, a log of wood noisily disintegrated in the open fire. Momentarily distracted by the sound, Miethe turned his head to look first at the fire and then at the decanter. Maria quickly reached out her hand and grabbed the revolver. She aimed the weapon at Miethe. I knew she had the guts to shoot, but would she?

It occurred to me that she must have been waiting for a chance like this for a very long time. Her hatred of him was centuries old. From the day he had murdered Kaspar von Karst and then raped her, he had forced her to take his side, tyrannized her and chased her when she attempted to flee. Every time she had managed to escape from him, he had found her and dragged her back. He had always remained vigilant lest she should decide to avenge herself. Now she was strong again though; Francis's blood had restored her old strength.

Miethe turned in her direction, and a halo of light appeared around his head. He raised both hands and with the power of his mind prevented her from pulling the trigger, but he could not force her to put the revolver down. Over the course of time, she too had learned the power of magic.

He was not thinking at all about me right now, and the presence of my monster had escaped his notice altogether.

Miethe's concern was certainly misdirected, for it might not be Maria at all who was the threat to him. Even if she made the attempt, she would probably not succeed anyway, for soon she would have used up all her strength, and then Miethe would simply take the weapon away from her.

I concentrated now with every fiber of my being, and Otto sprang like some jungle cat from hell. I heard his extended claws scratching the floor as he ran past me. With a mighty jump he flew over the table and landed on Miethe's back, burying his front claws in his flesh. His hind legs pumped up and down, tearing Miethe's clothes to shreds. Miethe staggered, and his halo began to fade until it was finally extinguished completely. The monster sunk his teeth into Miethe's neck, and together they collapsed onto the ground. Miethe started to scream. The impulses he transmitted now were so powerful that a cosmic whirlwind arose in the room, lifting old books and sending them smashing against the walls. I managed to keep myself upright but was thrown back a few yards with my feet dragging over the floor. Everywhere in the house doors began to bang open and shut, and a hellish drone became audible, as if the engines of all the automobiles in the cellar had been started at once and were running at full throttle.

Maria had dropped the revolver and moved back. She came too close to the open fire, and her clothes ignited. She slapped her hands against her skirt with a frenzied motion. The sealed decanters that were hanging burst, and a terrible stench filled the air. Toxic substances were released into the air that would have immediately killed normal mortals. All the work that had taken Miethe so many years to accomplish was now destroyed. The chains from which the pots and flasks hung began to swing and clang against each other.

Otto did not let go. His mighty jaws held fast on Miethe's neck, and his claws continued to do their bloody work. Miethe's time had come. He kicked violently, and his fingers moved spastically through the air, trying to catch hold of the monster's fur, but his efforts were futile. His powers were being drained, and he no longer had a grip on the environment around him.

I found that I could move again, and with four or five steps I was next to Otto, where I witnessed something that I had not seen the monster in Valencia do. Otto unhooked his lower jaw from the rest of his skull, in the same manner a snake does, revealing a cavernous mouth. Breathing heavily through his nostrils, he began to devour his macabre meal. His sharp teeth raked along Miethe's head, and the muscles in his throat began to make swallowing motions. He stretched out his hind legs, and his stomach began to sway to and fro. I heard Miethe's strangled voice but could not tell if he was screaming with fear, cursing us or using his last drop of strength to recite magical incantations, for his face and head had already disappeared into the throat of the beast, and the monster's mouth had already closed over Miethe's broad shoulders.

The floor was wet with the liquids that flowed from the broken kettles and decanters.

The shoulders and upper arms of Miethe were now inside, and everything was going much faster. Otto used his front paws now to pull in his prey. The last I saw of Rainer Miethe was his feet. The monster closed his mouth and slowly crept to the open fire. There, his belly swollen with his meal, he stretched out with a deep sigh and closed his eyes. He appeared twice as big as he had been; his long tongue hung lazily out from between his bloody teeth. Now was the time to let Otto rest; it was going to take a while to digest this meal.

Maria ran to me and held on tight. I buried my face in her long hair to block the awful stench surrounding us. There was no longer any sound in the house. All was deathly quiet.

After a while we looked at each other, and although we both sobbed, we did not cry. We had lived too long to be able to shed tears. With our heads raised and our mouths wide open, we looked up at the ceiling and made moaning, guttural sounds.

We cried as the wolves cry.

Without tears.

Wolf tears.

Intangible as life itself.

* * *

"Will he ever come back again?" asked Maria.

"Never again," I replied.

As soon as the time was ripe, I would change the monster back into a cat, and then Otto and I would be companions for all eternity.

Maria and I kissed each other, took one another's hand, and together we left the room, wading through the evil-smelling sludge that covered the floor. I wanted to find Francis as soon as possible; I knew he was close by. We went through the door that led to the hall filled with hospital equipment. At the back of this room was another door, behind which I knew I would find him. I also had to find Doctor Steiner and tell her that evil jesters no longer lay in wait for her along the corridors and in the halls, that never again would they attempt to drive her insane with their dancing and tumbling.

"Francis needs blood," I said. "My blood. He has to get well again as quickly as possible."

Francis lay flat on his bed, bound with broad straps. I was shocked when I saw how lean and pale his face was, but he laughed when he saw me.

"Paul. Paul. Are we safe?"

"Yes," I said, as I sat down carefully on the edge of the bed. "You don't have to worry about anything any longer."

"I heard a noise, but didn't have the strength to move my spirit. You were our last hope, Paul, and you came through admirably. Tell me exactly what happened."

I shook my head.

"Listen. Can you hold on a bit longer? One hour longer?"

"Of course. Now that I have seen you, I already feel my powers coming back."

"Then I must get to Doctor Steiner, she has to help me with a blood transfusion. And we both know she has experience with that now, so it will be just fine."

Francis laughed again, and I felt my emotions weaken. A short sob escaped me, but he did not see me cry, for wolf tears are invisible.

11 -Eternally Further

I held Doctor Steiner's hands for a long time. She sat on her bed in a scantily furnished room, and I got down on my knees in front of her. After I had told her that Rainer Miethe had vanished and that, with him gone, the specters of the jesters belonged to the past, she burst out in tears. But it soon became apparent how strong her character was.

"I thought I was a confident, secure woman and had myself under control, that nothing could happen to me. I was the one who helped people who needed physical healing and were in spiritual need," she said. "All of a sudden so many things happened that I couldn't comprehend, and I was confronted with my own anguish. The worst part of all was that I couldn't understand what I was seeing. But when I started to believe that everything that was happening to me was real, then I began to think differently about matters."

"It finally dawned on you that you were not insane after all and that there was an outside power that had entered your mind."

"I began to see the entire event as a scientific phenomenon that needed to be studied. No longer were the jesters my greatest fear; it was the fury of Miethe that would rain down on me if I attempted to escape. I was also warned by Francis Beck. He made it clear to me that Maria Delaruelle would eventually take my place in the world. A new life for her would mean death for me. That scared me so. I could envision her walking through my house, I could see Miethe visiting her and everyone in the street greeting her with 'Hello, Doctor Steiner.'"

She held her head to the side and looked at me with her dark eyes. The resemblance to Maria was striking.

"I have seen you before, both you and Francis. I was in a state of mind that was very much like dreaming."

It flashed through my mind that I had seen her too, when I was sitting at my workbench in Rotterdam, restringing a guitar, but I couldn't remember any of the details.

"Possibly," I said. "Francis has told me this also, but at the time I was not as susceptible to such contacts as I am now."

Hilde told me about the time she had spent in Miethe's house. She had assisted him with the blood transfusions, she had worked in the laboratory in his search for the elixir, and she had listened to what he had to tell her.

"Mentally, he was rather unstable. He needed me. As a doctor I could take care of his physical ailments, and my resemblance to Maria was also important, but the most important thing he needed from me was my knowledge of psychology. He had anguishes and doubts, and he wanted me to clear his mind, as if I was a witch doctor."

She started to cry again.

"I had seen his odd, syrupy blood. I was forced to give Francis's blood to the man whom I hated so much. As soon as he was well again, he brought me to see Maria. Never before had I seen anyone in such bad shape, but Miethe would have let her die if he had not been finished with Francis himself. He called Francis his fountain of life. Meanwhile, he confessed all his crimes to me. I was his private psychiatrist, and he cared not at all that I shuddered with fear at all those stories. The worst part about it was that I knew he spoke the truth. The elixir of Alexander, the man he murdered, was real. You are so old, so very, very old."

I let go of her hand so I could wipe the tears from her cheeks. We both remained silent for a moment or two.

"Will you help me?" she asked me then. "I need time to come to terms with all this and get a clear picture of these events. I need someone to talk to. I am afraid to be alone now."

"If you help me," I said. "We have to go to Francis. He is depending on us now."

We kept on talking for a while and it became clear that Hilde was afraid to leave that room, but she understood I had to go to Francis. I helped her up, and together we went to the door. She held on tight to my arm. In the corridor she suddenly fainted. I caught her just in time to prevent her from collapsing onto the hard floor.

"I am obviously not as unshakable as I thought," she said with a sigh. "Miethe has a cupboard full of medicines, and I wanted sedatives so badly, but he didn't allow me to take them. I am in urgent need of them now, though; I—I believe I can't even get up again—"

I bent down and helped her up, and she put her arms around me as if she were a little child. She began to cry once more, and her tears rolled down my neck. When we went through the laboratory, I advised her to keep her hand over her nose and mouth. It still reeked of the spilled liquids, which undoubtedly were poisonous as well as foul smelling. Looking above her forefinger, her lips pressed against her hand, she gazed round. Otto lay swollen and panting heavily by the fire. Hilde began to gag, and I quickly got her through the room.

"Was that—"

"The monster?" I said. "Yes. It is digesting the evil."

All of a sudden she was the scientist again.

"I saw scorched, burned books. It's a pity about all the information that has been lost forever here."

Maria sat on a chair next to Francis's bed. She had loosened the straps and stroked his forehead with her fingers. I knew they were in love with each other, and I was happy for my friend but could not help but feel disappointed that Maria, about whom I had dreamed throughout the ages, would never be my wife.

"You will feel strong again soon enough," I said to Francis.

"Strong and young," he said, his voice soft.

I saw his sunken chest moving quickly up and down. Hilde got up, talked to Maria for a while, and then, together, they rolled the bed into the other room. They pushed it next to another bed, on which I would lie. I took my shirt off, and saw Hilde pull a table near, on which was placed all kinds of equipment.

"Don't you want to take your sedatives first?" I asked her.

"Later," she answered. "Please, lie down. We must take care of Francis first."

* * *

Francis recovered quickly. My blood got him back on his feet. The first thing we did, once he was strong enough, was clean up the laboratory. A few books were still in reasonably good shape, and we brought them to the libraries.

We took my monster outside. Otto's stomach wasn't swollen any more, but he was still so big and heavy that it took two of us to move him.

My friend was eager to see how I would bring the transformation about.

I poured a mixture of different ingredients and magnetized water in a small circle that would determine the size of the cat. The grass was scorched where the liquid touched it, and the circle became blackened. I lay Otto over the circle and began to recite my incantations.

"The power that has been forged from matter and thought will leave this creature. Let all powers of heaven and earth go back to their origins. Let the divine comet leave this animal."

Otto swished his tail, raised his head and roared like a tiger. We saw his teeth grow smaller, his body shrink. When his nose and the tip of his tail touched the inner sides of the circle, there was once again a little cat lying in the grass, looking up at the sky with surprised, yellow eyes.

"My cat," I said. "My eternal companion. We will keep each other company forever."

I picked him up, took him in my arms and pushed my face into his sleek fur. Looking up, I saw Francis standing in front of me; he reached out his hand to stroke the cat's head.

"Maria and I will be staying together," he said.

"I already knew that," I replied. "I wish the both of you much luck. What are your plans?"

"We have a short time to arrange much. We want to stay here, but even though Miethe is gone, Paul, the danger might not be entirely over. If he has been in contact with scientists, who will do anything to get people like us, immortals, in their hands, then we will be watched constantly. Always keep your eyes open, wherever you are. Trust no one! I don't know if you plan to stay with us or not, but if you leave, you must always let me know where you are and how I can reach you."

"Haven't we always done it that way? Century after century?"

His hand slid from the head of the cat to my upper arm, and for a moment his fingers rested there. We looked at each other and nodded. Then we turned around and walked back to the house.

A new period in our long lives lay ahead of us.

New years.

The journey through time would go on and on for us. There was still no end in sight.

* * *

I could make monsters appear when pursued. I had scared the hell out of Walter Fabry by showing him grotesque figures. In Bärbel Körner's restaurant, I had made a traveling salesman appear. But what I could do was nothing compared to what Francis and Maria could do together. While I kept Hilde company and helped her to come to terms with the events that had transpired, they made Georg Wust appear through their concentrated power of thought. The fat, little man was made to receive, one by one, the men who had worked for Miethe. They were dismissed from their jobs and were paid a goodly amount of money for their efforts. Miethe had a lot of money in the house. In a safe we had found a great deal of cash and some gold.

Georg Wust disappeared the moment the last man was out the door with his pay.

Miethe had thought about everything; all his possessions were precisely listed in a book, and countless documents detailed how he had gathered his collections. We all knew that they were falsifications, but no one, outside of ourselves, could ever prove it. Francis and Maria went to see a notary in Karst, and when they returned, we were all fabulously wealthy.

"Bloch, the notary, has no doubt that it was Rainer Miethe who visited him a few years ago to arrange for our power of attorney over his possessions and the right, in his absence, to sell whatever we wish. He is also convinced that Miethe asked him to make us co-owners of the house. Only recently, he said, Miethe dropped by to arrange the papers that made us his partners in the hillside vineyards, cellars and buildings of the late Wilhelm Schwarzburg. All the contracts are safe in his vault."

"You stamped it on his memory, didn't you?" I said. "Messed around with his mind."

"You could say so, yes."

"But how did you ever convince him without Miethe being there, too?"

"We had him draw up all the necessary papers, and believe me, a man works surprisingly hard when he is in a trance! He wrote down the dates that were whispered in his ear, and time after time, he signed his name, with style, mind you, to all the documents. Miethe could not say enough nice things about him! The three of us dropped in on him, you see."

I pulled back in shock when Francis and Maria made a figure materialize between them that rapidly took on the looks of Rainier Miethe. It was definitely a shock to my system, and I could not help but think how good it was that Doctor Steiner did not happen to be present.

"Thank you very much, Mr. Bloch," said Miethe, his voice sounding exactly the same as it always had. "You have been an excellent help. I am a happy man now that my friends are my partners. Trust me, sir, I will reward you liberally."

Then Miethe simply vanished into thin air.

"That was quite an impressive spectacle, I suppose," I said.

"It was also very tiring," Maria remarked. "It cost us quite a lot of energy, and we still have to perform this play one more time. Rainer Miethe is going to make one more appearance: he will gather all the important people of Karst in a restaurant, for a formal dinner, and then he will announce his departure. Perhaps he is going to buy land in South America, or maybe he is going on a world tour, or maybe he will just retire to his yacht. Whatever it is, everyone will understand that he will be gone for a long, long time and that we will now conduct his business."

I could see it all before me: A full dining room at Bärbel Körner's, with Miethe at the head of the table, Maria and Francis at either side. He would be on his best behavior, and everyone would regret his departure.

"We will sell all the possessions of Schwarzburg to the winegrowers," said Francis. "That is, if you agree with it, Paul. After all, we are partners."

And we all laughed.

"I will leave it all up to you," I said. "Regardless of how long we live, we will never be able to spend all the money we'll get for the things in this house."

"Will you be there when we have this dinner with Miethe?" asked Maria.

"No, no. I'm going to leave you. It's such a pity that the great outer doors that lead to the cellar are bricked up; otherwise I would pick out a nice automobile for myself, put Otto in the back seat and drive away. Now I'll have to take my old Ford to the first dealer I see and buy myself another used car."

"You shall want for nothing," replied Francis. "You will leave a rich man."

"And Hilde? I'm sure you won't let her down."

"I've told her that we can wipe her most traumatic experiences completely from her memory," said Maria. "If Francis and I work together, we are capable of doing that. But she said no. She wants to deal with it and get over it in her own way, on her own strength."

"I know."

"I will have a talk with Leopold Kreher soon," said Francis. "He is the new town doctor who lives in Hilde's house. He won't be able to refuse the offer I'm going to make to him. If Hilde so desires, she can return to her house and her practice, I will see to it. I'll bet you that he will be standing there with his mouth wide open when he hears my offer."

* * *

I began to lead a roving life with Otto, the cat, as my traveling companion. I kept in touch with Francis and Maria. I heard that Hilde had resumed her practice in Karst and that she regularly she visited my friends. The three of them gathered in Miethe's old laboratory to continue the work on the elixir of life.

"We have all the time in the world to find it," Maria said to me during a telephone conversation. "But of course it would be fantastic if we could find it while Hilde is still alive."

One day, while I was living in a rented house in Spain and spending my days with Otto at the edge of a swimming pool in a beautiful garden, Francis called me up.

"We had such a strange experience yesterday, Paul," he said. "We had such a fright! Hilde was with us. We put a table and some chairs outside and decided to crack open a fine bottle of Karster Glut. The weather was beautiful, not a cloud in the sky. All of a sudden it started to hail. Not cold, white stones though. Thousands of copper and silver bells were raining down on us. Like jesters wear on their caps, sleeves and the toes of their shoes. They blanketed the grass, jingling and clanging as they came down. I have no explanation for it. Unless of course Miethe's ability to work miracles extends even beyond death."

"Was there anything special going on?" I wanted to know.

There was silence at the other side of the line for a moment, and then Francis said, "There was a damn good reason that I had decided to open a bottle of that excellent wine, Paul. That very morning Maria had gone to Hilde for an examination. Paul, my wife is expecting a baby!"

* * *

There is a photograph from 1932. Rotterdam. Francis and I are dressed in our old-fashioned clothes. We had been there together, but now I went back alone. I was not sure whether or not, once I was there, I would lose my memory again, or if I would continue to spend my life in the knowledge that my future was infinite.

Once, we had traveled in the company of Albrecht Dürer, and I had then gone on from Aachen by myself. Now I was driving from Karst to Rotterdam in an old Rolls-Royce Silver Wraith. The painting by Dürer in the back seat would fetch me a fortune once it was sold. It was strange to think that I had a picture that was so very old and that I had known the artist personally. I had also taken some antique violins along with me, three of which I had built myself.

Life was laughing at me, but I wasn't laughing back. More and more often I was beginning to feel dejected. As old as I was, I understood less about life than a mortal.

Once I was back in Rotterdam, I checked into an expensive hotel and went out each day to search for a house where my cat and I could live in comfort and happiness. Francis knew where I was, and one morning I received a card from him. I opened the envelope and read the message.

"With joy and pride we announce the birth of our son Paul. Maria and Francis Beck."

Under it he had written with a fountain pen, "We are eternally grateful to you."

Only I knew what that meant.

I sobbed.

My eyes though, did not become wet.

I cried wolf tears.

Afterword

For the inhabitants of Karst, many questions have remained unanswered. What had the old eyes of Vitus Weiss seen before they were caused to stare motionless into the valley of the Moselle? How had Wilhelm Schwarzburg gotten his neck stuck between the forked branches of the tree? Why did Hans-Jürgen Lins smash his speeding car into the cliff face? Not to mention all the grief that unexpectedly appearing jesters caused in the little village.

A man like Andreas Pallasch wears his heart on his sleeve, and it would be very interesting indeed to hear what he has to say when he is in his cups and talking perhaps a bit too much at Bärbel Körner's restaurant.

One cannot help but speculate that the beautiful hair of Doctor Steiner was turned prematurely gray by the sudden departure of her wealthy friend and patron, who left so spontaneously to go on a world tour.

On festival days, when the harvest queen passes through the streets on a float, followed by brass bands and cheerful villagers dressed in their finest clothes, there will never again be a jester present to dance along with his little bells ringing.

If Karster Glut does indeed exist, dear reader, I would like to invite you to come drink a couple of glasses with me. Somewhere between Koblenz and Trier we would see the hillside vineyards, where the white grapes grow that are harvested and pressed to make that exquisite vintage. We could sit back on a terrace with a view of the river or visit Bärbel Körner, who always has a good supply of this wonderful nectar in the house. Maybe later, as we take a walk through the old streets of Karst, we will run into little Paulus Beck. And as we look into his innocent brown eyes we can, filled with emotion fueled by the wine, wish the boy an eternal youth.

No time limit should be fixed to the wonders of life.

#

About the Author

Koos Verkaik is a literary whirlwind — author of over **seventy novels and children's books**, and a true master of **magic, mystery, and adventure**. Born in 1951 near Rotterdam, he penned his first stories at just **seven years old** and quickly rose to become **Europe's youngest comic strip writer**, contributing weekly to *Sjors* magazine.

By eighteen, his first novel *Adolar* was in print. Since then, his imagination has never rested. From writing **radio plays and international comic scripts** to working as an editor and copywriter, Verkaik's storytelling has taken on many forms — including secret pseudonyms and far-reaching projects across the globe.

His books have captivated readers from **the USA to India**, with his signature style blending the **supernatural with suspense, and fantasy with fast-paced thrills**. Whether for adults or children, every Koos Verkaik story promises a wild, unforgettable ride.

Step into his world at www.koosverkaik.com.

www.ingramcontent.com/pod-product-compliance
Lightning Source LLC
Chambersburg PA
CBHW072342020726
47506CB00004B/971